A DRIVE THROUGH TIME

ANDREI SAYGO

COPYRIGHT ©2021

ANDREI SAYGO

This book is a work of fiction. The names, characters, places, and incidents are the products of the author's imagination or are used fictitiously. Any resemblance to actual events, business establishments, locales, or persons, living or dead, is entirely coincidental.

All rights reserved. No part of this publication may be reproduced, stored in a retrieval system, or transmitted in any form or by any means (electronic, mechanical, photocopying, recording, or otherwise) without the prior written permission of the copyright owner. The only exception is brief quotations in printed reviews.

The scanning, uploading, and distribution of this book via the Internet or any other means without the permission of the author is illegal and punishable by law.

Please purchase only authorized electronic editions, and do not participate in or encourage electronic piracy of copyrighted materials. Your support of the author's rights is appreciated.

1

The three riders approached fast, their black capes fluttering in the wind, like they were sent by Sauron himself. Their blades glinted in the sunrise, poised to strike. I gulped. *I'm too young to die. I haven't even had a girlfriend. Or breakfast.*

Something about facing death on an empty stomach just isn't right. Especially if it happens not five minutes after you woke up in an unknown place. And I don't mean in an unfamiliar bed trying to recall what happened last night. I mean somewhere in the woods, facing three murderous, raging madmen screaming at you. And that's not even the strangest thing in the last five minutes. Let me rewind and tell you how my morning started.

I woke up thinking of the storm the night before, with winds rocking my RV like a dinghy in rough waters and the sky ignited by bolts of lightning. It had been the last Friday in

September, the night before my planned month-long vacation, and my colleagues had snuck a few crates of beers into the office to celebrate the end of my internship at CERN and wish me *bonne chance* on my journey around Switzerland and beyond. What happened afterward...my mind drew a blank. *Oh Duncan, why did you have to drink so much?*

Moving sluggishly, I rolled out of bed and strolled through the RV's narrow corridor to open the door and let in some fresh air. This was my first real hangover; a splitting headache and the desire to throw up assaulted me. I pressed on the handle, closed my eyes, and inhaled the morning's fresh, crisp air. The effect was instantaneous, like a cool breeze on a scorching day, and the invisible fog covering my mind dissipated—only the headache remained. I stepped out...right into something wet and mushy. My right shoe landed in a slimy, muddy puddle. It had rained last night. "What the—" I started, but my mouth froze open.

Instead of the expected CERN building, with its three-story-high mural depicting the ATLAS particle detector, what rose over me was the majestic Mont Salève, Geneva's impressive home mountain, its green forests and gray rocks a splash of contrasting color on the spotless sky.

I had admired the peak every day from my tiny apartment, hiked on it several times, and I was sure of what my eyes showed me. Instead of an almost empty parking lot, Mont Salève greeted me. Birds' chirping and the buzzing of insects bathing in the sun's rays were the only sounds. No cars, no traffic, no airplanes. Nada. Zilch.

I stared at the scenery for a while, in shock, unable to

comprehend what had happened. Myriad questions and thoughts filled my mind. *Should I pinch myself? How did I get here? Did I drunk-drive here last night? I need breakfast.*

I closed my eyes and took a few deep breaths. There had to be a logical explanation, and the most likely scenario was that my colleagues—Martin, Francesca, Etienne, and Sergio—had organized a prank. Sergio was the last one to join the party and didn't drink, as far as I could remember seeing. He'd said he still had some work to do, an experiment they had to start over the weekend while everyone was gone. *He must have arranged this trick to drive me into the middle of nowhere.* Stories about his pranks were legendary. Once he filled someone's office with Styrofoam. Another time, when a colleague of his was on vacation, Sergio transformed the person's office into a Western saloon, with batwing doors, a stand-up bar, and a good mix of alcoholic beverages.

I had no doubt he coordinated this. This was exactly what I told them I would do to celebrate the end of my internship: a month of living in my brand-new RV, off the grid, traveling and tracking the movement of the gray wolves from central Europe, to the northern parts, to the countries from the former Soviet bloc and even Russia.

I would have preferred to be the one choosing which place I would visit first, but Sergio had apparently made that choice for me. *He should have stopped by a pharmacy to get something for my headache.*

"Haha. Hey guys, this is not funny," I shouted, hoping one of them would appear from behind the trees surrounding the clearing. Silence. "Hey, anyone there? You can come out now." My voice dispersed through the field, but no one appeared.

I raised my leg and shook it hard a few times, trying to get the mud out of my shoe and pants. A few specks flew off, along with one of my shoes. Everything else remained stuck like it had been glued on. I cursed under my breath, hopped on one foot, and recovered the shoe, then thoughtfully took a few steps and went around my motor home.

A dark forest rose, not more than fifty meters from the RV. I did a 360-degree turn, taking in the natural beauty of the place—the vibrant green of the grass and forest, the looming dark silhouette of the mountain painted over the deep blue of the cloudless sky—and a chill swept over me from the utter beauty of the scenic expanse. A cool breeze blew against my cheek, the sweet perfume of flowers greeted my nostrils, and the sounds of tiny insects playing in the sun's rays circled my ears. Their noise drowned my thoughts. I was part of it; I belonged there, one more soul in a vast, flourishing arena.

The moment passed, and the logical portion of my brain started working again. Something was amiss. The RV tires looked brand new, with no mud on them and no tire tracks around, which should have been impossible with all the earth soaked by the rain. A boggy swamp would have been a more accurate description of where I was. *How did I get here?*

Shouts, screeches, and what sounded like a herd of deer trampling through the woods pulled me out of my thoughts, and I focused on the trees ahead. A two-wheeled cart pulled by a brown pony with silver dapples came rushing out of the woods from a path I hadn't realized was there. Two people rode in the cart: an older man, probably in his late fifties, with a whip in his hand, its brown color matching his tunic, and a young blond woman, her long, gray, plain-cut dress partially hidden by a wide strap holding a quiver full of arrows.

They hadn't seemed to notice me and kept looking back, searching for something, maybe the source of the approaching shouts. On the uneven road, the cart, along with the people inside, bounced jarringly each time the wheels hit a rock. With all the squeaks and rattles it made, I was sure it would disintegrate before my eyes, dropping both passengers into the mud.

Three figures on galloping horses shot through the trees at the forest's edge. Two of the riders had axes in their hands, the third one, a sword, its blade flashing with captured sun.

The cart hurriedly approached my RV, but the riders were gaining on them. Everything looked so ridiculous, I thought I must be on a movie set; people with cameras must be filming the entire thing. But no one shrieked, "Cut!"

The three riders with black capes streaming behind them as they charged released a chilling battle cry and brandished their weapons. I took a step back, fell on my backside, and froze; my breath stopped in my throat. I was a passenger in my body, seeing everything from behind my eyes, like watching a screen in a dark room with my arms and legs tied to the ground.

Now only thirty meters away from me, the cart creaked with each rotation of the wheels. The passengers turned their heads, their mouths open and eyes glued to my vehicle. The whip fell from the older man's hands. The woman was the first to recover, and her shout broke through my shock. I nearly jumped out of my pants.

The cart came straight at me—it showed no signs of slowing down—and she made frantic gestures for me to get out of their way.

I jumped out of my paralysis, stood, slipped, and bounced off the RV. It hurt. I got up and ran to the door. A sense of relief washed over me when I opened the door and set foot on the stairs.

For a second, I remained there, pondering what I should do. The easiest thing would be to close the door and ignore everything I'd just seen. It wasn't my fight, and I had no interest in the wrath of those three horsemen. Plus, the woman and the older man could have been thieves for all I knew. The smart option was to mind my own business.

But that's not what my dad taught me.

I turned and gestured for the two to follow me, then moved aside, leaving the door open so they could get in. I was sure if they made it inside, those three pursuers had no chance of getting in. Not with those weapons.

I looked out the windshield and watched what was happening, my heart thudding in my chest. When the man and the woman got in the RV, I would close and lock the door in a heartbeat. Meanwhile, their pursuers must have figured it out and forced their horses to gallop even faster, closing the distance with every passing second. I wasn't sure the two of them would make it. By the time they jumped out of the cart, they would be overrun by the three riders.

The distance shortened considerably, and I wasn't sure what to do; there was no time to help them. The wagon approached my vehicle and started slowing down, but one rider saw it as his chance and threw the ax. I watched, horrified, as the ax flew inches away from the man's head and buried itself deep in the ground in front of my door. The cart continued without stopping, and a couple seconds later, the riders had almost reached my RV. I didn't want to give them a chance to get in, so I clicked on the computer screen next to me and closed the door. I felt as if I was condemning the companions to death.

I made a phone gesture with my hand next to my ear, indicating I would call the police. It didn't faze them even one bit. So I honked.

Two horses made a quick change of direction, and the third one jumped sideways. All three men landed on the ground with heavy thuds, loud enough I heard them from inside the vehicle. The animals continued galloping back toward the forest, leaving the riders lying there, unmoving.

I grabbed my phone and hurried to the door, but before I stepped out, an arrow sailed right past me, followed by two more.

I took my phone out of my pocket to call the police, but I had no signal. For a few seconds, I remained standing there, waiting, and when nothing else happened, I cautiously peered outside, behind the door.

Three bodies, each with an arrow stuck in its chest, lay on the ground. The surrounding grass slowly changed color from green to red as blood trickled away from their open wounds. *There goes my appetite.*

The morbid need to stare at those lifeless bodies with their black capes torn to reveal maroon leather tunics and basil green trousers was overwhelming, and I didn't have the strength to take my eyes away. I knew I had to do something, call for help, or get my emergency kit, but I couldn't force myself to move.

"Thank you for saving us," said a feminine voice in English, with an accent I couldn't place.

I spun, facing the cart, which had stopped next to the door. The woman had a bow in her hand, and her gaze stopped for a moment over the three dead people before she fixed on me.

She wore no makeup, and freckles were liberally scattered on her high cheeks. Rich and lustrous hair fell in long waves past her shoulders. She held the bow with assurance and grace, and ice ran up my spine. *She's the one who skewered them.* It didn't seem to bother her at all.

I met her gaze, and she searched my face, biting her beautiful, plump rose lips, her forehead puckered. I had no idea what to say when a woman thanked you for helping her kill three men. *You're welcome? Any time? Happy to be of service?*

"We were fortunate to cross paths with you. What is your name, if I may ask?" asked the man next to her in a scratchy voice, wide eyes focused on my RV.

He looked younger than I'd initially thought. His shaggy gray hair and stubble had enough dark strands to put him in his late forties or early fifties. His gaze met mine, and his piercing black eyes narrowed as he spat into the mud at his feet.

I was taken aback because I understood the words—they were in English, with a strange accent—but the sounds were different, the way that when you're watching a dubbed film, you can see the words don't match the lip movement. His behavior seemed odd too.

"What happened? Why were they following you?" I asked, not wanting to give them my name just yet, not after everything I'd witnessed.

Both looked at me and my clothes as if I were an alien.

After a moment of hesitation, the man spoke, his gaze not meeting my eyes. "Very early this morning, a few women and children escaped from a couple of nearby villages and warned us that Orgetorix's men would attack us. They were pillaging and burning everything in their way. We were in one of the few settlements that refused to abandon our homes and start the journey to the southern plains. We took everything we could and ran, heading to Lord Ambenix's town, to safety. These three were scouts sent ahead to check the road and must have picked up our trail."

Who has names like Lord Ambenix or Orgetorix?

"Couldn't you just call the police? I'm pretty sure we're close to Geneva," I said, and pointed at the looming mountain.

He frowned, then shook his head and asked, "Geneva? I'm sorry, I don't mean to offend you, but I know of no such place."

"You know, Geneva...with the famous Jet d'Eau? The United Nations?" I was mildly irritated, but he shook his head again. "How can you not know this? Aren't you from Switzerland?"

"What is Switzerland?" the young woman asked.

What kind of question is that? I was alone, unarmed, with three dead bodies next to me, facing two dangerous people who seemed way too comfortable with murder. And they had no idea in which country they lived. *Duncan, stay cool, keep your calm.* There had to be a rational explanation. *Hmm, maybe Sergio crossed the border.*

"Switzerland is the country we're in, if I'm not mistaken—isn't it? Unless my colleagues dropped me somewhere in France." I glanced again at the mountain but couldn't tell for sure from this position if I were still next to Geneva or had crossed the border.

"I'm sorry, but we haven't heard of such places. We are just simple people heading toward Lord Ambenix's town, with the hope he will protect us," said the old man.

Why don't they know the name of the country they live in? Unless they were from a small, sheltered village or a closed community that lived detached from society, it made no sense.

"Do they have a police station there? We need to report what happened here." I pointed to the three bodies. "I can definitely testify it was self-defense." I hoped my assurance was enough, and they wouldn't think of murdering me too.

"What is police?" asked the woman, her brows furrowed.

"People that protect the area to make sure everyone is safe." *Duh.*

She seemed to consider this, then nodded.

"Yes, they have a militia, but they won't care about these three. They'll probably be glad we did it."

Maybe it was the way she said it, as if the murder of three people was the most banal thing in the world and the "militia" would totally ignore it, or maybe it was because I hit my head and couldn't think straight, but I couldn't stop myself. I laughed. It was a nervous laugh. I found it bizarre that someone wouldn't know about the police or would believe they'd ignore a triple murder. These were the most peculiar people I'd ever encountered, and since leaving the U.S. and coming to Europe for my studies, I'd seen my fair share of absurd. I would have continued laughing, but the young woman's brown eyes threw daggers in my direction.

I inhaled, the crisp air spreading through my body, chilling my mood and bringing me back to reality. I didn't want to be the fourth man skewered by her arrows.

"Look, I'm sorry, but this is just unbelievable." I raised my hands, palms facing them, in a pacifying gesture. "I'll be on my way, and I would appreciate it if you could point me to the nearest town."

"The closest town is now probably in the hands of Orgetorix's men."

I frowned and was getting ready to give him a piece of my mind, but the woman intervened.

"Father, he isn't from around here, and he may not know—" she started, but the old man raised a hand to stop her, then turned toward me, meeting my eyes.

"We owe you our lives, so trust my advice," the man said. "You have to run. Otherwise, before the sun sets, you will be surrounded by Orgetorix's army, and they will kill you. You seem to have . . ." He glanced at my RV before continuing, "Powers I have neither seen nor heard of, but you won't be able to stop them."

I would have categorized him as a lunatic and left, trying to find the way back all by myself. But then I glanced at the three unmoving bodies, and I shuddered. This wasn't a joke, no matter how much I wanted it to be. *Where am I? Why is everything so different? What was the woman going to say I don't know? I just want to go home.*

At what must have been a dumb look on my face, he continued, "We need to get going if we want to get there before nightfall." His tone brooked no argument, and he turned to take the reins.

"You are free to join us . . ." interjected his daughter, but she was quickly reduced to silence by a look from her father.

What should I do? I could tell them goodbye and trust I would find a way out, or I could follow them and see where they were going. Someone was bound to know more than those two. And there was something in his words that surprised me. He suggested I had powers he had never seen before, and my RV would have made a good deterrent against any attackers. *Why did he say that?* When I thought I understood his reasoning, I wanted to laugh. They were scared of me when actually, I feared them. I had an expensive vehicle, and people had been murdered for less.

My phone wasn't working, I didn't know where I was, and I needed them to get me to the nearest city and hopefully to civilization. There, I would let the police sort things out and finally enjoy my vacation. *The sight of those three bodies will probably haunt me for days to come.*

"I graciously accept your offer," I said, not without a touch of irony, my gaze fixed on the woman's father. A flash of anger swept over his features, and his jaw tightened.

"You are free to walk along with us, but the cart will be too heavy if . . ." started the girl's father. I raised a hand to stop him.

Hopping in their cart wasn't my intention. Instead, I preferred to remain where I felt safe, inside my RV.

"Thank you, but I have my *cart* here." I patted the steel door.

"I can follow you," I continued, not trusting enough to invite them inside. Not after she just killed three people in cold blood, self-defense or not. The man breathed a sigh of relief.

"But you don't have any horses—how would you pull that after you?" asked the daughter, gesturing toward my vehicle.

My first intention was to laugh, but I stifled it quickly. "Don't worry, this baby has a few hundred horses under the hood." I gave her a polite smile.

"That's foolish."

"Alana!" said her father in a sharp tone, turning to his daughter, who blushed and looked at her feet.

"Excuse me," Alana said in an apologetic tone, not meeting my eyes.

"Don't worry about it," I said easily, not wanting to get on their bad side. "My vehicle doesn't need horses. I have gas and electricity, and even if the tank is empty, with this sun, I just need to extend the solar panels, and soon this beauty will be ready to drive." They looked at me as if I were speaking in a foreign language.

"Please excuse our ignorance, but we don't know what these words mean. Did my old ears hear that you have a hundred horses there?" His brows creased.

I grinned. "Something like that."

He gave me a calculated look, the one usually reserved for rabid dogs you're considering putting down. I averted my eyes, and my gaze fell on the spreading pool of blood surrounding the three bodies. I shuddered at the grisly sight, and when I inhaled, the metallic smell of blood assaulted my nostrils. Now I was glad I had an empty stomach. "So, what are we going to do with them? We can't just leave them here." I didn't feel comfortable leaving the corpses at the mercy of whatever animals patrolled these woods.

"We don't have the time to bury the bodies, and their people will soon find them," Alana's father said, glancing at the sky. "By sundown, at the latest. We must get going. We have already spent too much time in this place. If you wish to, you can follow us," he finished halfheartedly, giving me an odd look, like he wished I wouldn't.

I went inside the RV with a shred of hope dancing in my chest and checked the fifteen-inch tablet next to my driver's seat, wanting to get the GPS location. It was dead, with no signal from a cell tower or a satellite. Frustrated, I inspected the fuel levels. The gas tank was almost empty, and the batteries had less than thirty percent charge. I wanted to punch something. *Couldn't Sergio have dropped me near a gas station?* I had less than fifty miles left until the battery was depleted, but only if I kept my electric consumption to a minimum and used a paved road. In my current conditions, I estimated I had thirty, maybe thirty-five miles left. I took a paper map I kept next to my seat, the one I bought the first time I went hiking on Mont Salève, and tried to find my location on it. No luck. I could have been anywhere between Geneva and France. An urge to tear the map to pieces overwhelmed me. Instead, I folded it and put it in my back pocket as I stared through the windshield at the moving cart. With all my heart, I hoped they would bring me back to civilization; otherwise, I would remain stuck in whatever place this was.

These people were bonkers, and I didn't want to have

anything to do with a triple homicide. *If my phone will just get a signal soon...* I was planning to turn Alana and her father in. The evidence was clear. The arrows must have had the woman's fingerprints all over them. I would testify as a witness and let them know it was self-defense, but I couldn't let them off the hook and drag me into whatever feud they had.

I started the electric engine, and the RV responded immediately when I pressed on the accelerator. I had been afraid I'd have problems getting out of the swamp, but the wheels had a good grip. Ahead, the cart stopped, and both Alana and her father stared at me, their eyes bulging and mouths agape.

What now? I made a gesture for them to keep going, and they eventually did, reluctantly, sneaking glances every few seconds, talking between themselves, and pointing toward my car. Truth be told, weirdly, a part of me was pleased. Not many people had seen an RV such as mine. It was a luxury recreational vehicle, and with the improvements I'd requested, unique. A white, top-of-the-line deluxe motorhome, it had sports-car design lines; a panoramic helicopter-like windshield; tires, engine, and frame that allowed it to operate on extreme off-road terrains; and at my request, enough Dyneema, polycarbonate, and steel to give a tank a run for its money. I had heard stories about sketchy areas in Eastern Europe, so I wanted to be prepared for any eventuality. My father always told me to bring a gun to a knife fight.

The RV was probably the one thing my father would be proud of, since I hadn't followed in his footsteps and joined the army. He had taken me with him every time he was stationed in a different city or country, and I had been grateful to him for not sending me to a boarding school, even though I didn't make any lasting friendships. But he had my future planned out for me, and that was where our opinions diverged.

Over the years, having been exposed to military life, daily training, and weekly trips to the shooting range, I grew to like computers more than guns. I hadn't enjoyed being pressured into doing something, even though my father said I was good at it. But then again, that's what all parents say. We had some heated conversations, and when I didn't back away, he did. My father hadn't told me in so many words, but I didn't think he would ever forgive me in his heart.

I sighed and forced those thoughts out of my head. If I wanted to get back to Geneva, I needed information; I needed to know my location. I was driving at a turtle's pace, on a trail barely wide enough for my vehicle, with branches hitting and scraping the frame and windshield. It was annoying, but it gave me plenty of time to open the Maps app and recheck my GPS.

Unfortunately, even though the seller had assured me it was the best and most reliable brand, my phone remained dead with no connectivity.

I followed the man and woman at a safe distance, munching on a protein bar and analyzing my situation.

There were two, maybe three possibilities. One was that Sergio had played a prank on me. The second was that somehow, I had driven here by myself. And third, the most unlikely one, was that I had traveled back in time. I almost laughed out loud at my thoughts.

From those three, the only one that made some sense was that Sergio was involved. Maybe, with some incredible luck, driving here by myself was possible, too. I wasn't great at holding down my liquor.

Time travel, on the other hand, was possible only in movies and books. In the real world, I knew of at least one paradox that stood in its way: the grandfather paradox. One cannot change the past without altering the future. If such a thing were possible, then if I stepped on an insect, it might throw the world and its future into chaos. No, I had to follow the Occam's razor principle—the simplest explanation was most likely correct. As Theodore Woodward once said, "When you hear hoofbeats, think of horses, not zebras." My hypothetical horse here was the unfortunate prank that had left me in the middle of the forest next to Mont Salève.

It was the simplest, but a few details didn't fit. *Why were the three riders wearing those clothes and wielding those weapons? Why did Alana and her father seem so surprised when they saw my RV? Why is their behavior so strange? It's like they're from a different time.*

I remembered the conversation my colleagues and I had the night before. I had been utterly fascinated by my colleagues' discussions about Geneva's history, especially as Francesca, a Ph.D. in physics with a background in history, loved to contradict Etienne every time he said something inaccurate. Etienne was French but had been raised in the Geneva canton. However, he must have not paid attention to his history classes, because Francesca found holes in his stories and things to add every time Etienne described the city's rich history.

"Since the first century, Geneva had been an independent settlement occupied by the Celts . . ." Etienne had explained.

"Actually, Etienne, Caesar had conquered it decades before. In fact, in the year 58 BCE, he changed his mind from attacking Romania for its precious metals, and he destroyed the bridge over the lower Rhône at Geneva, which he then established as a Roman city," Francesca had said, interrupting Etienne's explanation, her sparkling eyes staring straight at him, making him blush.

Something about this discussion nagged at me, but I couldn't put my finger on what.

As I asked myself those questions, a theory presented itself. What if they were Amish? Or Amish-like? Maybe they were part of a group of people who lived in isolation from the outside world. I tried to remember what I knew about the Amish lifestyle. I knew they preferred plain clothes that didn't attract attention to the wearer, and they didn't use electricity, phones, computers, cars, or anything else I considered modern. They were also peaceful people, and what I witnessed earlier had been anything but that.

With questions cornering me at every step, I gave up and asked the onboard computer to open up Spotify. I selected a playlist I'd downloaded in advance and tried to enjoy driving my RV, following two people who behaved as if they hadn't seen a car in their entire lives.

I would have enjoyed it even more if not for my constant headache. Without that, and without the image of the three bodies popping up in my head, I would have appreciated the quiet, peaceful forest, exactly how I imagined my vacation to be. But my mind didn't want to relax; it wanted to go back to the earlier events. The harder I tried to bury them, the more things popped up, exacerbating my headache and inviting dread into my heart. Exhausted, I gave in.

My dad used to tell me stories about the various places he was stationed with the army, but he skipped over the gory details of injuries and deaths. I thought I would freak out the first time I saw someone die, but that wasn't the case now. In my mind's eye I saw it on their faces—the malicious glee when they wanted to kill Alana and her father—and I understood why Alana did what she did. It was the survival instinct, the one we all have in us.

A few hours later, Alana and her father stopped their cart near a small clearing, traversed by a narrow river, to give the pony time to rest. He leapt from the cart like he was a man ten years younger, went to the back, and took out a piece of gray cloth. Through the windshield, I saw him unwrap stale bread and share half with Alana.

I extended the RV's solar panels to trickle some energy into the batteries. *Should I offer them some of my food?* During the last few hours, I hadn't noticed any murderous tendencies. They almost looked like a couple of regular folks, barring their clothes, bow, and the quiver full of arrows. Better to offer an olive branch. Kindness could go a long way. I took a bottle of water and two protein bars and went out of the vehicle. Tyrenn pinned me down with a look that raised the hair on the back of my head. If looks could kill, I would be feast for the crows. *What's wrong with this guy?* I climbed on the roof.

At that height, the view was spectacular. A carpet made of fifty shades of green lay ahead of me, hiding a multitude of living things underneath it, judging by the sounds they made. It was a peaceful and mesmerizing concert, enriched by the mist rising from inside the forest, like smoke from a sleeping dragon's nostrils. It felt surreal, as if I had stepped into a storybook of times long forgotten.

But that wasn't the main reason I'd climbed up there. With my hands trembling, I took the phone out of my pocket and raised it above my head. Nothing. No signal at all. *Where are all the satellites, the cell towers?*

"How did you scare their horses?" asked Alana when I climbed down. Her father was by the stream, looking after the pony, and she was tidying up the things in their cart.

"Oh, I just honked," I answered, a little sheepish.

"Honked?"

"The RV has a horn inside. I press on a button, and the RV makes that sound."

"Is this something you made?"

"The RV or the horn?" She pointed to the RV. "No, I just bought it."

"Where? I haven't seen or heard of anything like this."

I had told no one how I gained the money to afford such a thing. My colleagues assumed my family was wealthy, and I didn't correct them. But being here, lost in the woods, with no trace of civilization around me, made me think I could get this off my chest. It bothered me that I couldn't tell anyone how in my first month at CERN, by using the facility's computing power and prediction models, I had applied advanced machine learning algorithms to "guess" the lotto numbers two weeks in a row. Across three different countries. Combined with my Bitcoin mining, using CERN's powerful processors, I gained a sizable fortune in a relatively short time. I was careful to run everything only in the wee hours of the night, and only when the systems were crunching data from various experiments.

"Are you familiar with lotto, Bitcoin mining, or machine learning?" I guessed the answer by the puzzled expression on her face.

"You speak with strange words, and your clothes are like nothing I've seen before," Alana said after a few moments of silence. "What are you?"

I wanted to laugh, but I understood why she asked. To her, I was out of place, like the latest mobile phone model in an antique shop. Instead, I kept quiet and shrugged. *Let her think whatever she wants. The faster I return to a civilized city, the easier it will be to sort all this out and get back to my vacation.* She kept looking at me expectantly, so I borrowed a page from the Greek legend of Odysseus and the Cyclops.

"Don't mind me, I'm Nobody. Can I ask you something?" I needed to detour the conversation to something that was bothering me. She seemed willing to talk, unlike her father, who hadn't said a word to me since we left the clearing.

"Of course."

"Why are you speaking to me? I mean, your father doesn't seem to want to have anything to do with me, unless I misjudged him."

"My father…isn't afraid of many things, but is cautious of what he cannot understand." She looked down at her feet. "He said you command an ancient spirit bound to your carriage and thinks that what we heard was the scream of the spirit, who sucked the life out of those men and horses. My father is afraid you might do the same to us."

"Do what?"

"Sacrifice us to Donn, the god of death, and bind our souls to do your bidding."

I laughed. "I can promise you I command no spirits. And you? Aren't you afraid too?"

She paused for a moment. "I'm not afraid of you." Alana's gaze met mine, and her brown eyes had an intensity I had not noticed before. "I know I should be, but I'm not. I have heard tales, and once, I saw a shaman passing by our village. You do not resemble one of them. Your carriage isn't black, nor do you have skulls and dead plants hanging around it. Your smell is that of the sweet flowers, and your eyes don't have the haunted look of one who deals with the souls of the dead."

"Thank you, I guess, and you're right, I'm not one of those shamans." Those guys didn't sound friendly at all. *Are they morticians?*

"Then, what are you?"

Not what, but who. "I'm a human, like you. I just come from a part of the world more advanced than what I've seen here."

"From the Delightful Plain, where there is no sickness, people are always young, and happiness lasts forever?"

If only. I smiled. "Not exactly. Look, I meant to ask you something. Where are we? If I show you a map, can you tell me?"

"A map?"

"Let me show you." I unfolded the paper map. "I think we're in France, probably somewhere here, near Beaumont. See, it's this mountain," I said, pointing to where the map displayed Salève. "The green areas are forests and grass. Do you know where we are?"

Her eyes remained glued to it, like a baby seeing colors for the first time in her life.

An idea came to me, picked a nearby branch and started drawing on the ground. It didn't take long, and I had a rough map of the area at my feet. I was no van Gogh, but I hoped she would understand.

To her credit, she recovered quickly.

"My father taught me how to write and draw on thin leaves of wood and the bark of trees, but this . . ." she said, studying my map without touching it. "I've never imagined anything like it." She glanced at my scribbles and at the mountain, which was clearly visible through the trees. "If that's the one"—she pointed to the looming mountain—"you are correct. We are here." Her finger hovered where I drew the border with France.

"Then, we're in France?" *Finally, I have an answer.*

"I don't know where France is, but I know we're on Lord Ambenix's lands."

Again with this name. "Then how come you speak English and not French or some other language?"

"I don't know what English or French is, but I speak the same language you do. Except when you use odd words I'm not familiar with."

A thought occurred to me, and I decided to see if she was telling the truth.

"Bonjour, comment allez-vous?"

"Hello to you, too, I'm fine," she replied with a smile.

"See, so you know French," I said triumphantly.

"I told you, I do not know what that is. You just said hello and asked how I was," Alana's smile was gone.

"Yes, but I asked you in another language, not this one we're using right now."

"No, you spoke the same tongue."

I nodded, disappointed I couldn't confirm even this basic thing. Back to square one.

At that moment, my headache spiked, and I had to close my eyes, gently rubbing my temples.

"Are you injured?" Alana's voice betrayed concern.

I tried to shake my head—a big mistake. My brain was swimming and banging to the sides of my skull, and pain flared as if something had exploded inside my head. I groaned. "Just this damn headache. I'm not even sure how much I drank last night. Should have known better." I moaned in pain and sat on the cold, damp ground.

I heard her move away but didn't open my eyes. I continued pressing my temples with my thumbs to ease the pain.

"Try this." Carefully, I peered through one half-open eyelid. She held a brown clay bowl in her hands.

"What is it?" I studied the small bowl filled with a creamy liquid, the color of dark-red wine.

"It will help."

I hoped it wasn't poison, but if she wanted to kill me, she had already had plenty of chances. Plus, the concoction didn't smell too bad. It had a rich, earthy scent, like grass after a rain, combined with a fruity aroma, similar to blueberries. I drank it. It tasted exactly how it smelled. The sweet flavor of fruits, combined with an unusual flavor from grass, mushrooms, and some vegetables I didn't recognize, enveloped my taste buds. My body grew tense, waiting for something to happen. The pain receded, but the concoction didn't seem to have any other immediate effect.

"Thank you." I handed Alana back the bowl. She placed it next to her but kept her eyes on me.

"May I try something?"

I nodded, curious to see what she wanted to do.

She placed her palms to my ears and gently pressed her icy fingers to my temples. With circular motions, she started rubbing, and I closed my eyes. It felt heavenly, like a coiled spring set loose. Her palms smelled of herbs, and her fingers felt like the most natural thing, a perfect fit in the hollows on my temples. My body relaxed, and my mind drifted away, scattered like dust in a whirlwind. But I soon snapped back, like a rubber band, when she stopped and pulled her hands away from my temples.

"It will take some time, but your pain will be gone." Her tone was full of confidence, like a seasoned doctor giving a diagnosis.

I stared at her. This person was totally different from the Amazonian woman from earlier.

Maybe it was the fact she helped me, or the way she talked, but I decided to trust her and extended my hand. "I'm Duncan. Duncan Drake." Alana studied it for a moment, then gripped my hand and shook it. Her skin was delicate, but I felt the strength behind her grip. She raised her gaze, and her breath caught when her eyes met mine. Seconds passed, and her touch grew warmer. Her dark chocolate eyes were hypnotic, and they pulled me in, like a metal caught by an invisible magnetic force.

"Alana, it's time to leave this place," her father's sharp voice broke the spell. Alana's face grew pink, and she rushed to her father's side, on top of the cart.

For a short time, I remained there, a knot in my stomach. It was a strange feeling, one I had never felt before and didn't know how to interpret it. It was like I was drawn to her. Not wanting to lose sight of the cart, I went back into my RV and continued following Alana on the lovely rhythms of "Time" by Hans Zimmer. When I'd reached the last song on the playlist, my headache was gone.

2

The trees opened up, and an emerald green field emerged ahead, its vibrant color one I'd seen in paintings from long ago. Rickety wooden houses spread across the grassland, all the way to a fort surrounded by a wooden wall, its silhouette illuminated by the red disc of the setting sun. Golden hay, green crops, and brown sheds stood empty on both sides of the RV. I expected children and adults to run toward the car, shouting, pointing, waving, but it was eerily quiet—only a dog's bark here and there.

My hopes of finding a working phone or a Wi-Fi signal to find my way out to civilization came spiraling down. The farms looked deserted, like the villagers had run away in a hurry, leaving everything abandoned. A few stray dogs rummaged for food, content to growl in warning and let me know this was now their territory.

When I approached the fortification, the farm animals'

cacophony became loud and clear, as if all the beasts from the village had been moved inside the fort.

I took a moment to study the entrance and the protective wooden wall. The front gate was embedded between two inward-angled exterior walls and didn't look wide enough to drive through. A raised platform filled with archers stood atop the gate. People with spears and bows along its walls gawked, shouting and gesticulating in my direction.

What's wrong with them? Haven't they seen someone with an RV before?

Alana's father stopped the cart, turned, and motioned for me to follow them on foot. I gave him a thumbs up, but the expectant look on his face didn't change. I went past them and parked the RV next to the farmhouse closest to the gate. The front yard was big enough to fit my entire vehicle.

I turned off the engine, pocketed my phone and keys, then grabbed a jacket to ward off the evening's chill, along with a backpack containing a few things I thought would be useful. Prepared, I joined the two people waiting for me. By the time I exited the vehicle, their cart was already next to the entrance.

From above the gates, the incredulous eyes of people craning their necks over the sharp wooden spikes watched my every move.

"Let's go inside," said Alana's father, ignoring the archers on each side of the two walls. I followed them, trying to spy on the people above without being obvious. After the day I'd had, I thought nothing could surprise me anymore. I was wrong.

A pungent smell hit me like a rock, and my first thought was that I had stepped into a latrine. It reeked of odors I couldn't name and didn't even want to think about. Covering my nose with my jacket and inhaling slowly didn't help much; I still had the urge to throw up.

In an instant, a group of tall, bearded, unkempt men surrounded us, immediately intensifying the aroma. They wore brown tunics, green trousers, and pointed brown leather sandals. Swords and short axes dangled at their belts. Their aggressiveness made me queasy, frightened of what they would do next. Afraid to uncover my nose, I made no move to defend myself, but pulled my backpack closer in case they decided to be hostile. I had a knife inside, though I doubted I would survive long enough to pull it out if one of them wanted to skewer me.

"Are you some kind of shaman? How did you make that thing move without horses?" thundered one man in a harsh, basso voice. His square face hid behind a red, shaggy beard and bushy eyebrows.

I kept my mouth shut; otherwise, I would have laughed at the absurdity of his question. People from the village gathered around in a larger circle, all whispering and pointing at me and the gates, where my RV was.

"He is a powerful shaman, and came with us after we fled our village," answered Alana, looking over the crowd.

"And you are?" asked the same booming voice.

"My name is Tyrenn," replied Alana's father in a conciliatory tone. "Together with my daughter and this young man, we seek shelter from Orgetorix's army. We received word that his people were pillaging and burning the nearby villages on their way here."

"We know all that, old man." The man was built like an ox, with broad shoulders and arms thicker than some trees I'd seen on my way there. His right hand moved to his ax, although he didn't need one to break me in two like a rotten board. "He doesn't look like a powerful shaman. And even if he is, his kind is not welcomed here. In fact, we kill his kind if they step on our lands."

Tyrenn placed himself between the ox and me, his stance relaxed. He'd seemed more afraid of me than he was of this brute.

Alana stepped next to her father. "He helped us defeat three of Orgetorix's men. His carriage moves without horses, and what else but a spirit can do that? And who can command the spirits but a shaman? He can help us fight them," she said, as if schooling a child.

Murmurs of agreement rose from the surrounding crowd, and to my surprise, the big man's hand left the proximity of the ax. I understood why Alana wanted them to fear me. Having people afraid of you is a good method to be left alone and unchallenged. I hoped her bluff would work; otherwise, I would have been hard-pressed to impress them. What I didn't like was her insinuation I would help anyone in a fight. My primary goal was to go back home, and I had no interest in taking sides. This place didn't seem like it had any telephone or computer, and I wanted nothing more than to go back to my RV, but I doubted the archers above would let me take two steps outside the village.

For a moment, no one said anything, and several of the men surrounding me took a step back, fear written on their faces.

"Let's get him to Ambenix; he'll know what to do," said another rough voice from behind. Someone pushed me forward, and I almost fell face-first into the excrement-rich mud, eliciting laughs.

An arm stopped my descent and kept me from completely losing my balance. Alana's pale hand was thinner than mine, but her grip was firm, and her reflexes were as swift as a mongoose's strike. She was studying me, a thoughtful look on her face.

A sudden flash of insight made me realize this was the first moment she saw me for who I was: a young man out of his depth, vulnerable and scared.

I nodded my thanks and continued the forced march, escorted through what I thought was the main street, under the scrutiny of the people working their small gardens, feeding the pigs, or locking the chickens in haphazard sheds. Very few buildings resembled houses. Most looked like ramshackle wooden cottages and adobe huts, built from the same mix as the bog I stepped on. Separating them were dark alleys where packs of ownerless dogs rooted through the trash. A few beasts barked at me, and I moved closer to Alana' side. I could swear the dogs looked more vicious here than in any other place I'd visited.

Several minutes later, I arrived in front of a sizable wooden building, two stories high with a massive door. Four people stood next to it, each with an ax hanging on their belts, scrutinizing me. They wore the same clothes as my honor guard, except all four had a small, round, wooden shield, hanging by their brawny arms. Two of them, barely straining, opened the doors for Alana, her father, and I to enter. The ginger man and three others followed me inside.

The air was a tad more breathable here; it only smelled like dirty feet. Happily, I took a few deep breaths to ease my burning lungs from the strain they'd had to endure.

I was in a medium-sized room, similar to a CERN conference room, where you could seat maybe thirty people, except it didn't have a whiteboard, projector, padded chairs, electricity, or proper ventilation. Two square holes in the walls let in a trickle of light, illuminating the wooden benches and a large table where three people engaged in a heated discussion. On the other side of the table facing me sat a mountain of a man. He had black curly hair, a square jaw, a black beard in desperate need of a trim, and steely gray eyes that focused on me, ignoring everything else. A curtain of silence settled around the room.

"My Lord Ambenix," said the ginger with the basso voice, "these three have come to ask for our protection from Orgetorix's men, who are attacking our lands, raping and murdering our women and children." His tone revealed bitterness, and the hate was palpable.

What if this is just one giant renaissance fair? A small voice inside me whispered to be careful; they weren't playing by the same rules I was used to.

"Who are you?" asked Ambenix, his voice like rumbling thunder, ending my contemplation.

"My lord, my name is Tyrenn," said Alana's father with a bow, while one of the men surrounding me approached and leaned to whisper something in Ambenix's ear. "This is my daughter Alana, and this young man is Duncan, a shaman we've encountered on our way here. We came because—"

"I didn't ask why you came; I know why you're here. For protection, like all the others. Tell me, Tyrenn, can you fight? Can your daughter fight?"

"Yes, my lord, I've trained my daughter with both bow and sword."

"Good, we'll need you both if we are to prevail in the battle. Orgetorix's army will be upon us in the morning. You," he said, studying me with his cold gray eyes. "You say you're a shaman? My men told me you command a spirit that pulls a large carriage? Is that true?"

"I didn't say I was anything," I replied. I didn't want to confirm something I wasn't, but I didn't want to destroy the persona created by Alana and her father either. I hesitated for a moment, unsure of how to continue. I knew they couldn't help me, but a shred of hope forced me to at least try.

"Now, I don't want to be part of whatever you have going on here. If you could lend me a phone that works, a computer, a radio, anything I can use to communicate with the police or point me to the nearest highway, to civilization, I would much appreciate it." My heart raced, and I felt sweat trickling down my spine. My last hopes hung on his next words.

Whatever Ambenix expected me to say, I don't think this was it; his eyebrows rose, and his gaze moved to Tyrenn, who just shrugged.

C'mon on people. No one heard of a phone?

"I know you live away from everyone else, but surely you

must have heard of these things." I turned away from Ambenix to face the people around me. "Look, if I can just—"

I didn't have time to finish my sentence because something slammed into my back, and the force of the blow drove me to my knees. I turned my head to see who did it and Ambenix's cold eyes met mine.

"Your words mean nothing. I know how your kind is. You expect to be treated like kings, for people to give you everything you desire. Then you repay them with plague and madness. Let me tell you, the only thing you'll receive here is a swift death."

His eyes blazed, and his voice raged like a stormy sea crashing to the shore. A sharp crack reverberated through the room when he slammed his fist on the wooden table. I flinched. His penetrating gaze fixed on me like a rifle's scope, and I felt sweat pouring from every pore of my body. We stayed like that for a moment, him waiting for a reply, me trembling where I stood. My mind froze, unable to process what was going on. He took a deep breath and leaned back in his chair.

"If you're not able to help us, if you don't want to fight, then I'll grant you a quick death and burn your body and the carriage you came with. We can't spare anyone to guard you, and we can't let you go either. You'll be caught, tortured for whatever scraps of information you can provide, and killed, so better to be done now. It will be a mercy compared to the other fate waiting for you."

He gave a quick nod to someone behind me, and I felt cold steel at my throat. I saw no mercy in Ambenix's eyes, just an icy determination. He was ready to have my head cut off.

What is wrong with everyone? I was on my knees, about to

have my head chopped off, because I asked for a phone. Energy had left my body; my lips were dry, and I felt like fainting. *What have I done to deserve this? God, I promise I will do anything if I survive. I won't ever mine bitcoin again.*

"Don't kill him! He can help me—he'll be my varlet," cried Alana.

Energy coursed through me again, ignited by her words. I focused my gaze on her but didn't turn my head, afraid I would cut myself with the steel touching my neck. Alana's pale cheeks reddened like a strawberry, but she didn't avert her eyes from Ambenix.

He seemed to consider her request, and a few moments later, drew in a sharp breath. His steely eyes swept over me, made a small nod, and the blade moved away from my throat. I let go of the breath I was holding. *I've never been so close to dying.* A feeling of immense gratitude swept over me. I owed Alana my life.

"You know what this means—he will be your responsibility," Ambenix said gravely. "One wrong step and you both die, if not by my hand, then by the enemy's hand."

"Yes, my lord," replied Alana and bowed.

"You," said Ambenix, looking straight into my eyes, "should consider yourself lucky such a brave woman protected you. In her place, I would have fed you to the dogs. From now on, you follow all her instructions; otherwise, I have a pack of hungry dogs waiting for you outside. Is that clear?"

I nodded, too stunned to think of a reply. I didn't want to go anywhere near the dogs in these parts. Alana came next to me and pulled my arm, urging me to follow her.

Outside, the smell wasn't as bad as I remembered. I must have gotten used to it, or it seemed less important after my close encounter with death.

"So, what now?" I asked, my voice trembling slightly.

"Now, we need to find a place to rest and eat something. Tomorrow's going to be a long day," replied Alana and headed after her father, who seemed to know the town.

A few minutes later I was back at the front gate, where Tyrenn and Alana had left their cart. My heart leaped when I saw the massive doors. On the other side was my home. Safety. A longing sensation I'd never experienced before embraced me. I was like a flea on a dog's fur. One scratch and my life would be over. However, if I made it to my RV, Ambenix's threats would soon become a thing of the past.

But the gates were closed and immovable as a mountain, with spearmen and archers guarding them, and my hopes sank into the depths of Tartarus.

With no other option, I accompanied Alana and Tyrenn through the muddy streets. Each step, each roll of the wheels, grew the seed of fear within me.

Once again, alone among strangers. I was used to it, but at least at home, I knew the rules. Here, apparently even asking for a telephone could result in a death sentence.

I looked up and asked silently for a way out, but no answer came. The splendor above hypnotized me. I stared in admiration at the artistic colors painted over the vast celestial arena as the sun set behind the blush wine sky.

"Are you coming?" Alana asked, pulling my sleeve. With a silent sigh, I lowered my gaze and continued my walk.

The town wasn't big, and most of the ramshackle houses were square shaped and made of ill-fitting wooden planks with thatched roofs of straw and mud. Chickens, sheep, and cows cluttered the place, all crammed together along the streets and in barns and sheds. Everywhere, I saw people dressed in rags, children crying, and men with defeated looks on their faces. *No one thinks they'll survive tomorrow.*

Tyrenn, who hadn't said a word since we left the hall, led Alana and me through dark alleys where even the light was afraid to enter. A few times, my heart jumped out of my chest when I heard people begging or laughing maniacally from the darkness. Tyrenn stopped in front of a shabby-looking shed. From inside came loud voices, shouting, and a strong smell of alcohol. I assumed this was the town's version of a restaurant.

Tyrenn guided the cart next to a rundown-looking stable situated across the tavern. Inside were two stalls large enough to hold a wagon and a horse. Two children, a woman, and a man occupied a wagon in one of the stalls. The children and the woman covered some hay with a cloth to make a bed. The man looked me over with suspicion but said nothing.

With practiced movements, Tyrenn took the harness off the pony and led it and the cart inside the empty stall.

"We must buy some food. I'll see if they have any bread and spice soup, and then we can have a meal together." Tyrenn pulled out a short sword from the cart, where it had been concealed behind a threadbare bag. In the folds of his cloak, it disappeared as if swallowed by quicksand. Everything happened so fast, if I had blinked, I would have missed it. His movements had been agile for a man of his age, far nimbler than I could be.

Tyrenn's attitude had changed since we'd exited Ambenix's place. He seemed warmer toward me, and I thought I understood why. When I first met him, he had been afraid of me, fearful of what I could do. But when I had been a moment away from dying, he must have taken pity on me. Or he realized I was no threat, and his attitude had shifted.

"Duncan, please forgive me," he said. "I shouldn't have let some old wives' tales affect my judgment. I'm glad Alana did what she did."

All my resentment melted at his words, and I inclined my head.

"You are free to join us, young man. We'll share the few things we have."

My stomach turned at the thought of the food I had seen while I walked through the town as I imagined how it was cooked. Then it growled, reminding me I hadn't eaten since morning. Alana lit a small candle, the only source of light in the stall, and put it on top of a square rag, which I assumed was the table.

"Thank you for saving my life," I told them. "I appreciate your offer and willingness to share your food with me, but I already have some, and I can share it. I think it might be better than what they have there," I said in a polite tone, pointing to the tavern. Inside my backpack, I had several protein bars and water bottles, which I pulled out and spread on the cloth lying on the ground. Each bar had at least twenty grams of protein, five grams of fiber, and several hundred calories.

Both looked at me, unsure of what to do.

"Oh, right, you've never seen anything like this before, have you?" Neither of them replied. "Let me show you." I opened one of the protein bars and handed it to Alana. I took one and motioned for Tyrenn to take one too. Alana studied it like it was something found in the woods behind a tree. I wanted to laugh but decided against it; I was alive thanks to her. I took a bite out of mine to show them it wasn't poisoned and started chewing. Alana's face lit up, eyes closed, as she savored her first reluctant bite.

"It tastes sweet. What kind of food is this?" Her tone was full of admiration.

"It has dates, peanuts, and eggs," I answered. Alana shrugged and continued chewing.

Tyrenn unwrapped his with a forceful movement, almost spilling its content on the ground. He took the protein bar between his thumb and forefinger, looked at it, sniffed it, then started chewing. He grimaced and spat it out.

"What's wrong? It isn't good?" I asked, worried it had gone past the expiration date.

"It is sweeter than honey," he said, after taking a few swigs from the waterskin he'd filled at the stream earlier.

I had a replacement for that, too. "This is bottled water, and it's safe to drink. Here you go, take one." I handed them a bottle each. "You just need to unscrew the cap and drink it. When you're done, put the cap back like this." I took one bottle, twisted the cap, took a sip, and then screwed it back on.

Alana was the first to try. Her eyes were gleaming, and her face radiated with pleasure.

"It tastes like water from a mountain spring," she exclaimed. "And look, it even has a drawing of a mountain."

"I have more in my RV if you're interested," I said nonchalantly, secretly hoping she would help me get outside the town.

Her father frowned. "You can't go outside. It's late, and they won't open the gate," said Tyrenn, guessing my intention. "We were lucky they allowed us in. By now, Orgetorix's scouts must be in the forest, circling around like vultures, searching for a way in."

He went to the cart and took out the bag where they kept their food. It had only half of a round bread and two apples. At his unspoken question, Alana shook her head and continued munching at the protein bar, her finger tracing the contour of the letters on the wrapping.

I pondered over the events I'd been thrust into since morning. Unease crept up on me. There was no sign of technology nor civilization. People here behaved strangely—killing someone seemed to be a part of their daily lives. *Am I part of a weird experiment?*

"Do you know what year this is?" I asked Alana.

She shrugged and shook her head.

Of course she doesn't know.

"We should rest. It's getting dark, and tomorrow we'll need all our strength," Tyrenn said and handed me the empty bottle. He stood, then moved closer to where the pony ate the hay spread on the ground, patted its neck, and lay down on the hay.

I pulled the phone out of my pocket to check the time. The screen displayed Saturday, 20:53.

"What is that?" asked Alana, peering over my shoulder, a

quizzical smile on her face. "How can it make light? Does it have a fire inside?"

"No, it doesn't have a fire inside," I replied, amused by her question and conscious of her proximity. Her breath tickled my ear, and I briefly forgot I was in a God-forsaken village with no prospects of getting home.

"Then how does it make light?"

"There's a battery that converts chemical energy to electrical energy. The electrical energy powers up this device."

She frowned. "And what do you do with it?"

"You can use it to make calls and talk to people."

"But can't you just talk like we do right now?"

"Not if the other person is far away. A phone allows you to talk to someone like they were here, next to you, no matter where they are."

"Can you talk to someone now?"

"Not now, because I don't have a signal."

"Signal?"

I tapped at the top of the screen. "You see, to use it, you need a cell tower that relays the data back and forth. The tower is the thing that provides the signal."

"Like that tower?" She pointed at a tall wooden structure, a platform raised above the wall surrounding the town. With so many twists and turns, I had lost my sense of direction. *I'm not far from the entrance.* This gave me hope. Maybe when everyone was asleep, I would have a chance to get out.

"Not exactly," I replied, my thoughts exploring different escape possibilities.

"I think I should clean my weapons," she said after a while and moved farther away.

From the cart, she pulled out a bow and a quiver of arrows, then a short sword, the blade gleaming in the light filtering through the tavern's windows. She made a few swift movements with it, as if fighting invisible enemies. They were smooth and precise, and I realized that she had been doing this all her life.

Panic gripped me at the foreignness of it all, at how alone I was. I needed to escape, to go to my RV and find my way back to civilization, if that was even possible. *Maybe during the battle tomorrow I will have an opportunity.*

Once Alana finished her moves, she placed the sword in her lap and started sharpening it on a stone she got from a torn leather bag. The scraping sound of metal on rock made my teeth hurt.

I pulled out my headphones and went to lie down by the wall with the backpack under my head. I put one earbud in my ear and selected a playlist on my phone to drown out the blade's harsh noise. I closed my eyes to the undulating sounds of "Blood Sweat and Tears" from the *Leap!* soundtrack. I wished for all this to be just a dream, and that when I awoke, I would be home, back in my apartment.

3

I jolted in panic at screams and shouts in the semi-darkness of the room. Rolled on my side, I reached for the bedside lamp and groaned at the dull pain in my back. Alana and Tyrenn were standing, swords in hands, focused on the entrance like some invisible enemy was ready to attack.

I was in a stable, and it hadn't been a dream.

"Hey, what's going on?"

Alana gestured for me to keep quiet.

A faint voice came through the stable's wall behind me.

"Captain Lann, our watchmen found three scouts. One was killed. They are bringing the other two in." Heavy footsteps followed the words.

Tyrenn and Alana darted toward the stable's exit at the sound of the footsteps. I grabbed my backpack and scrambled after them. By the city gates, a group of guards brought in two limping men. An arrow protruded from one man's arm.

Ambenix, along with three guards, headed straight for the newcomers. The moment Ambenix reached them, the one with only an injured leg lunged toward him, a small blade in his hand.

A fraction of a second later, two blades flashed, the steel gleaming in the surrounding torchlight. One severed the man's hand, and the other one decapitated the attacker. The body fell backward, lifeless, with blood spurting from the stump, and the head rolled at Ambenix's feet.

My blood ran cold. This man wasn't bluffing about killing. Whatever doubts I had lurking in the dark corners of my mind evaporated. This wasn't a joke; it was real, and these people were insane.

It was the first time I had ever seen someone dying such a violent death, and I felt sick. I braced myself to stop the tremble in my hands. The pungent metallic air closed in on me. I shut my eyes. My mind kept replaying the moment the head rolled to the ground, eyes open and unblinking. I needed air, fresh air. I needed to get out; I would asphyxiate if I stayed there a moment longer.

"It will pass," Alana said, her hand on my shoulder. "Is this your first time seeing someone decapitated?"

Is this your first time? What kind of question is that? I nodded, not trusting my voice. The familiar sour taste of bile filled my mouth.

"He attacked Ambenix; he attacked us. You don't want them to kill us, do you?"

I focused on taking small breaths, ignoring the foul smells until things settled inside me. "Of course not," I replied through my clenched jaw.

"Good. Now hold on to that anger and don't let go. It will help you overcome this," Alana assured me in a knowing tone. *How many decapitations had she witnessed?*

I took a deep breath—a big mistake, because the smell of excrement combined with blood plunged into my nostrils, and I started coughing. Alana guided me behind a barn, putting the gruesome scene behind me.

"You keep on helping me," I said, once I had my wits back. "First with my headache and now with this. Why is that?"

She shrugged. "You look like a young man who needs help."

"So, I'm not the scary shaman you're telling everyone about?"

That made her smile. "No. You're something I've never seen or heard of before, but you're not one of them. They have something that makes my skin crawl. You don't."

"Fair enough." I looked past her shoulder to the crowd, which was now dispersing, the soldiers climbing the ladders to reach the wall's top.

"Do you think they'll attack now?"

She shrugged. "Probably not. I'm not sure if those two were scouts or assassins. There may be a few more sent to observe what happened and gather information about our defenses. They'll be more careful, and it won't be easy to catch them."

Too bad I don't have access to a satellite. Then another thought struck me, and I wanted to slap myself for not thinking of it sooner. I could have used a drone to check where the nearest city was. At least during the night, it should have been easier to spot the city lights. I only needed a moment by myself, away from prying eyes. And once I knew where to go, I needed to get back to my vehicle. *What if I played my role as a shaman and helped them find the spies? Would they let me get back to the RV?*

"Hey, I have an idea, but we need to find a place without too many people and less light."

"I can ask my father, but what do you want to do?"

"I think I can help detect when someone is coming, but I have to try it first before I can be sure."

"Wait here," she said and went back to speak to Tyrenn. Plans started forming in my mind, on both finding the alleged scouts and finding a way out. If I gained their trust, maybe I could fool them into letting me out of the village. *And then, bye bye, suckers.*

"Come with me," Alana commanded. I would have preferred to do this by myself, but I needed her.

We walked farther away into the village, always keeping left.

"Is this good?" Alana pointed to a patch by the wall, obscured by two trees.

"Yes, it's great." I knelt, opened my backpack, and found the object I was looking for. I pulled out a black plastic case containing a top-of-the-line drone and its controller. I had bought it to spy on the nightlife at night, so I'd opted for thermal and infrared cameras and a transmission distance of a few kilometers. It was excellent for what I had in mind.

A chilly breeze caressed my cheek. The sky, illuminated by thousands of tiny dots of diffuse light, was perfect for what I intended. I connected my phone to the controller, opened the app, turned off the beacon, unfolded the propellers, and launched the quadcopter. It hovered in front of me, waiting for my commands and humming like a small swarm of bees.

A gasp escaped Alana's lips. I turned to face her, and a cold metal poked at my throat. Her face, barely visible, was hard, her eyes full of anger.

"You lied to me. You do control spirits. Is that why you told me to come along with you? To take mine?"

"No, wait," I said, trying to lift my arms, but the cold steel pressed into my throat. "It's not a spirit. It's a drone," I exclaimed.

She bit her lips, then the pressure of the steel recessed. Alana took a step back but kept the unwavering blade in front of me.

"What *is* that, if not a spirit?"

"I haven't lied to you. It's just a device that uses a battery, like my phone. It uses electricity, just like lightning—"

"Lightning is sent by the gods when they are angry. And I see no storm or clouds above us." Her voice was devoid of any warmth.

It was my turn to remain quiet. My mind rushed through several explanations, but I couldn't come up with anything believable.

"Let me show you. I promise no harm will come to you."

"And how do I know you'll keep your promise?"

"Well, you have your sword ready to cut through me if I don't. Right now, I'm going to press on this," I lifted my left hand holding the phone, "and the drone will lift up above the trees. Then it will go around the camp and search for scouts."

She nodded, and I breathed a sigh of relief. I pressed a button, and the drone shot straight up until it reached an altitude of thirty meters, way above the tree line. I didn't want to push it more, afraid the wind would pick up and interfere with my plan.

Heart hammering in my chest, I turned the drone in a 360-degree arc. Twice. Then three times. I pushed it higher another ten meters and repeated the process. I got the same result. Pitch black, like a veil of darkness, covered the entire area. Everything around the village was black as tar.

My heart sank, all traces of hope gone. I wasn't in Kansas anymore. *But where am I?*

I recalled the drone to a lower altitude, programmed it to follow a circular pattern, and sent it to patrol around the camp. The drone disappeared into the blackness of night. All this time, Alana said nothing, watching me. I put down the controller, and she lowered the sword.

"Magic," she whispered, her fingers covering her mouth. "I've never seen a bird like that. It sounded like a horde of flies."

"We call this a drone. It will fly around the camp and send us what it sees."

"But it's night," she argued.

"This one can see very well into the night."

"Like a cat?"

"Exactly," I agreed with a smile, happy she was willing to listen. "Let me show you."

I switched to the drone's thermal camera and arranged the phone so Alana could watch it.

"What is this?" She pointed at my phone, the screen

displaying the trees below with small blue and purple spots, depicting nocturnal animals.

"Through it, we can see what the drone sees. You can come closer; I promise it won't bite."

"What are those colors?"

"Small animals. A person or a larger animal would be orange or yellow. Look, if I read this map right, it will be over us in a few seconds." True to my guess, two bright yellow dots, close to each other, showed up on the screen. I paused the drone and turned to face Alana.

"Move back two steps."

She threw me a suspicious look but said nothing and did as I asked. One dot moved slightly on my screen.

"Now come back," I said and pointed to the display. The dot moved again.

"You hold it, and I'll move."

The arm holding the blade lifted a few centimeters but then stopped, and she extended her left hand, palm up. I placed the phone in her open hand and moved back, my shoulders touching the wooden wall.

"It moved," she exclaimed.

"I know," I replied, moving toward her, and lifting the device from her outstretched hand, careful not to impale myself on her sword.

"See? Nothing hurt you, like I promised. Let me set it to start patrolling again."

"I'm sorry for not believing you," she said, her voice tight. My gaze moved back to her. The sword had disappeared from her hand.

"No, it's my fault. I should have explained what I wanted to do."

She shook her head. "You told me before you come from a world different from mine. I never imagined how much different. You're doing things I've never even dreamed of."

"Well, now maybe you will," I said, glad to have earned her trust. "Let's see what we can find."

Alana leaned her head next to mine, a few strands of her hair touching my cheek. The heat of her skin warmed me like a blanket on a winter night. I didn't dare move or look at her because I was afraid she'd leave, so I stayed as unmoving as a statue, enjoying her proximity.

"Look," exclaimed Alana.

With great reluctance, I opened my eyes to view three big orange dots painted on my phone's screen. Based on their position, they were in the surrounding forest, north of my location.

"What should we do?" I asked, excited, all my fantasies replaced by a surge of adrenaline.

"Are those people?"

"Yes, those three are definitely people, and they are outside the walls, in the forest."

"Let's go tell Ambenix," said Alana, and pulled me after her. I barely had time to set the drone to follow one of the targets.

I approached the largest structure in the camp where I almost got my head chopped off. *Not again.* The four guards positioned themselves to block my way in.

"We need to see Ambenix," demanded Alana, her voice firm. I was still trying to catch my breath.

"No one is allowed in," thundered one guard.

"Maybe we should wait here," I said, panting. She ignored me.

"He divined the location of the enemy scouts." Alana jerked her thumb in my direction.

Before the guard had time to answer, the door opened. The man who'd cut the arm and head of the assassin stepped out, and in a booming voice asked, "What's this ruckus?"

"Sorry, Captain Lann. These two wanted to get in," replied the guard.

His gaze settled on me. "Oh, it's you again. What do you want? The dogs are still hungry."

Alana didn't seem worried by Lann's words. "We need to see Ambenix. We know where the enemy spies are."

He moved his gaze to her and raised his eyebrows. His tall, lean figure and neatly trimmed short beard gave him an air of superiority among the unkempt barbarians in his company. The deep blue eyes, dark hair tied in a ponytail, and two swords at his belt reminded me of the covers of the romance novels my colleague Francesca hid in her office drawer.

"How do you know?"

"Like we've said, he is a shaman. He has a spirit flying over them as we speak."

Lann and the guards turned to stare at me, expectantly. "Like she said, I have a spirit," I replied stupidly. Lann's frown deepened, and I had the impression Alana rolled her eyes. "I mean, it can observe someone in the woods during nighttime. There are three of them, right here." Using my finger, I drew on the ground an approximation of the camp and the three scouts' location. *I really need to wash my hands with industrial detergent.*

Lann studied the drawing for a few seconds, then turned and headed back.

"Make sure they remain here," he said to the four guards as he stepped inside.

"Yes, Captain Lann," replied the four men in unison.

A minute later, Lann came out and started running toward a group of people gathered around a campfire near the gate.

"If it's a trap, kill them," Lann shouted over his shoulder, just as I was breathing a sigh of relief.

People—mostly men, but some women and children as well—had gathered around to see what was happening, and some snickered at Lann's words. *Is everyone so eager to see people killed? Can't they find some other form of entertainment?*

The warriors spread into two groups and headed out the gates in the direction I showed them. I took the controller from my pocket, bumped Alana's elbow to get her attention, and I settled in to watch what was happening. Ten orange dots slowly encircled the three spies I'd located.

"What trouble have you gotten yourselves into this time?" asked Tyrenn as he joined Alana. She explained briefly, based on her understanding, what was happening. The four guards listened intently. Alana used words like "magic," "spirits," and "summoning." I wasn't sure if she believed everything or said them to impress the audience. I smiled to myself and continued watching the ten dots encircle the other three. There might have been a struggle—orange bubbles came together—but soon, thirteen dots headed toward the village.

"They're coming back with the spies," I told Alana, loud enough for the people surrounding me to hear. The four guards and Tyrenn looked surprised, but Alana nodded knowingly. She was the only one who'd seen the drone up close and understood the images on my phone.

Several minutes later, a group of people, surrounding three men bound and gagged, marched toward the building behind me. Whispers from the bug-eyed crowd replaced the silent anticipation.

"Looks like you won't be food for dogs," commented Lann in passing, heading toward the doors. Our four guards rushed to open them, leaving us unsupervised. The group carrying the bound enemies followed Lann inside, leaving me alone with Alana and Tyrenn in front of the city hall.

"Can we leave now?" I shouted at his back. He waved a hand, and I took that as a yes. No one stopped me from leaving.

"That was very good, Duncan." Alana's face radiated joy, and she seemed pleased with the outcome.

"You did very well." Her father had a smile on his face.

"I didn't do much. I just found the people hiding in the bushes." I stopped next to an empty alley and guided the drone hovering twenty meters above me to land, and put it back in my backpack; its battery was almost depleted.

Tyrenn's eyes widened when he saw it but didn't say anything.

"Having captured their scouts will give us more time to prepare," said Alana, and I wondered how she knew all those things. Before I had a chance to ask, someone shouted her name. A boy, no older than twelve, dark hair, skinny, clothes in tatters, ran toward us.

"Miss Alana? Master Tyrenn?"

"What is it?" she asked in a soft voice.

"The captain sent me to bring all three of you back. Lord Ambenix has a few questions for you."

"What's your name?"

"My name is Madoc, my lady," said the boy, and I noticed a blush.

"Very well, Madoc, show us the way."

The boy led us back to the city hall, where I passed the guards at the door and stopped in front of Ambenix. Lann was there, along with a few other people I didn't recognize. The prisoners were gone. Dark puddles expanded on the wooden floor.

"My apologies, young shaman," Ambenix rumbled. "My first impression of you may have been rushed. Lann here says you can communicate with the bird spirits, and that's how you found those men. Is that true?"

I wanted to make sure this time I put my best foot forward. "First, I must also make apologies for earlier—my statements were without thought." Ambenix seemed pleased at my words, and a smile cracked his stoic face. "About the spirits, yes. I have under my command three of those things you call bird spirits, and they can inform me when the enemy is nearby, especially during the night."

"I need you to ask them to fly around the camp and alert us when they find the enemy. Can you do that?" he asked, his eyebrows raised.

"I will do as you command, but I need to go to my...cart."

He frowned. "Why?"

I took a deep breath and clenched my teeth to stop the smile I knew threatened to creep onto my face.

"I only had one of them with me; the other ones are there. The spirit of the bird I have with me is tired and hungry, and I need to feed it my special potion. Also, my magic circle is there, and I need it to summon and talk with all three spirits." It amazed me how I kept a straight face through all my outrageous explanations.

There was no need to explain about Wi-Fi, Bluetooth, and other things he didn't know or care about. If I did, I knew his answer would have been no. Or worse.

If I wanted to monitor all the drones simultaneously, I needed to connect them to one of my laptops. But the real reason for my request was that I wanted to get back to my vehicle. There I would be safe, and I could ignore all the crazy people and their death threats.

"So be it. But I'll send my guards with you, for your protection, in case your bird spirits missed any other enemies." He motioned to two of his men to accompany me. *For my protection! Funny.*

I glanced toward Alana, and my heart sank. A long-forgotten sentiment of chivalry or something else made knots in my stomach, nudging me to remember that without her, I would have been dead, by the hands of the same people who now asked for my help.

"I'll also need Alana."

Ambenix studied me, then nodded in approval. He didn't ask why, but I assumed he intended to appear like he understood how these things worked. Or maybe in their folklore, a shaman needed a beautiful young woman to help him in his activities.

We were soon past the gates with my escorts' help, and I fished in my pocket for the keys to the RV. I pressed the button to unlock it; a beeping sound and a quick flash of the headlights followed. The guards gasped behind me.

Alana had seen me lock it earlier, and she wasn't taken by surprise, but I caught the look of awe in her eyes when I opened the door, showing the illuminated set of stairs. I invited her to go in first, and just as I was thinking how to ask the guards to remain outside, one of them spoke.

"We'll remain here for your protection." He stopped a few feet away from the door, his back to the vehicle's front porch. The man probably thought I had nowhere to go, that he could get through the door with a kick or his sword if the need arose. *Yeah, good luck with that, buddy.*

I inclined my head in agreement, keeping a straight face, not wanting to betray the delight I felt, then locked the door behind me. *Finally.* I breathed deeply, the stench from the camp replaced by the new car smell.

I turned on the interior lights. Alana stopped, and the bag she carried in her hand dropped to the floor. Her head darted left and right, taking in her surroundings.

She spun, her movement a blur, and for the second time that evening, she had the blade at my throat.

My original fear came crashing down like an avalanche. Had she only saved me because she wanted to get inside the RV, and now she would kill me? The rational part of my brain reminded me that I was the one who asked her to come.

"If you try your magic on me, I will kill you." Her tone wasn't threatening; instead, it was cold and very matter-of-fact, like she was talking about the weather.

"Please, I promise I won't do anything to you. I only want to help," I said, raising my hands. She seemed to consider my words, and a moment later she put the sword back in its sheath, keeping a hand on the hilt.

I let out my breath and put a hand over my forehead. It felt cold and damp. *Man, I really need a shower.* I took off one of my shoes.

"What are you doing?"

"I'll leave my shoes here, at the entrance. I don't want to spread dirt all over the place," I said, intending to burn them. There was no way I could clean the muck up, not even with the best laundry detergent.

"Wait. In my tribe, we follow the rules set by the host." She took off her pair of shoes and laid them next to mine. Hers were made from brown leather, with no heel, and stitched with threads of the same color. I placed both pair in a plastic bag I got from a bin nearby, tied it in an overhand knot, dropped the sack in the biohazard container, and shut it.

"Do you want anything to drink?" I asked, motioning for her to take a seat on the couch. She nodded, her focus on the surrounding lights. I opened the fridge across from her and took out two cans of Cherry Coke. It was past midnight, but I was sure I would not get any more sleep, not anytime soon, and I needed some sugar and caffeine. She looked at the can, studying it, but didn't make a move to touch it.

"I've never seen colors and writings like this. What do they mean?"

"Well, here in front, it's the name of the drink. These words tell us what it contains, and these ones on the side tell us who made it. It's perfectly safe, I promise." To show her, I opened mine and took a sip.

She narrowed her eyes, studying my face for a few moments. I took another sip.

Her shoulders sagged. "I'm sorry. I didn't mean to offend you, but I've heard stories about shamans and what they do to people."

"Everyone keeps on saying that. Who are these shamans?"

"It's a story best left for another time," she said and took the can in hand. "It's cold."

"Ah, yes, it was in the fridge...oh, right, you don't know what that is. It's a container that keeps food and drinks cold. With it, you can keep the food for longer periods without it getting spoiled."

"Like a root cellar!"

"Indeed. Now, let me help you open it."

She put her ear next to it, then looked inside, sniffed it, took a quick sip, and shouted in surprise.

"It feels like...like something pinches my mouth! It has a delightful taste, like ripe cherries at the end of spring." She took another mouthful and smacked her lips.

I smiled, amused by her description. For someone who hadn't tasted anything carbonated before, her reaction was quite pleasant. In this familiar environment, with plenty of light, I had time to study her. Her honey-blond hair was pulled back in a ponytail. Adorable dimples complemented her oval face when she smiled, and her expression filled me with a strange sensation, one I couldn't put my finger on. She wore a patched-up long gray dress with long sleeves. It was a rag, but mostly clean, perhaps the only piece of clothing she had left. Her body was well toned and lean.

"How did you learn to handle a sword? "

"My father and my uncle. They taught me how to fight." Her eyes glistened.

"Look, I don't know what is going on, but why are people talking about war? When we first met, Tyrenn said something about Orgetorix and his army pillaging villages? Why?"

"What do all men who have power want?"

"More power, I guess."

She nodded. "There are rumors among the tribes of resettlement. Orgetorix wants everyone to move south. He promises rich fields and plenty of food for everyone."

"Well, that doesn't sound so bad."

"His words are lies," she said through clenched teeth. "He doesn't care about us or our homes. Whoever stands in his way is murdered. My father…"

"Tyrenn?"

She took a deep breath, and the passion and bitterness in her voice disappeared, replaced by a haughty tone.

"Thank you for the drink; it was very kind of you. Now let's get to work. How can I help you with your birds?"

It was the last thing I wanted to do, and it must have shown on my face as her look darkened.

"You asked me here to help you, and I did, even though I

could have refused. I came because of my father, Ambenix, and all the people in the village. Do you still intend to help them?" she asked, her tone as icy as the drink she held.

"Yes, definitely, let me charge the drones," I said with forced sincerity. "In the meantime, if you need anything, let me know. Oh, and the bathroom is over there," I said and pointed to the door across the kitchen. "You can freshen up, wash hands, things like that. You can even take a shower if you wish."

"What is a shower?"

"Yes, it's like a bath, but you can't lie down, you have to stand, and the water comes from above you. Come with me, I'll show you how it works."

Out of everything, the thing that impressed her the most was that I had hot water on tap. She also flushed the toilet a few times, said the toilet paper was too thin, and admired herself in the mirror. But nothing compared to the hot water. She turned it on, then off, then on again, and exclaimed each time she had warm water trickling between her fingers.

I asked her if she wanted some of my clothes, and she agreed to examine them. I had a few jerseys and long tights I used during the summer to ride my bike around Lake Geneva. Those were the only things I had with a good chance of fitting her. I also added two of my T-shirts and a pair of sneakers to the bundle.

"Unfortunately, we left in a hurry, and these are my only clothes," she said, looking down at her ragged dress. "Yet none of the clothes I have, or had, matches the fabric, the seams of the ones you've shown me. Look at this pair of pants—it's so soft! The ones I left behind were similar in length but weren't as soft as these. They seem very expensive."

"Well, I have plenty more, so don't worry about that. And they're not expensive at all, not where I come from." I put down the bundle of clothing. "I'll leave these here, and you can decide which ones you want to try."

She closed the door, and soon the dripping sound of water started.

I entered my lair, a medium-sized office composed of a desk, a stand with drawers filled with three laptops, a rack full of hard drives, four monitors on two of the walls, and some other equipment, including the two additional drones I'd promised to put to work. One of the two walls with monitors was dedicated to all the cameras mounted around my RV. I turned them on. The two guards were in the same spot where I'd left them.

For a few moments, I remained there, exploring the possibilities.

I could leave, but I had nowhere to go. No lights meant no civilization nearby and no one to help me get back—assuming I could *find* my way back. And if what Alana, Tyrenn, and the others said was true? Then if I tried to leave, I would face an army. I was caught between the hammer and the anvil, with no other option than to take part in a war I knew nothing about. I could be helping the wrong side, but something told me that wasn't the case. Not when villagers who couldn't defend themselves needed my help. There was only one option.

I took out the drone from my backpack, connected it to my portable power bank, grabbed the others from a drawer, and plugged them into one of my power strips. I opened my laptop and loaded the program I used to configure the drones. It was easy enough to set up a flight path for them to follow, to cover most of the area around the fort, and add a couple of triggers. One was to send me an alert if they detected a heat source, and the second was to return and recharge when their battery reached fifteen percent. Last, I redirected their feeds to one of my mounted screens to monitor what was happening.

A knock on the open office door interrupted my work. I swiveled the chair, and my mouth fell open at the sight of sculpted legs covered in black tights, an oversized T-shirt with the CERN logo covering two perky breasts. The scent of peppermint lingered in the room. If I had met her in these clothes in Geneva or any other part of the civilized world, I would have mistaken her for a beautiful yoga or fitness instructor. My heart raced, and my cheeks grew hot, like someone had lit a fire next to them.

"Thank you for the clothes," said Alana, interrupting my thoughts.

"Sure...no problem," I mumbled, taking a few slow, deep breaths to regain my composure. "I'm almost done setting up the drones. Do you want to come with me and launch them?"

"Yes," she said, and her face lit up, joy dancing in her eyes.

"Perfect. We need to wait a few more minutes for them to charge, but in the meantime, I can show you some of the things I have here." I motioned toward the monitors on the walls.

Her eyes told me the story behind her thoughts, especially after discovering those devices were not windows. Amazement, disbelief, curiosity, and wonder all played over her face.

"They're ready," I said once the three drones had a full charge. "Let's go on the roof. We can use the internal stairwell."

I reached out to the ceiling in the kitchen, pulled down a staircase, and flipped a switch inside my RV's phone app. The roof panel slid back to provide access, and an automatic lift system raised it up to create a walled-in roof deck, along with an L-shaped couch and a table. I went first and extended my hand to help Alana climb. Her hand felt warm.

"It's so peaceful and beautiful up here," she said, coming closer to me, still holding my hand in hers.

The unearthly beauty the cosmos offered, painted by the Milky Way with its stars casting their light onto Alana like celestial diamonds, made me forget where I was. It was a sight I'd never seen before; the sheer number of visible stars was astonishing, and for a moment, I experienced a profound sense of clarity. I realized how small and unimportant I was, like a grain of sand on a vast beach.

The hoot of an owl in the distance brought me out of the trance, and Alana moved away slightly, taking with her the warmth of her body.

I cleared my throat. "Let me set these things up first, and we can watch more later."

After plugging the wireless charger into a socket embedded on the couch's side, I released the three drones. With a barely audible hum, they disappeared into the night.

Alana was still looking up at the beauty that is the visible universe.

"I always imagined my mother is somewhere there, watching over me," she said, her voice barely above a whisper.

She came closer and took my hand in hers, enough to feel her warmth again, but she didn't continue, and I remained quiet, respecting her silence and thoughts. I let my mind drift through the stars and through memories, and it came back with an astonishing insight. This was my perfect moment. Away from everything and everyone I knew, away from civilization, lost in space and time, I felt whole. I felt I had a purpose, that I could make a difference in the life of someone important to me. Someone I cared about—more than I realized.

Later, when the cold air couldn't be ignored anymore, Alana and I climbed down the stairs, to prepare for a war I knew nothing about.

4

Years spent around army types helped make me the person I was—a hoarder of everything survival and military: tactical gear, weapons, and books. My plan to travel to Eastern Europe and Russia to track the gray wolves' movements had only intensified my desire to stay prepared for extreme situations. While Switzerland had similar laws as the U.S. regarding guns, I wasn't entirely sure if my permit would hold in other countries. To avoid any issues with law enforcement, I had a safe installed in the RV where I kept my handgun and ammunition. From what I'd read on forums, there were sections in Eastern Europe that had armed gangs, and there were many cases of people robbed of all their possessions in remote areas, where help wasn't readily available. I knew my expensive RV made me a target, and I had no inclination to let something like that happen. But I wasn't prepared for war.

I browsed through the files on my computer, looking for

something to give me an idea of how to help those people. When I found it, wished I hadn't. It was a document with detailed instructions on making a so-called fertilizer explosive, based on something I found in abundance around here. Manure.

But I was faced with a dilemma. If I acted upon this finding and helped create it, I was responsible for the massacre. If it worked, it could kill many people. *Who am I to make that decision? And what about the police?* But there were no police; there was no civilization. They decapitated people without trial, without arrests. The laws I knew didn't apply here.

I accepted that I wasn't where I thought I was. Or when. Maybe I was in an alternate universe. Perhaps I went back in time. Conceivably aliens had kidnapped and sent me to a distant planet. *No, that doesn't make sense. I recognize the constellations.* Or maybe there was another, more straightforward explanation I was missing.

I closed my eyes and rested my head in my palms, willing the thoughts to stop swirling in my head.

Alana's soft fingers brushed the back of my neck, and I felt goosebumps all over my arms. All my ideas vanished like a puff of smoke, and my brain was a calm sea once again.

"What happened?" she asked, her voice soothing.

"I found something that could help, that might give a chance to the townsfolk, but if I do this, it could kill many people. I would be responsible for a lot of deaths, and I don't think I can live with that."

"Duncan, look at me." I did, and she took a step back, her

gaze focused on me. Alana's eyes were sparkling, and a tear ran along her cheek and dropped to the ground.

"These men have killed my family, my betrothed, my friends. Orgetorix sent them to kill, to butcher, to enslave. You didn't see what they did." Her voice became bitter. "You didn't see newborns forcefully removed from their mothers' hands, thrown in the mud, and left there to die. You didn't see the women stripped of all their clothes and raped. Trust me, when they come here, they will do the same to us. Men will be forced to watch their children beheaded and their wives used by Orgetorix's soldiers."

My mind created vivid pictures from her words, and my body tensed. That kind of people I would happily pound to dust.

She took in a sharp breath. "If you have the power to stop them, you must use it. Otherwise, you will be responsible for all that will happen."

She knelt in front of me and put her palms over my knees.

"I know you don't like killing. I saw it in your eyes when we first met." Her voice was soft. "I don't like it either, but there is nowhere else to go. There is no other place to hide. We would be found and killed."

She closed her eyes. "Would you let that happen, or would you help us?"

For a long moment, I said nothing. I stared at her, and past her, into the future events. I had no idea if she was trying to manipulate me, but she spoke the truth. I knew that much. The past few hours had offered a glimpse into this brutal way of life.

Soldiers fight wars because they are ready to die. They may not want to die, but ultimately, when they engage in a fight, they might. And they do it so they can protect their loved ones—their families, mothers, fathers, sisters, brothers, and friends.

I cupped Alana's face in my palms. She opened her eyes, stared at me and my decision cemented.

"I will help." I poured every ounce of determination into my voice.

"Thank you," she whispered and kissed my palm, her soft lips sending shivers down my spine.

I looked again through the document, but unfortunately, I was missing a way to extract the ammonium nitrate in large quantities, and the book had a few vague mentions about the compound's stability.

But it put me on the right track, and soon I found details on how to make good old gunpowder based on potassium nitrate —also referred to as saltpeter—sulfur, and charcoal. There was plenty of charcoal available—I had seen it around the campfires—and the ingredients for saltpeter were simple: urine and organic material, such as straw. The only catch was it had to be in a place protected from rain and sun, plus it had to sit there for many weeks. *It looks like I have to find a latrine.*

Following the smell didn't work in this case; the entire village was, in my opinion, one big toilet, so Alana had to ask around.

There were several communal latrines around the place, and I started with the one closest to the gate, because I had forwarded the drone alerts to my phone and didn't want to lose the RV's Wi-Fi signal. As expected, no one volunteered to help, and Alana and I spent until dawn filtering the mixture and crushing everything into a black powder. Without access to sulfur, I only mixed it with charcoal. The difference with sulfur would have been in the reaction time; with sulfur, it ignited faster.

The other concern was the burning torches. I chose a place further away from the walls and buildings to lower the risk of blowing up. The two guards kept their distance, the stench too overpowering even for their acclimated noses. Alana and I used several disposable medical masks sprayed with my cologne, but they only took the edge off.

As the sky took on a shade of red, I added the last cup to a small cauldron filled to the brim with black powder. Exhausted, filthy, and immune to all but the most horrible odors, all I wanted was sleep. For a week. Unfortunately, the work wasn't done yet. I had to test it, then find the best way to use the explosive during the upcoming battle. But first, I needed a shower and a change of clothes.

I warned the guards to keep everyone away from the cauldron, and Alana asked Captain Lann for more people to guard it, especially against anyone dumb enough to carry a source of fire near it. I read the disbelief and skepticism on their faces, but they listened to their orders.

This might not work. After all, it is just a big pile of dung with some charcoal in it. No, I had to trust what I read.

I took a small amount of the black smelly powder in a wood container; I didn't want to use anything that conducted static electricity and could create a spark. I went to the RV to clean up and test the black powder. The two guards followed, but I observed they kept their distance and tried not to walk downwind behind Alana and me.

Once inside, I started to undress.

"What are you doing?" Alana's voice had a sharp tone to it.

I looked at the clothes I held in one hand.

"I don't think there is any point in trying to wash these, so I'll burn them. I would suggest you give me yours, and I'll find you new ones."

"Sorry, I thought..." Without another word, she went into the bathroom, and a few seconds later, a white, freckled hand sneaked out, holding the clothes I gave her earlier: tights, jersey, T-shirt, and hoodie.

Already holding everything except my underwear, it took some juggling on my part to get hold of hers. I went to the back of the RV, where I had a small portable incinerator, dumped the pile of clothes in it, set the timer, and closed the door to the crackling and sizzling of the roaring blaze.

I fished for more clothes and shoes in my closet and handed some of them to Alana, who accepted them with a wet hand. Tired and filthy as I was, I still felt a jolt at the sight of her wet, naked skin.

When she came out, she stopped in her tracks, her eyes wide when she saw me, and the blood rushed to her cheeks.

"I'm telling you, this city needs proper sanitation. They need to build pipes to have the water wash away all the muck." After hours spent digging through their filth, I missed the cleanliness brought by civilization.

"Would you mind covering...that?" she pointed to my waist.

I looked down at the towel I was holding next to my black boxer brief.

"Ohhh, you mean this?" I gestured toward my underwear and hurried to put the towel in front to make her more comfortable. Alana didn't look down; she just stared at me. "I was going to take a shower, that's all. Sorry if I gave you the wrong impression. I didn't even think of how it may seem to you. I definitely wasn't thinking about...you know, not that I wouldn't, unless you want to, of course, but I was just..."

She brushed past me toward the couch, where she had left her bag of weapons.

I quickly crept into the shower, and a second later, locked the door, just in case she had any murderous thoughts. When nothing happened, I relaxed and turned on the hot water.

I scrubbed until my skin turned red. It felt like all the clean, soapy smell had coated and penetrated my skin, surrounding me like a cocoon.

"Much better," I said to the clean face staring at me from the bathroom mirror. I looked around and groaned. *Dang, I forgot to get new clothes.*

"Alana, I need to search for some clothes. Please don't do anything...violent, okay?" I came out with only a towel covering my waist.

She sat on the couch, sword in her lap and an amused expression on her face. Alana didn't say a word, just watched me as I walked to the bedroom closet.

"So, back to work?" I asked once I was dressed in more decent attire.

She nodded, still watching me intently, then a moment

later, put the sword back in the bag and gently picked up the box with the gunpowder from the table. I followed her outside and asked one of the guards to bring a cup of the oil they used to keep the torches burning the whole night, along with a rope, and I chose a spot for bomb testing.

Less than twenty meters from the RV, Alana carefully deployed the wooden box, her hands steadier than mine would have been. I took the rope, coated it with oil, fixed one end inside the container, and gradually unrolled the string until it reached the RV.

Soon Ambenix and Lann were up on the walls, along with half of the town, looking intently in my direction. Alana and I took shelter behind the armored vehicle, and I took a lighter out of my pocket and lit it. The fire followed the line, like a serpent going for its prey.

What am I doing? I'm no demolition expert. What if I haven't used the proper quantities? What if—

Suddenly, a loud BOOM resounded and the ground trembled. A cloud of smoke, dirt, and other debris landed smoothly on the ground, covering the newly formed crater. *It worked.* I could hardly believe it. *I might have used more powder than necessary.*

A loud cheer erupted from up on the walls. People had their swords, axes, and fists up in the air and shouted a cacophony of unintelligible sounds. I was as surprised as they were. Alana's eyes shone brightly, radiating with joy, and a feral smile stretched across her face.

"We will win," she declared, leaning close in to give me a peck on the cheek. I felt my cheeks ignite.

The moment Alana and I stepped inside the village, people started cheering and chanting. Their cheerful spirit was infectious. My face broke into a smile, and I waved. People who were close by scattered in all directions, like rabbits running away from a fox.

"Don't do that. They're afraid you'll do something to them," Alana whispered in my ear.

"But I didn't do anything."

She shrugged and continued walking.

When I arrived to take the cauldron, I found it encircled by twice as many soldiers as before.

Ambenix came to join me, followed by Lann, Tyrenn, and two other people. Behind them, a lot of warriors shouted and made gestures of encouragement. Tyrenn's eyes were shining brightly. He seemed ten years younger, and his manner had changed. A sword was attached to his belt, and he wore a proud expression on his face, no doubt directed toward Alana.

"You have done well, shaman," said Ambenix, a touch of awe in his voice. His eyes were fixed on the black cauldron, like it was filled with gold, not with dung.

I liked praise, but I didn't know how to respond to someone congratulating me for making a bomb.

"Come, let's meet and discuss the best way to use this thing you have made."

I followed him and his people to the same building as before, the one I suspected served the role of city hall to this village, and I spent the better part of an hour explaining how the explosive worked and the best usage for it. It was exhausting. After having spent an entire night digging through their muck, I was more than fed up with their lack of knowledge.

"Look, just spread the black powder next to the front wall and add hay in front of the gates," I told Ambenix, Lann and half a dozen other warriors who formed some sort of a war council. "You can then send fire arrows to the hay and the powder, and I'll call my earth spirit to swallow the army." I suggested hay to create some sort of a wall of fire to block and consume the attackers. Or at the very least to distract them.

Once they had everything they needed, I left them to put my ideas into action, and this time, no escort joined me on the way to the RV. Carts with hay kept coming from inside the village, and people deposited the hay in front of the wall. I ignored them and continued forward, to my RV, where Alana was waiting for me.

I recalled the drones, then drove around the encampment and parked next to the wall at the back of the village, in a secluded area, less likely to be used by the attackers because of the thick vegetation surrounding it. I extended the solar panels and hoped for the sun to emerge. It was cloudy, and I didn't want to run out of power.

Alana had been on the passenger seat the whole time I drove, but she didn't say a word, her hands gripping the arms of the chair tightly.

"How did you move us without horses? What spirit do you command that can do such a thing?" Her hand loosened on the arm. "And this chair is as soft as a horse's mane."

Seeing Alana dressed in modern clothes had made me forget about her upbringing.

"First, it's not a spirit. It's called an engine, and it spins those four big wheels. As long as it has energy, it can keep them in motion and get us wherever we need to go. Second, I'm happy you like the chair, but I've never felt a horse's mane, so I'll have to trust you on this."

"Never?" she asked, a surprised expression on her face.

"No, I mean, I've seen horses, but never been close enough to touch one."

For a few seconds, she said nothing, the wheels spinning in her head, and I recognized the look. She had an idea.

"When this is over, I'll teach you how to ride a horse."

"That would be interesting." I wasn't entirely comfortable with her idea. It was a nice thought, but I just couldn't see myself on a horse. I would be a laughingstock if I fell off the animal, and while I didn't care much about anyone else's opinion, I cared about Alana's. When I left this place, I was going to miss her. Something in my chest constricted, making it hard to breathe.

"Tell me about where you come from? How is it there?" Alana's question surprised me, but I was glad to tell her about my world.

"Well, I'm from a country called the United States, but I traveled a lot. My dad was deployed on various army bases all over the country. We never stayed for more than a year in one place. Later, we moved to the United Kingdom during high school, as he got a position at a base there. It was easier than I expected, thanks to my dual citizenship from my mother's side, which also helped me later get an intern position at CERN."

Alana pursed her lips. "I don't know what many of these words mean."

"Well..." My stomach took that moment to erupt in a loud growl.

She laughed.

"Hey, what do you say about an early breakfast?" I forced a smile on my face to hide my embarrassment.

"But I have more questions."

"I'll answer them while we eat."

I wasn't a magnificent cook, or even a modest one, but there were two things I knew how to make well—scrambled eggs and fries.

It didn't take long for me to ready an omelet with ham, cheese, and a dash of pepper; I left the fries for lunch. During the entire time it took me to prepare it, she watched me like a hawk without saying a word.

I waited for her questions, but she ate in silence. *What is she thinking? Does she like my food?*

Thoughts swirled in my head. She had been very sure of herself earlier, when she told me about the scouts and when the attackers would arrive.

"Why do you know so much about war?" I asked, breaking the silence.

"My father taught me the art of war. He showed me how to fight with a sword, how to shoot with a bow, how to ride horses. He told me many stories from his earlier life before I was born, stories about how armies fight, strategies, and some of the things he did."

"But I thought your father was just a farmer?"

She stared at me for a couple of seconds. "He had been a captain in his chieftain's army, much like Lann is for Ambenix. When I was five, he made a wooden sword for me, and from then on, every morning and evening, he gave me lessons on how to parry, thrust, counter, disarm, or kill a foe. Several years later, we started dueling with real metal swords. He took me along each time he went hunting, and that's how I learned to shoot with a bow."

That explains her skills.

"I was not allowed supper if my shot was less than perfect," she remembered with far better humor than I would have had. "But shooting is not everything. I had to be silent and careful to stay downwind, otherwise the animals could smell my presence and run. The first time Father took me hunting, I had a shot aligned with a deer's body, but I felt a breeze swishing past me moments before releasing the arrow. The wind must have carried my scent, and in an instant, the deer disappeared, and my arrow buried itself in the trunk of a tree. That evening, I had no supper."

She stopped, her eyes unfocused, staring somewhere past me, probably recalling other things from her childhood.

I felt sorry for her and for the experiences she must have had. And I thought my life was difficult as a military brat. My dad required me to keep everything clean, to do my chores, but nothing as bad as what Alana described.

"I think you should get some rest," I said after I finished the meal.

"What about you?"

"I have something I need to look into." If I was going to be part of a war, I had to better prepare myself.

She put the sword in her lap, took a piece of cloth from her bag, and started cleaning it. I cleaned the dishes and went to my office.

My phone beeped just as I finished working. *Finally, I have a signal!* Instead, it was an alert from one of the drones, together with an image it took. *Wow, that's a lot of people.* Time was up. The war was upon us.

"I'm going to the gates. Stay here," Alana said after I told her what I'd seen.

It was time to choose. Fight or flight. Stay and help these people, or drive off, letting them defend themselves. My conscience was clean; I'd already given them the gunpowder. They had a fighting chance. Slim though, because, from what I discerned from the drone's footage, they were outnumbered four or five to one. Almost a thousand people were coming to attack several hundred men, women, and children in the village.

"Alana, wait." For a brief second, I considered asking her if she wanted to come with me, but I knew she wouldn't do it. Her father was here. "I'll come with you. Let me grab a few things."

"No, Duncan. Please remain here. I've already lost people I cared about, and I don't want to lose you, too." A warm feeling engulfed me. *She cares about me.* I didn't know how much or what I meant for her, but I was glad she didn't see me as the guy who almost fainted when he saw a man decapitated. Or I hoped she didn't.

Remaining in the RV was the safest thing to do, but it wasn't the honorable thing to do. And maybe I could help her; after all, she had saved my life.

"You won't. I have to come with you. I can't hide here in good conscience while you're out there." I gestured in the direction of the incoming army.

She studied me for a moment, then nodded.

"Very well, but promise me you will stay close to me and do everything I say."

"I promise."

A few moments later, I took the small entrance at the back of the town and ran through the mud toward the gates packed with warriors. A mass of bodies stood on the parapets surrounding the wall, probably three or four hundred people altogether. I had no idea where Ambenix had gotten so many warriors.

Inside, it was eerily quiet, without even the soothing crackle of the campfires and torches, which were now all extinguished. *Where are all the animals, the chickens?* On the other side of the wall, I heard people, horses, and carts, but no yells, no shouts, no battle cries. It was totally different than what I imagined the beginning of a battle would be.

"In the name of Orgetorix, open the gates," someone shouted from beyond the wall. "If you lay down your weapons, no harm will come to you. If you resist, your bodies will be food for crows."

A mountain of a man stood tall and proud atop the palisades. Ambenix. "I heard what you have done to the poor women and children to whom you promised no harm. If Orgetorix wants this land, let him come get it. I have spoken."

Not even a minute had gone by when a deafening cry from hundreds of chests reverberated across the sky. A shadow raised to block the sun's rays, and hundreds of arrows came like a deathly rain upon the village. Alana swiftly pulled me away from the main street, and I stumbled and landed face-first in a haystack, inside a stable. Dozens of arrows buried themselves into the earth where my feet had been seconds earlier.

"Thanks for that," I murmured. It was the second time Alana saved my life.

"Just make sure you stay close to me and do what I do," she reminded me.

Shouts, cries of agony, the clang of steel on steel, and above all, the metallic smell of blood told of the carnage happening outside. A shudder ran down my spine. This was real, and people were dying. *Why isn't Ambenix blowing them up?*

I peeked through the half-opened door. I could see fighting on the parapet; the tops of ladders connected everywhere across the wall, and people swarmed over them like ants on a piece of bread. Ambenix still had people on the walls, but most were just sitting there. One of them was hit by a few arrows in the head and fell. Except it wasn't a man, it was a wooden log dressed like a man. That's when I realized Ambenix had planned for this to happen. He wanted them to climb over the walls and enter inside the encampment with minimal resistance; unfortunately, the defenders left there were sacrificed, and they knew it.

The defenders put up an immense effort to keep the enemies at bay, but they were outnumbered, and for every enemy they slew, two more climbed to take their place.

A couple of them pushed down a ladder full of people. It must have been an inhuman effort, and their struggle was soon repaid by arrows extruding from their chests. The parapets were now full of enemies, and they were climbing down, some jumping from the ramparts to join a fierce fight, where fewer than a hundred people faced hundreds of enemies.

Ambenix wielded an enormous ax, sweeping everyone in his way. His movements were mighty and swift, and no opponent had time to get close before the unforgiving steel cut meaty chunks from them. Heads, hands, and other body parts littered the mud in front of him. On his right, Lann's blades were like lightning, cutting, piercing, shredding everything they came in contact with. No adversary withstood his whirling blades for more than a few seconds. Most of the attackers had only one long sword, which they wielded with two hands, but they were no match for Lann's speed. His shorter, lighter blades were like a tornado, delivering a thousand cuts from a thousand directions.

On Ambenix's left, to my tremendous surprise, was no other than Alana's father. His movements weren't as powerful as Ambenix's or as fast as Lann's—one might say he was a tad slower than everyone around him—but each time the enemy's blade came close to stab him, it missed, and a second later, Tyrenn's blade protruded from the attacker's chest or throat. He was never in one place. He moved like a man twenty years younger on a dance floor. His technique was even more impressive than that of Ambenix or Lann. With every attack, I expected the enemy's sword to pierce him, but it never happened. He was always victorious, though only by a small margin.

Unfortunately, the field was now clogged with dead people, body parts, and weapons, and when a more zealous attacker jumped with his blade ready for a down cut, Tyrenn tripped and almost fell. I watched as the attacker's blade descended on Tyrenn's unprotected side, but before he brought it down, an arrow struck him in the throat, and the enemy fell to the side. Next to me, Alana lowered her bow, eyes focused on her father.

But no matter how many people they killed, more attackers poured in. Slowly, wave after wave, the enemies pushed back the entire line of people that had Ambenix at its center. The brave defenders were now close to half their initial number, fifty people, maybe less, and they started retreating, gradually, toward me. That's when the gates opened, and a loud cheer erupted from the outside. The encampment was breached, and people on horses appeared at the gates, spears in hand, ready for attack.

5

The enemies charged, pouring like water through cracks in a wall. The villagers fought with desperation, but it wasn't long until the left flank collapsed under the attackers' momentum. The line of defenders started retreating faster, but not in disarray. They kept the same cadence, helping each other when needed, closing all the gaps, not giving the enemy an inch more than they had to. But the outcome was inevitable. They were fighting a brave fight, but many were swallowed by the tumultuous sea of foes.

Alana pulled me with her, and I sprinted toward the other end of the city, where another line of a hundred warriors was waiting, no doubt to make a last stand.

Two of them quickly parted to let us through, then went back to their original positions. I recognized our guards, who had been assigned to protect and keep an eye on me. This time, however, their attention was on the advancing horde. I wanted to ask Alana why they didn't go help, but I kept my mouth shut. I assumed they had their reasons.

Not long after, what remained from the first line of defense arrived and was quickly replaced by the second line of people, who were fresh and looked eager to fight.

Alana went straight to her father, but with all the cries, screams, and people dying around me, I didn't hear what they said.

Ambenix climbed atop a cart, ax in his right hand, and pointed forward. "Now!" he roared. A dozen fiery arrows took off toward the gate, like comets blazing through the sky. They glided past the walls, and a curtain of fire erupted in front of the now open doors, the hay burning fiercely, unnaturally fast, igniting the soldiers nearby. Dozens found their demise trampled by the hooves of the scared horses or in the hot embrace of the wild flames.

"Again," shouted Ambenix. Several comets flew again, this time heading toward the wall.

I'm not sure how many of them found their mark, but at least one did. The ground moved beneath my feet, and the shockwave, like a strong wind, pushed me back a few steps. Next came a massive explosion, a giant plume of smoke rising high into the blue sky. In a blink of an eye, hundreds of people and horses were incinerated or blasted away, their internal organs liquefied. Tons of logs, rocks, shrapnel, and dirt rained upon whoever was close enough to the blast site, now a smoldering crater. The entire front wall was gone, and through the smoke and flames, I saw the field and the road we'd arrived on. When the blast happened, all the attackers must have been close to the gates, because the area was now filled with parts of unmoving, burning corpses.

Everyone stood back for a breathing spell, too stunned to continue, including me. I never expected such an explosion.

Ambenix, the first to recover, charged into the dazed enemies. His warriors, including Alana and her father, joined him. The remaining attackers formed a defensive line, but there weren't too many, only enough to make this a fair fight.

I had never seen such viciousness and rage as when the two armies collided. The attackers had nowhere to retreat, nowhere to run, so they poured everything they had into a fight for their lives. The warriors fought with a ferocious intensity, but Ambenix's people matched them in anger. They were fighting for their families, their children.

Alana's blade wove a net of death around her, her style similar to her father's but more energetic. She didn't wait for the enemies to get too close before her blade slashed their bodies, leaving them staring with empty eyes at the red mud.

She was already fighting two big brutes when a third one killed the man next to her and headed in her direction, blade held high, ready for a strike. A shout would have done her no good; she couldn't spare any more time battling a new opponent, and everyone around Alana was busy fighting.

I raised my Maxim 9 handgun, the one I'd taken from the RV, and sent three shots in quick succession, two to the body and one to the head. Each bullet was capable of 550 foot-pounds of muzzle energy, and Alana's attacker dropped to the ground like a rock. For once, I was grateful to my dad for the weekly target practice I had growing up.

This was my first kill. Until then, I had only ever shot paper, cans, and bottles. I knew very well what I had done, and I braced myself for the sick feeling I had when the scout was decapitated by Lann, but nothing came.

When I was old enough to fully realize what it meant to shoot someone, I remember asking my dad if soldiers felt any remorse when they killed people. He explained to me that, in most cases, yes. The only time when death didn't have a powerful impact on someone's conscience was during a battle when the situation was "kill or be killed." During those moments, the brain could quickly compartmentalize and let you move to the next attacker to keep you alive. With all the death around me, I must have switched to that mode of thinking.

My target dropped to the ground, a bullet hole protruding from his skull. Alana didn't lose a moment and skewered her last opponent, who died with a puzzled expression on his face. She turned toward me, frowned, nodded, and went back into the fight.

I barely registered what she did; I was in the "zone." In my pockets were only three spare magazines, so I shot only when I was sure of the outcome. No need to waste any bullets. My focus was on the gun and my targets, and a moment later, I had two more headshots. One was attacking Alana's father; another one, Lann.

That's when the hounds of hell were unleashed. A group of twenty or thirty dogs, all barking madly, lunged to bite and tear through the attackers. It was a gruesome sight. One of the dogs clamped its teeth over a man's arm; another one sank its fangs in the man's leg, and when the attacker fell to his knees, another dog jumped and ripped out the man's exposed throat. In other cases, the fangs met the steel blades or the skull-crushing axes, but the attack gave our defenders a moment to catch their breaths, and with renewed energy, they jumped back into the vicious fight.

Slowly, the tide of the battle started changing, and by the time my gun clicked empty, it was clear the victory was on our side.

My mind switched modes again, and I could analyze the situation before me. *What did I do? I have killed so many people.*

The few remaining enemy soldiers, no more than twenty, were fighting back-to-back in a tight circle when Ambenix raised his ax and roared, a sound so animalistic coming from his throat, it made my blood run cold. Everyone stopped, the enemies' faces betraying confusion and fear.

"Enough!" cried Ambenix, his eyes on the last group of enemies, surrounded by four times their number. "You are brave warriors and have fought a great battle, but make no mistake, you will die here, and crows will feast on your flesh—unless you put the sword down, kneel, and swear allegiance to me," he said, head held high.

I was taken aback by his words. *Just like that he will forgive them?*

The men looked at each other, then one by one, they threw their swords down, to Ambenix's feet, and knelt...all except one.

Ambenix surveyed the group, then focused on the only man who still had his sword in hand. He was a bearded man, somewhere between thirty and forty years of age, brownish hair, black and cold eyes, broad shoulders, and arms laden with muscles.

"Who are you?"

"My name is Culann, the captain of this army, and I will not bow to anyone except my lord."

Ambenix seemed to consider that, then nodded, more to himself.

"Very well, I can appreciate a man of honor. Now kill everyone else. I don't like traitors," he shouted to his people, and dozens of arrows pierced the unarmed enemies.

That was more in line with what I expected from Ambenix. *What a cold, heartless, iron fisted ruler.*

Silence fell, and Culann remained the only one standing, surrounded by the bodies of his comrades.

Ambenix struck the ground with his ax, the blade sinking deep in the red mud. "You can choose to fight anyone here, to the death, and if you win, you are free."

Culann nodded and started looking around, as if searching for someone. I glanced around me, at the faces eager for a fight. *Hmm, I'm surrounded by bloodthirsty warriors.*

I moved my gaze back to him, and his eyes met mine. "I want to fight him." His finger pointed in my direction, and I looked behind me, but there was no one there.

"Who, me? Are you kidding?" My mind couldn't comprehend the idea. The war was supposed to be over, the danger eliminated.

I looked toward Ambenix, his expression unreadable. *I'm no warrior. Surely he wouldn't...*

"Agreed," said Ambenix, a sadistic smile creeping over his

face. *Oh, what a fool I am.* Now, after I'd saved him and his entire village and Ambenix no longer needed my services, I was expendable. No gratitude, no nothing.

Alana was next to me, her eyes sparkling in the sun's light.

"You will win, Duncan. I'm sure of it."

"I have no idea what I'm supposed to do," I said and was surprised by my own voice, an octave higher than usual. Somehow, my subconscious must have realized the peril long before I had time to fully comprehend what was happening. *How did I get to this point, to this death match?*

"You will fight with knives; do you have one?"

I nodded, my brain still frozen. It was an odd sensation. I knew the danger but hadn't fully registered it. Like when you observe a car speeding toward you. You see it, but the only thing you can do is watch and hope nothing terrible will happen, even though some part of your mind knows and screams at you to get out of the way, to run, a scream for deaf ears.

"Good. You have a very good chance. He's tired after all this fighting, and you will be faster. He will try to end this quickly, so stay away from his blade. Move around him. Don't let him pin you down." I looked at her, at her face, at the way her lips moved. Even though what I heard didn't match her lips' movement, I didn't care. Her lips were a shade of pink, closer to white, probably due to exhaustion after the fight. I remembered I had some water in my backpack, and I offered her a bottle.

Everything was so surreal, like I was in a dream, and my brain was stuck, not wanting to accept my future. I wanted to spend the last few moments of my life watching Alana's face, her hands, which gently cupped mine, her yoga instructor outfit, which made both of us stand out in this crowd of brown leather mixed with red blood. She still had the jacket I'd given her, and I discerned a few droplets of blood on it—nothing that couldn't be washed.

"Duncan, look at me," she said urgently. I raised my gaze and met her brown eyes, the color of autumn's dressing gown. "You need to ignore everything else and focus on what lies ahead." Her eyes bored into mine, drawing me closer and closer.

"I don't think..." I started, but my voice was weak, and my brain refused to go any further.

She bit her lower lip, probably in frustration, and then a moment later, her warm lips touched mine. It was soft, like silk slowly caressing my lips, with the promise of more to come. I closed my eyes and let that feeling fill my mind. My body reacted; my heart started pumping faster, wanting to burst out of my chest, like water pressing on a dam. I felt the energy coursing through my veins. I had a reason to live. I needed to win. When I opened my eyes, she was gazing intently at me. I'm not sure what she saw there, but a small smile appeared on her face.

"You are a shaman," was all she said and moved away, my backpack in her hands. She joined her father in the large circle of people surrounding my challenger and me. My opponent already had a long knife in his right hand, and his face stretched into a sneer.

In my hand, I had a CRK Mark IV that my father gifted me after I finished college. He had given me training on how to use it, but until today, I only pulled it out from its sheath to admire it. It was the first time I had it in my hand with a real purpose: to kill someone else and save my life.

Culann took a step forward, his knees and arms bent, like a cobra, ready to strike. People started cheering, and Ambenix said something, but I tuned everyone out. My only focus was on the man right in front of me, approaching with sinuous movements. Everything in me screamed to run and not look back.

His hand moved like lightning in an arc toward me. I leaped back but must have been too slow, and I felt a sharp pain, as though I'd touched hot iron, flaring on my left shoulder. He continued his momentum with another slash, aimed for my belly, but I moved around him, and his blade cut through the air.

We circled one another, which was good because it gave me a moment to catch my breath. This hadn't started well at all. I was wounded after the first strike. He feinted attacks a few more times but didn't follow through; however, each time, my heart leaped, fearing another wound. Doubt crept into my mind, and I realized he was toying with me. His technique was better, probably the experience he had from hacking people. On top of it, the pain in my shoulder was growing, but I couldn't spare any time inspecting my wound, even though I felt the blood pouring out of it, down my arm. My strength was slowly ebbing away, drop by drop.

A thought flashed through my brain, and desperation must have shown on my face when I understood what he was after. He wasn't playing a game. He was waiting for me to bleed more, to have my reactions slow down so he could finish me off. He must have interpreted it as fear, and a malicious grin spread across his face.

My time was up. I couldn't wait any longer; I had to act and take the initiative. I felt my arm shake, probably from the tight grip I had on the handle, and I had to force myself to relax for a few seconds before my first attack.

That's when he lunged at me. I should have remained coiled, ready, and shouldn't have relaxed in the middle of a fight to the death. I jumped backward, barely avoiding the tip of the blade, but he must have seen I was unbalanced and followed up with a kick that sent me tumbling to the ground. In a second, he was on top of me. I tried to grip his wrist with my left hand, but he quickly threw the knife to his other hand and planted it right into my chest. I felt the blow deep in my heart.

"You took the life of many of my men. Now it's your turn to die," he growled.

Luck accompanies those who are prepared. Besides grabbing the handgun, I also had made a makeshift slash-proof vest while Alana cleaned her weapons. I taped some ceramic and aluminum dishes together with duct tape, added a few sponges and pieces of cloth with more duct tape, and then used string and glue to affix them to one of my hunting vests, which I kept under my jacket.

It stopped the blade, and my right hand, still holding the knife, curved and struck the back of his neck at the base of the skull, then yanked the blade toward the spine. I must have severed his spinal cord because all his movements ceased, and he fell like a rock on top of me. I twisted his body away from the blade. Otherwise, he could have pushed it right through my chest. His unblinking eyes were full of pure hatred, and for a few seconds, we stared at each other. I watched his life draining away, leaving two empty sockets. It was the last image I had of him, and it rocked me to the core.

All the other kills I'd made that day weren't personal, but this was. I'd stabbed a man and watched him die. The image was forever engraved into my brain. The rational part of me made a good case. It was self-defense; he chose to fight me, and he would have killed me. But none of it mattered. I had killed someone in one of the most intimate ways possible. He wasn't ten or twenty meters away, like the others I'd shot. He was at less than an arm's length when I stuck my blade into his neck. On my face, I felt his dying breath.

The face of a blond angel, with tears rolling down her cheeks, greeted my eyes.

"I'm fine," I said in a gruff voice, and her sad eyes lit with joy.

She helped pull me up and guided me through the crowd, who parted before me like the Red Sea before Moses.

Some shouted and cheered, but most were quiet, their faces expressing awe and fear. I was too tired and wounded, both on the outside and on the inside, to care, and relented to follow Alana wherever she led, leaving a trail of blood behind me.

I wasn't surprised when we arrived back at the RV. Once seated on the couch, she helped get my jacket, vest, and shirt off and inspected the wound. My entire shoulder pounded like it had a built-in pneumatic drill. Exhausted, I asked her to bring me a drink from the fridge; I needed the sugar to avoid passing out. I pulled out a medical kit from my backpack, which I kept mostly for situations like this: bruises, scrapes, and lacerations from murderous knife wielders.

Alana came back with a can of Coke and took the wipes from my hand. I let her continue cleaning the wound while I focused on the drink. It felt reinvigorating, like giving water to a thirsty man in the Sahara Desert. After a few sips, I touched the ice-cold can to my feverish forehead and let the chill spread over my body and my thoughts. Over my wound, Alana spread an ointment with a summery smell, like flowers, plants, and grass after a rain, and applied the dressings. I felt the pain and heat recede immediately, like a fire put out by an extinguisher, then gradually, my shoulder went numb.

"Thank you," I said when she was done. Alana said nothing, just nodded, and went to the kitchen to wash her hands of my blood. It looked like I was going to survive, and an immense feeling of gratitude inundated me. I was tired but happy to be alive. I needed rest, and my eyes dropped closed. I'd stay here for just a second.

6

I woke up with a stiff neck. Everything around me was bathed in fiery red light and quiet like a tomb. *I hope I'm not dead.* A look outside the window showed the red sky on fire, lit by the setting sun. Inside my RV, everything was clean, spotless, with no dirt or blood traces—even my clothes and vest, which lay on the table next to me, were clean, but Alana was nowhere to be seen. Only her bag waited on the kitchen counter.

I decided to shower; I had to remove all the sweat and crusted blood and change my bandage. The wound was healing up nicely, faster than I would have expected. I didn't know what ointment Alana used, but the edges around the gash were pink with almost no trace of a scar. It was unbelievable. Nothing I knew of could heal a wound this quickly.

I didn't dare use the hot water, afraid it would take too much from my already drained batteries, so I had a quick cold shower, and a few minutes later, I made myself a few sandwiches, hoping Alana would return soon. Hours passed, and she didn't.

With nothing else left to do to occupy my time waiting for her, I had to make the decision I dreaded. I needed to leave this place and find a way back home.

I made excuses to avoid just going. I told myself Alana knew the area, and without her, I would be lost and would roam for days, even weeks, until I could find a city. But the truth was another reason, stronger than all the others. I remembered her kiss, her warm lips on mine and the feeling it gave me, and I wanted more. I let out a deep breath and opened the door. With a new change of clothes and a backpack on my uninjured shoulder, I went to find her.

There was only one sentry at the back door, and he let me pass, but gave me a strange look of both fear and awe. It wasn't hostile, but it wasn't friendly either.

The village was bursting with activity. Women were coming and going, each carrying large sacks filled with vegetables; children carried water or herded sheep; dogs barked incessantly. *Where did they hide them?* Everyone stopped to stare and wave when I passed near them. Except for the dogs. They rummaged all over the dirt for human flesh. It was sickening.

I marched through the village with a purpose, keeping on the main road until I reached the place where the second line of defense had made their stand. Most of the bodies were gone, but the blood was still there, soaking the earth and giving off a metallic stench. In front of me, a wall of wooden stakes was being raised by more than a hundred workers. All the stakes were in the ground, not all the same height, but they were tall enough, and the only thing missing was the door. I was amazed at how fast the people worked to build it.

A smoldering pile of bodies attracted my attention. Those were the attacker's corpses; I recognized their uniforms. They were headless. A group of people, both men and women, poured some sort of brown liquid over the severed heads and placed them on a smaller mound nearby. Disgust swept through me at the grotesque sight.

"She's not here," said a young voice.

I turned to see Madoc, the boy we'd met the day before. He wore the same ragged clothes, and he seemed even thinner than before.

"Do you know where she is?"

I didn't want to go around the city looking for her. Ambenix had been quite clear when he allowed Culann to challenge me. He wanted me dead. For what reason, I didn't know, but I suspected it was because he thought I undermined his power. People were now more afraid of me than him.

"She went with her father and a few other warriors to hunt."

"Which direction?"

He raised his hand, which trembled slightly, and pointed beyond the wall, back toward the forest where we'd come from yesterday. The same place where the enemy came from as well.

"Are you feeling all right?"

"Yes, shaman," he said and looked down at his feet.

"Something tells me you're not telling the truth. What is it?"

He was quiet for a few moments; then, in a low, embarrassed voice, he said, "During the battle, the barn where we kept the food took fire, and we lost most of it."

"And you don't have anything to eat?"

Madoc shook his head. I looked at him, the way he stood on his bare feet, his torn clothes, his thin frame. *He's famished.* I reached into my backpack for my last protein bar and unwrapped it. "Here you go."

He glanced up, and I read the confusion on his face.

"This is food. You can eat it." I mimicked the act of chewing.

Madoc looked at me, suspicion in his eyes, but the hunger must have been greater than his aversion for shamans.

"Thank you," Madoc said and took it from my outstretched hand. Tears rolled down his cheeks, and with a quiet "thank you," he started running and turned into an alley, close to the crater formed near the newly built wall.

I looked around, wanting to engrave the sight into my memory. My gunpowder caused so much destruction, and so many lives lost, but I saved innocent lives too. I wanted, no, I needed to remember what my actions could do.

But there was no reason to stay anymore. If Alana left, I could and should go as well, and maybe I would see her again. My hopes swelled at the thought.

I owed nothing to anyone here. Instead, they owed me their lives and freedom. My skills had saved the village, but I wanted nothing from them. The only thing I needed were instructions on how to get back home to civilization, which they didn't have.

With one last glance at the people working on the palisade, I threw the backpack over my shoulder and departed.

After not even a hundred steps, I heard people running behind me. I should have stopped, but instead, I hurried up. The closer I was to the RV, the safer I felt.

"Shaman!" someone shouted. I walked faster. "Stop!" I was almost running now, the door in the wall drawing nearer. Then the sentinel appeared and posted himself right in front of it, his right hand on the hilt of the sword. His face bore a worried expression. He didn't seem too keen to fight me, but I knew if I tried to push my way through, he would. I slowed down, and my pursuers caught up with me. They were four big men, all of them with dirty short black beards and axes in their hands.

"Shaman, Lord Ambenix demands to see you," said a basso voice I recognized from the day before.

I knew that if I went with them, I would be at Ambenix's mercy once more. He was unpredictable, and I preferred not to find out his true motives.

"I'm busy now," I replied, my right hand moving closer to the backpack, where I kept my gun.

"It's not a request, shaman," he replied, an evil grin spreading across his face.

They were closer to me than felt comfortable. Two in front, two on my sides, and the sentinel in the back. Not an ideal position. I probably could have shot three of them until one of their axes chopped my head. I'd seen how they used them in battle and wasn't too keen to see them in action against me. *To live, I have to obey them.* Unless I could be the shaman they all thought I was.

"If you don't want all of you to go up in flames, like the wall this morning, you need to let me get to my carriage." Surprise flashed on his face, but I could tell he wasn't entirely convinced. "You've seen what it can do," I pressed. "I'm brewing a more powerful potion that we can use if anyone attacks us again, but unless you let me get back, it will destroy half of the town. Us with it. Well, I may live, but you will all die."

He seemed hesitant now, and I knew I had the hook in.

"You can come with me if you wish. There is nowhere else for me to go," I said and spread my arms, palms open.

"Walk," he said after a few moments.

With a relieved breath, I headed toward the RV, past the guard who was kind enough to open the door for my escorts and me.

I had hoped all of them would stay behind as the previous guards did, but when I put my hand on the doorknob, the basso voice chilled my blood. "I'm coming with you."

This was not the plan. If he stepped inside, it would be almost impossible to flee.

"Sure," I replied in what I hoped was a reassuring voice and turned my head to nod. At the same time, I took note of where the other people were. Lucky for me, they kept their distance, probably three or four meters away from the RV. His hands grabbed the door when I opened it, presumably to make sure I wouldn't close it on his nose. I took two steps on the stairs, and when I thought he had one leg up in the air, ready to climb on the first step, with a quick movement, I lowered myself, turned my head, and planted a back kick, straight into his chest.

Instead of catapulting him into the vegetation surrounding the RV, he staggered and took a step back. *I'll need a wrecking ball to move this guy.* But it was enough for me. I swiftly shut the door over his fingers. His howl of pain filled my ears. I locked it and slumped to the floor. *You're safe Duncan. Breathe.*

The next moment, I heard a heavy thud, followed by two more. They were trying to get in.

Unfortunately for them, they had no weapons capable of getting through the vehicle's armor. I didn't want to give them too much time to figure out other attack methods or slash my tires, so I rushed straight to the driver's seat and pressed on the ignition button. The dashboard and the tablet immediately lit up, and a second later, the status showed green and ready to drive. The solar panels I had extended before the battle had charged the battery enough, but it was still a long way from full. Even with their advanced capabilities, there was only so much they could do. I sent the command to pull them in, and I sped up, following the same road along the walls.

I switched to my rearview camera and saw the men running after me, but it didn't take long to leave them behind, and I was back on the road I had first traveled, a night and a war ago.

I didn't dare push the acceleration too much. I was not willing to risk bumping into anything and damaging the vehicle, not when I had no idea where a car repair shop was.

Soon, the silhouette of the village, with its half built front wall, disappeared, hidden by the trees.

After almost an hour of driving, I encountered something I didn't want to see ever again. Night had fallen over the forest, and my headlights illuminated horses and people lying on the ground, unmoving, arrows protruding from their bodies. I recognized one face, his unblinking eyes glinting in the white light. He was one of the people who had been escorting Alana and me around the camp last night.

A feeling of dread washed over me, and I felt a bolt of ice

going down my spine. This was the hunting party. I was afraid, not for me, but for Alana. I didn't want to see her face, her lovely brown eyes, staring lifelessly at the sky.

I took my damaged vest, jacket, and gun and carefully stepped outside in the chilly night's air. It was jarringly quiet; only the leaves moved in the crisp breeze. At first, I hadn't noticed, but farther away were other bodies, their features hidden by the shadows. I held my breath, afraid of what I might see. Corpses littered the ground; most had the same dark green pants and tunics our attackers had worn earlier. *There must have been some survivors who ran after they saw the explosion.* I spent several minutes looking around but found nothing else, just some lines in the dirt and holes that looked like they were made by horses' hooves. Or maybe they were made by the wind for all I knew. I was no tracker, and I had no clue what I was looking at. Good thing I had help.

Back at the RV, I took a few minutes to program a drone's flight path to search for groups of people, then set it to scout forward, at the limit of the Wi-Fi range. I hoped it would find something, a trail I could follow. I wanted to be ready and leave as soon as the drone spotted something, so I gritted my teeth and set about doing the morbid task of moving away some of the bodies, which lay directly on the path. I could have gone over them, but that didn't feel right. It wasn't challenging from a physical perspective, but my psyche endured a veritable assault. The darkness surrounding the small pool of light amplified even the smallest of noises, and the blank stares I received from the lifeless eyes made my skin crawl. My heart thumped in my chest, and each beat felt like a strike on a drum in my ears. I half expected one of the dead bodies to wake up and grab me. Fortunately, there weren't too many bodies to move, but it was an experience I would never forget for as long as I lived.

As I washed my hands after that gruesome labor, my phone beeped. As I threw away the paper towel I used to dry my hands, I noticed the half-full bin still contained the bag with my sneakers and Alana's original shoes, the ones I forgot to dispose of.

The thermal camera identified a small area, not too far from my location, with a few large spots emanating a lot of heat. I couldn't distinguish how many people were there, but I deduced those were campfires.

I turned off the headlights and cautiously drove forward. When I thought I had traveled enough, I stopped the RV, turned off all the lights, and went on the roof to relaunch the drone at a lower altitude and check the surroundings. It identified the campfires and several yellow-red dots around them, either guards or prisoners.

I put on the damaged vest and jacket, and I grabbed the knife, gun, ammunition, and my binoculars. I had planned to use their night vision to track gray wolves; instead, I looked through the windshield to check the surroundings and assess their capabilities. The green tint that pixelated my vision wasn't the best to help identify everything around me, but it was better than nothing. I carefully stepped out of the vehicle, locked the door, and disappeared into the inky green.

I knew the general direction, but there were so many things around me—trees, vegetation, roots, fallen branches—that I needed to stop every few steps and choose the best and quietest path. I didn't see any sentries, but it didn't mean there weren't any. Night vision equipment was useful but couldn't replace daylight. People could be hiding behind the trees or through the bushes.

With each stop I made, I strained to listen to the surrounding noises. Every rustle of leaves had me on edge, my heart racing, waiting for an attack. Slowly and steadily I advanced, until a growing dot of light appeared in front of me. The closer I got, the more I felt and heard my heart thumping louder in my chest—so loud, I worried it could be overheard by someone nearby. After what felt like hours, I found a place behind a bush to observe the small clearing where two bonfires illuminated a dozen people and horses.

My heart constricted when my gaze landed on one person tied to a tree. It was too far to distinguish who it was, his face half turned away, but the body's contour read as masculine. Alana was nowhere to be seen, and fear spread through me. What if she had been killed? I could have missed her body when I searched for her. Unintentionally, I felt my hand getting closer to the trigger. If she were dead, I would kill them all, no matter the consequences.

Overtaken by a desire for revenge, I lifted the gun and set my sights on the people near the campfire. In daylight, from this distance, I could take out three, maybe four before everyone else had a chance to take cover. However, with darkness all around me, I could only hope for one, maybe two head shots. If I started shooting, my position would soon be overrun with enemies. I had enough bullets to take them all out, but if I missed or didn't inflict a mortal wound and had to reload, things could get dicey.

A thought flashed through my mind, and hope gained ground, stopping me from doing something impulsive. Maybe the person tied to the tree knew what had happened to Alana. If he confirmed my fears, then I would make all of them pay for what they did. If not, it meant she was somewhere in the woods, all alone, and needed my help.

I looked around the campsite to assess potential ways in. I saw only one man standing next to the tree where the prisoner was. If I was quiet enough, I had a chance to silence him with my knife and free the prisoner.

Silently, I made my way through the forest and took position behind a tree, ten meters or so behind where the prisoner was. I drew the knife out from its sheath and kept it close to me, ready to strike. I took a step and peered behind the tree, but the sentry wasn't there anymore.

Behind me, a noise like someone stepping on dried leaves made me turn my head and—BAM! Everything started spinning, and I fell to the ground.

7

Someone sat on top of me and rummaged through my front vest pockets. I fluttered my eyes open to see a man looking intently at my lighter. I didn't know if he had alerted someone else or kept this for himself until he could rob me of whatever possessions he found, but I had no time to waste. My fingertips grabbed the handle of the knife sheathed on my leg, and in one swift movement, I planted it inside the man's temple. It penetrated with a satisfying crunching sound. Simultaneously, I pushed with my hips to roll him on the side, followed his movement, and with my right fist, I struck his Adam's apple. He made some gurgling sounds, then his spasms slowly decreased in intensity, and the man stopped moving. Everything was still again—even my heart.

From one perspective, this kill was more gruesome than my first, but no nausea, no sick feeling enveloped me, just a cold determination. I looked up behind the tree. People were still around the fire, eating and talking. No one else had heard anything.

Crawling on my elbows and knees, I approached the tree where the prisoner was tied. My heart started racing again as I got closer to my goal. I didn't know how much time I had until people noticed the sentinel's disappearance, so I had to act quickly. I extended my hand and touched the prisoner, hoping he wouldn't scream.

"It's me, Duncan," I whispered.

"What are you doing here?" he murmured back. I recognized Lann's voice, and hope swelled inside me.

"I'm here to save you," I half-lied. "Can you run if I untie you?"

He was quiet for a fraction of a second, then replied back, "Yes."

"Good. What happened? And where are Alana and her father?" My breath, my heart, stopped, waiting for his next words.

"They ambushed us when we went hunting for food. Only Tyrenn, Alana, and I survived. The bastards took them to Orgetorix's castle for interrogation. Would have taken me too, but I was injured."

A warm feeling of joy and happiness washed through me, unclenching the invisible hand that gripped my heart. *Alana is alive.*

"Be ready. I will cut your ropes." I didn't wait for an answer and sliced through the ropes holding him to the tree. I then edged forward and cut the ones binding his hands. I had to be careful not to injure him by mistake, but he never moved a muscle.

"Hey," I heard a shout, and my blood turned cold. "What are you doing there?"

One of the men from the bonfire closest to me stood and pointed in my direction. Others rose as well.

"Let's go." In one swift movement, I rose and sprang in the direction of the RV. I glanced back and saw a dozen men running in two different directions, some following me and some Lann, who'd taken another course toward the horses. He reached the edge of the camp across from me when one of the sentries jumped in front of him, brandishing a long sword. The sentry lunged, but Lann evaded the cut, twisting his body around the blade, and punched his attacker in the throat. The man dropped the sword and staggered back, but Lann caught it before it reached the ground. Using an upward slash, he cut his attacker's chest, hand, and half of his face. Lann glanced back toward me and sprinted into the black forest. *Why didn't he follow me?* It was too late now, and I had to trust Lann would find a way to escape his pursuers and get back to the village. *He probably knows these woods better than they do.*

I heard people shouting and saw the light of torches peering from behind the trees, but I was outside their range. Within the forest's gloom, I used the binocular's night vision to find my way between the fallen trunks and around the limbs and roots emerging from the ground until I recognized the white silhouette of my RV.

I swiftly got in but didn't dare turn on the interior lights until I was in my small office, where I had no windows, only computer screens.

Back in safety, I could think this through. I had no idea where to go, and the only person who could help me, Lann, hadn't followed me.

If I went back to Ambenix's village to get some help, he would keep me there as his slave—unless he found a reason to kill me, even though I had saved him and his entire village.

Something inside my chest urged me to help Alana. I didn't know why, but she felt special, and I was attracted to her like iron to a magnet. It wasn't only a physical attraction; it felt like there was something more, like I was destined to help her.

Then I remembered when I first met her, Saturday morning, running away from Orgetorix's men. She had come from a path through the woods, followed by the three riders. *What if that path led to where Alana was being taken?* It was a long shot, but it was the only lead I had, and I needed to follow it. I wasn't sure it would take me directly to Orgetorix's castle, but it was my only choice.

A shred of hope remained in my heart that maybe going back to where it all began would somehow teleport me back home, wherever or whenever home was.

I found it challenging to drive at night, through the woods, without headlights. Instead of looking through the windshield with my binoculars, I opted to navigate by starlight. When my eyes couldn't stay open anymore, I stopped, put the RV in lockdown mode, and caught a few hours of sleep.

I arrived at the clearing early in the morning. My phone showed it was Monday, 7:23 a.m., and the sky got brighter as orange and yellow flames leaped across the horizon to herald the beginning of a new day.

I stopped the car and looked around. The clearing was empty as the day I first arrived, except in one of the bushes, I thought I saw some movement. I turned off the engine, grabbed my emergency bag, and exited the RV.

When I saw him, I stopped dead in my tracks. I recognized the clothes, which passed for a uniform in Orgetorix's army. The soldier lay in a pool of blood, a deep cut across his stomach gushing out blood, and an arrow stuck in his right shoulder.

"Water." His voice was barely above a whisper.

I didn't know what to do. *Should I leave the poor man here to die or try to save him? Hmm, maybe he can help me with information.* I took out a bottle of water from the bag.

"Save your strength. Here, drink some water. I'll wrap your wounds, but tell me first—have you seen a young woman with golden hair?" I hated to use my help as a bargaining chip, but I had to know.

He nodded weakly.

Hope flourished inside my chest. "Do you know where she was taken?"

"To the castle. With another man...they wanted to know what happened, how everything—" A violent cough stopped his words, and he started spitting blood.

"Take it easy. One more question, and I'll bandage you. How can I get there?"

He lifted a trembling hand and pointed to the road I'd first seen Alana coming from. "I can take you there..." He started coughing again.

I hurried to put the water bottle back in the backpack and grab a medical kit.

A whizzing sound flew past my ear, and when I turned back, a new arrow was stuck into the man's chest. His lifeless eyes kept staring at me; any other answers lost on his lips. I stood and turned, ready to run, when the tip of a blade came to rest on my chest.

8

Lann, along with half a dozen people, surrounded me.

"Shaman, Lord Ambenix requests your presence." Lann's tone was courteous, his sword unwavering.

"I cannot do that. Alana has been captured, and I need to find her."

He glanced at the body lying at my feet. "You saved me when I was taken prisoner, and for that, I have a debt of honor I must repay, but I cannot let you go. However, I will make you a promise. If you come with us peacefully, I will make every effort to aid you in your quest to find Alana."

I had nothing to negotiate with. My weapon was inside the RV, and I had no other way to defend myself against all of them. But I couldn't just abandon Alana.

He must have sensed my indecision, because he continued, "Even if I let you go, you don't know where she's been taken, and you have no idea where to go. Come with me, and I promise you, I'll find out where she is."

It seemed like I didn't have a choice—I had to trust him. Something in his voice told me Lann did speak the truth and he would keep his promise. But how long Ambenix wanted me for, I didn't know, and if I went with them, who knew when I'd be back?

"I'll come with you, but I need to know when I'll start my search for Alana."

"That I cannot say," Lann said, which made me begrudgingly trust him more, "but the sooner we make haste, the sooner it will be."

With no other options, I inclined my head and headed to my RV, hoping they would think I gave up.

Two of Lann's men blocked my way. "Your carriage remains here," Lann insisted. "You'll ride with us."

I'd half expected this, but I still had a nervous feeling in the pit of my stomach, like I was facing a bear armed with only a baseball bat. With no other option, I followed Lann to the edge of the forest, where they had left their horses.

"I've never actually ridden a horse," I told Lann. I wished I'd spent more time with Alana so she could teach me how to ride. My throat constricted at the thought of her.

"You'll learn," he said dismissively, swinging onto his own mount.

It looked easy, his movement so effortless, and I thought I could give it a try. The first time, I almost fell on my back. Getting up on a horse was no easy task. One of Lann's men took pity and helped me get up. Unfortunately, that had been the mildest part. Once I was on the saddle, my horse started moving, and with each step, I had the feeling I was going to fall. It was nothing like I thought it would be.

Lann shouted something, and suddenly, everything was in motion: me, the saddle, the horse, the ground, the sky—my fear of falling increased tenfold.

We weren't going fast, but for me, it felt like a gallop. The riders seemed relaxed, and I studied their posture to mimic it. I moved to the lowest part of the saddle, kept my back straight and not slouched forward, aligned my heels with the back of my head so they were on a straight line, and relaxed my shoulders. It made a world of difference. I wasn't in the same league as the others, but I wasn't afraid for my life with every step the horse took.

I turned my head, just as my RV, my one hope for safety, disappeared behind the trees. I glanced around, but no one seemed to be paying any attention to me. I took the phone out of my jacket pocket and pressed a few icons to extend the solar panels located on the roof to charge the battery, so the RV would be ready when I got in. Assuming I would be back. I briefly wondered why they didn't confiscate my medical bag and what I had in my pockets. *Maybe they're afraid of me—or whatever a shaman represents—and they're worried I'll curse them or something.*

The ride seemed excruciatingly long, even though Lann took another path through the woods and stopped twice. The first time was at the place where Lann had been held captive. It looked different from last night, mostly because there was no one there anymore. Lann's tracker, a slender man named Brennan, reported that the men were headed back toward Orgetorix's castle, and we took a different route, parallel to the one we'd been on.

The second stop was at the place where I'd first seen the dead bodies the previous night. Here the soldiers cleared the road and made a pyre for the corpses. No one asked me anything, and I didn't offer to help them.

By the time I got back to the village, I was sore, sweaty, and exhausted. The bright blue sky disappeared under a carpet of clouds, and twilight was upon me. With no energy left to remain upright, I slid off the horse. I would have landed face first in the mud if Lann's hand hadn't been there to push me back in the saddle.

"Thank you," I murmured. Even my lips were too tired to move.

Lann gave me a brief look, possibly to make sure I wouldn't fall again, then nodded. After I passed through the newly installed gate, he gave the order for everyone to dismount. It was the best news I'd heard all day. My triumphant dismount turned into a glide, and I had to throw my arms over my horse's neck to stop myself from landing butt first in the slimy mud. My horse wasn't in a cooperative mood and bent his head, dropping me with a splash in the bog.

Argh, I hate this place.

"May I take your horse?" asked a familiar boyish voice. Madoc had a hand on the reins.

I was glad to see someone that didn't want to kill me.

"Yes, thank you. How are things with you and your family?"

He grinned. "Very good, shaman."

"Glad to hear that."

"Come on, we don't have the whole day," said one of Lann's men. The warrior suggestively grabbed the handle of his ax.

If only I still had my gun with me.

"This way, shaman." Lann motioned toward the familiar town hall, with its two massive doors, guarded this time only by two soldiers. I followed him inside.

"There you are," said Ambenix in an amused tone. "Leaving without giving us the chance to say goodbye, shaman?"

"Alana has been taken and…"

"Spare me your lamentations. I need you to make more of that dark powder you made."

Ah, so that's why you want me here. It was the last thing I wanted to do: stay in the filth and smell of a latrine.

"I'm sorry, but I cannot do that."

"Why?" Ambenix's eyes narrowed to slits.

I was too tired and wanted to give him a piece of my mind, but my brain came with an alternative. One that had less chances to result in my decapitation.

"I used most of the material last time, and it takes somewhere between three and four months to get new ones," I answered, maintaining eye contact. I remembered reading somewhere that not looking away makes the other person think you're telling the truth.

"But we have more. We make turds every day." Ambenix started laughing, the other people joining him. I didn't. They were annoying, and I had to use most of my already depleted reserves of energy not to say something regrettable. And fatal.

"Yes, but I also used all my potions, and I don't have the ingredients to make more." The laughter died down.

"I see," said Ambenix after a few moments of silence. "Then what about our defenses? Do you have any ideas?"

The question took me by surprise. I hadn't expected Ambenix to believe me. *Now if only I can convince him to let me get to my vehicle.*

"I'll need to check in my...carriage," I almost used the term *RV*, which I was sure had no meaning for him. "I left it—"

"No. Everything you need to do, you'll do it here."

My brief hope faded away.

"But I won't be able to help—"

"Then if you can't help, I have no use for you anymore, and like I told you, my dogs are hungry."

Again with the dogs? I'd seen the vicious animals in a fight, and I had no desire to see them up close. I remembered how they tore huge chunks of meat from the men they attacked. It had been a gut-wrenching sight.

"But I helped you and your entire town defeat the army!"

Ambenix smiled, but it didn't reach his eyes. "Only because you would have died too, shaman. And if you don't help us again, the outcome of the next battle will be entirely different. As opposed to you, I care about this village and its people."

He was right. There was no way they could have stopped another attack, not without help. But I wasn't interested in spending my time there, preparing for an attack, which might or might not come. Not while Alana was in danger.

"So, what shall it be?" Ambenix's powerful voice whipped me back to reality.

Without any other options, I nodded my acceptance to help him. I needed to buy some time to think and find a way to escape and go after Alana. "I will inspect your defenses and prepare something truly magical."

"You have until sunrise to show me what you plan to do. I have spoken." With that, he made a dismissive gesture toward me.

It was my cue to leave, and I hurried out of the building.

"Hey, shaman," came Lann's voice from behind, and I slowed my pace to let him catch up. "Thank you for what you did yesterday," he said quietly. "I know you were there to save Alana; nevertheless, your actions saved me as well. Madoc will guide you around town, and if you need anything, send him to me. I've also assigned two guards to make sure you're…protected."

"You mean to make sure I won't try to leave." He just shrugged, and a sardonic smile stretched across his face. We walked like that for a few minutes in silence. My eyes darted to the shadows, trying to find gaps I could use. People had worked hard to restore the destroyed front wall, and unfortunately, they had done a good job. Sentries were placed at the few remaining gaps in the wall to make sure no one entered. Or left.

"And here is Madoc," announced Lann as I reached an old, battered wooden house. "Boy, I put you in charge of our shaman. You'll guide him through the town and answer any questions he may have. If anyone gives you a hard time, you let me know."

"Yes, Captain Lann," said Madoc, and assumed a straight position in front of the door.

Lann turned to face me. "I'll see you at sunrise." He turned on his heels and left.

Two people remained a few paces behind me—my guards.

"How can I help you, shaman?" I detected eagerness in Madoc's voice. He seemed to truly want to please me.

"Please stop calling me shaman. My name is Duncan Drake."

"As you say, sham—Sir Drake. If you don't mind me asking, are you all right? You look a little pale."

Well, after riding and not eating anything the entire day, how do you want me to look? I sighed. There was no point in being angry at his words. The kid only wanted to help.

"I'm fine, it's just I...it doesn't matter. I guess it's time to think about how to defend this little village. Madoc, by any chance, do you know what year this is?"

"I'm sorry, Sir Drake, I do not."

"Yeah, I didn't think you would. And don't call me Sir Drake. It makes me feel old. The age difference isn't that big between us, so please call me Duncan." Even though I was almost double the boy's age, having him call me "sir" made me feel old, and I didn't like it. Plus, I wanted to create a rapport between us, which could help me more than having him fear me.

"Yes, Duncan."

"Better. Fine, let's see what we need to do; otherwise, those two gents won't be happy." I gestured behind me at the two shadows. "Tell me, Madoc, do you know what a catapult is? Or a ballista?"

"No, sham—I mean no, Duncan."

"All right then, let's see if I can figure out how to build one. Do you know where I can find a place to stay?"

"You can stay at my house. My parents will be happy to have you as our guest. Everyone knows what you did for us."

"What do you mean?"

"With your magic, you saved us all when the earth erupted and killed those attacking us."

Yeah, I had saved him, his family, and many other people in this city, but at what cost? Hundreds died because of me. *Was it worth it?*

Madoc gestured toward the house. "We don't have much food, but we'll share what we have."

I looked at him, at his tarnished clothes, ruffled black hair, anemic body, and the excitement on his face. *Maybe it was worth it.*

"Lead the way."

A glance behind me told me that my guards went farther away, next to a barn filled with chickens. From there, they had a good view of the front door.

Madoc invited me to step in. The light emanating from the fireplace showed a modest room built out of wood and a thatched roof with straws hanging from the ceiling. Bowls of different shapes and sizes were spread around the house, and in the middle lay a low circular table made of wood. Next to it were a few bales of hay, which I assumed were used as chairs. On one of them, with her back to me, sat a woman, her silhouette barely visible in the semi-darkness.

"Mom, the shaman is here," he announced.

The woman rose and approached me. She wore a short gray

shirt tucked into a long skirt of the same color. Her eyes shone brightly, illuminated by the dancing fire, but the years hadn't been kind to her. The white streaks in her auburn hair and the wrinkles on her face told of a hard life. She might have been beautiful once, possibly not too long ago, but it had faded away. She was thin and as anemic as Madoc.

"I'm really sorry. I don't want to impose."

"Shaman, my name is Gwenn, and you're doing us great honor," she said, her voice as faded as her beauty. "All of us owe you our lives. We will be happy to share with you the little that we have." She did a small curtsey.

In any other situation I would have laughed, but now, I felt embarrassed. She was older than me, probably the age my mum would have been if she were still alive.

"Thank you very much for your hospitality."

A convulsive cough resonated from a corner of the house, hidden behind a curtain.

"I'm sorry. My husband is not feeling well." I detected a hint of sadness in her tone. I thought I understood why. Here, without medicine, any disease could be fatal.

"What does he have?" *Maybe I can help them somehow.*

"The doctor doesn't know," intervened Madoc. "He came here twice but said he can't help my dad."

"Can I see him?"

Madoc gazed at his mother, who nodded, and I discerned a glimmer of hope in her eyes.

In a corner, hidden by the shadows, a man lay on a hay bed covered by a dark cloak. Once my eyes adjusted, I could see a pale and sweaty face, half-hidden by a black beard.

"My name is Duncan Drake," I introduced myself.

"Shaman, I'm Noland—" he started, but another round of coughing made him stop.

"Don't talk. I'll ask you some questions, and you can just nod." I put my hand on his forehead; it burned to the touch. After checking for any visible wounds, I gently pressed under the jaw and each side of the neck. "When I pressed with my fingers, did it hurt?" He nodded, his glassy eyes fixed on me.

"I'm not a doctor, but your high fever and those swollen lymph nodes indicate you may have an infection. I don't have any antibiotics with me. They are in my RV—my carriage," I corrected myself, "but I have some Tylenol. It should help reduce your fever and pain." All three looked at me like I'd spoken a different language. I searched through my medical kit and took out two pills.

"Do you have some water for him? He needs to swallow this." Apparently, this was easier to understand, and Madoc's mother went to get a cup filled with a murky liquid, took the pills from my hand, and helped her husband raise his head to take a sip and swallow them.

Too bad I don't have another bottle of water.

"It should help with the fever and the pain for a few hours, but I can't do anything more, at least not with what I have on me. He will also need some food and tea."

"Thank you," Gwenn bowed her head. "I'll go prepare something to eat for all of us."

My stomach chose that moment to rumble. I hadn't had anything to eat since morning. My gaze fell on the ceramic pot in which she prepared a thin soup, and my eyes misted. From the little they had, they were willing to share it with me.

I took the bowl Gwenn offered and thanked her. They didn't have any spoons, so I put it to my lips and took a sip. It was a warm, watered-down version of a vegetable soup, and I caught a hint of cabbage and carrots.

Madoc inched closer. "Shaman," he started, and when I arched an eyebrow, he started over. "Duncan, you said earlier you can help my dad if you could get to your carriage?" His voice was a whisper, barely audible even for me.

"Yes, why?"

"If you could get to it, could you make my dad better?"

"Possibly," I said thoughtfully, hope rising in my chest. "I have some medicine that should fight whatever infection your father has."

"I know you're supposed to stay here, and those men outside are there to ensure that, but if you could get out, would you promise me you will help him?"

I didn't want to appear too eager, so I spent a few moments in silence. "I promise, but I don't think those two outside will allow it."

Madoc's eyes shone brightly. "I know of a way out. There is a small hole in the north wall covered by a tree, and there are no guards around. No one will see us." He seemed eager to help me escape, and I understood his reason. *The boy just wants to help his dad.*

"There are a couple of problems," I pointed out. "First, they will see us as soon as we open the door."

"But we won't go through the front door," he said with a

smirk. "There are two removable slats that can help us get out through the back. Where did you leave your carriage?"

"That's the second problem." I described to him the road I took to get here.

"I know these woods like the back of my hand," he replied, his voice excited. "We can get there before the moon is above our heads. Let me tell my mum."

Yes. I would finally be free to help Alana.

9

I followed Madoc through the hole in the back wall and then through some dark, narrow streets. He stayed in the shadows and away from the torches blazing on the palisades. After a few turns, I arrived at the base of an enormous tree. Judging by how thick the trunk was, it must have been hundreds of years old.

"Here," Madoc said and pointed to an area at the base of the wall. I couldn't see anything; there were bushes everywhere. The tree's thick branches kept all the yellow glow of the nearby torches or the white moonlight from reaching beneath. Madoc parted the vegetation and disappeared into the night. I crouched in the same spot, extended my arm through the leaves, and brushed my hands over the cold, harsh wooden fence until my fingers found a hole big enough for a man to get through. I took the medical kit in my hands and pushed it through the hole. It landed with a thud. I followed suit, and a moment later, I was on the other side.

"Follow me," Madoc whispered. Trees loomed in front of us, and a couple hundred meters to my right, people worked at the front wall while guards patrolled the area. There were a few on top of the walls, but their attention was focused on the workers.

Madoc moved at a snail's pace, keeping low through the thick grass. I was at the point of asking him to move faster when I realized why he did it. A rapid movement would have attracted the attention of the guards on top of the walls. This way, whatever they saw would appear like grass swaying in the gentle breeze of the chilly night's air. *Smart kid.*

Madoc went deep into the forest until he found a narrow trail. Every minute felt like an hour, without a flashlight, surrounded by the menacing rustle of leaves and ominous hoots of owls. The only light was the silver moon, which illuminated the path enough to make out the contours of larger bushes and rocks. Madoc walked in front, his movements sure and swift.

Why isn't he afraid? The smallest noise made my heart rate spike. *I wish I had my gun with me.*

Somewhere in the distance, a howl ripped through the heavy silence. The hair on my back rose, but I judged the wolf was too far away to be threatening. *For the moment.* I remembered reading about different types of howls. There are differences between species and subspecies that share geography and body size. The European wolf has a deep and steady style that drifts away into the night. *Just like it did now.* I wished I had the time and the means to study more about it.

I became interested in wolves at age twelve when my father took me on our first hunting trip in Alaska. One day on that trip, I had an experience that stayed with me my whole life. We had been walking in the forest for an hour when my father decided I should rest. Shadows danced all around me, and the leaves rustled, voicing a danger lurking nearby. With no warning, I felt my father's heavy hand push me behind him. In the same movement, he raised his rifle. Less than twenty meters away, at the base of a spruce, stood a gray wolf, unblinking and unmoving. The beast wasn't afraid; it seemed relaxed, like it owned the place. It raised its head and howled. The blood chilled in my veins, and I wanted to run, to get away from the awful sound, but my dad's grip intensified, and in a low, sharp voice, he told me not to move. "Do not let fear conquer you. Do not run from a predator. Let it know you're not easy prey," he said. The wolf continued to watch us, its gleaming eyes fixed on me. I stared back until a gust of wind blew in my face and I blinked. When I opened my eyes, the gray wolf had disappeared. Those moments remained forever engraved in my mind.

The fear the howl induced fascinated me, and I wanted to know more about wolves. Like my father said, "To conquer fear, you have to understand it. The more you know, the less you'll be afraid of."

That was why I had made plans to study and learn more about *Canis lupus*. I read a lot about how they hunt, what drives them, but I needed to see them in the wild, to prove to myself I wasn't afraid anymore. And to prove it to my dad. He had always been there to protect me.

That's when I realized Madoc felt safe because of the shaman who had saved him and his people. I was the one who had walked from a fight to the death with a knife in his chest.

The fear I had of confronting the wild animal subsided, and a part of me felt ashamed I'd ever had that thought.

I passed a shallow stream and walked for another twenty or thirty minutes until a familiar sight greeted my eyes: the RV's shape, waiting silently for my arrival.

"How did we arrive here so quickly?" I asked, not believing my eyes.

"Well, if you cut straight through the woods, the distance isn't that great."

I couldn't resist any longer; I ran. I wanted to feel the handle in my hand, to open the door, lock it, and feel safe in my home. I wanted to eat, drink, take a shower, rest, and forget about everything and everyone else. But I made a promise, and I had to keep it. I opened the door, turned on the lights, and motioned to Madoc to get in. He shook his head, a frightened look in his eyes.

"It's safer here than there." My words didn't seem to convince him. I couldn't understand how a boy who wasn't afraid of going through the woods at night was fearful of getting into an RV. "Look, nothing will happen to you. I give you my word. You will be perfectly safe." It took him a few moments to decide, but in the end, he nodded, probably to himself, and stepped up the ladder and into the vehicle. The door closed gently behind him. His face grew even paler, and his expression changed to one of fear.

"Don't worry. I just closed the door because I don't want

wild animals to come in. Now, do you want anything to eat or drink?" I asked, opening the fridge.

He shook his head vehemently.

"Do you at least want to take a seat on the couch?" Same answer. "Let me grab something to drink, and I'll search for the medicine."

It didn't take long, and I found what I was looking for. I was on my way to hand him the container with Tylenol when a thought struck me. Both he and his parents appeared to be suffering from anemia.

A few moments later, I returned to find Madoc in the same place, with his back leaning on the door. He hadn't taken a single step.

"This bag has the medicine your father needs. Tell your mother to give him one in the morning and one in the evening for the next five days. Do you understand?" He nodded, still without saying a word. "Good. Now, in this other bag, there are pills for you and your parents. You all need to take one in the morning. It will help provide some of the vitamins, nutrients, and minerals you're missing. This third bag has a few other things to eat."

"Thank you, shaman," said Madoc, his eyes moist.

"You're welcome," I replied and smiled at him. "One more thing. Lann will probably be very upset when he realizes I'm no longer there. Here are some sheets of paper with drawings for what he needs to build. The machinery pictured here should give Ambenix an edge defending the village again. Tell him to show this to a carpenter or someone skilled at crafts."

Madoc's eyes went wide when he saw the drawings, and he

almost dropped the bags on the floor, but I grabbed them before they slipped from his hand.

"Be careful with these so you don't spill them. Now, please let me at least give you a ride back. Sounds good?" His unblinking eyes were staring straight at me. "I will take your silence as a yes," I said and headed toward the driver's seat.

I drove until I saw the lights of the flaming torches on top of the palisades. For the entire time I spent driving, Madoc didn't move from where he was, with the papers and the bags in one hand and the other on the door, supporting himself.

"It's up to you if you want to go straight to the gates or go back through the same way we came." I pushed a button and opened the door. Madoc quickly stepped out, started to run, then stopped and turned to face me.

"Thank you very much, shaman, for not killing me. I've heard stories about your kind, about how not to come close to a shaman's home, about people who will never come back if they go in. But you're not like that. You are kind and true to your word." He disappeared into the woods, quiet and stealthy like a cat, not seeing the moisture in my eyes. *I hope Madoc will be all right and won't be punished for my escape.*

I did a three-point turn and drove until I reached the meadow, then parked behind some trees, away from the main road, where I thought I would be safe from detection. After a sigh of relief, I went to fulfill my dream: shower, eat, drink, and sleep. My last thought was of Madoc and his parents.

The next morning found me in the driver's seat. I already had a drone up in the air, scouting ahead, when suddenly, an alert popped up on my monitor. The photo showed a group of houses clustered together, forming a small village. It looked deserted, with no sight of people. I parked at the edge of the forest, took a few things with me, and proceeded on foot.

There were signs of a struggle everywhere. Broken wooden window shutters hung in their hinges, constructions had been partially knocked down, and black smoke rose from smoldering buildings like a ghostly tower. A fight had clearly happened there not too long ago.

I walked the dusty road, my nerves jumping at every squirrel looking through the rubble, until I arrived in a central square. All around me, the houses had their doors broken, dislodged, or wide open for anyone to view inside. There was no one there, not even a cat or a dog. It was like everyone had disappeared. *No wonder the squirrels aren't afraid.* I decided to enter one of the few remaining houses that hadn't been touched by the fire. *Maybe there are people still alive.* The door lay at my feet with a hole in the middle, like a giant hammer had gone through it.

Inside were broken vases, pots, an empty bed frame, and a wooden table split in half. Clothes lay on the floor, along with hay, dirt, and soot.

The sound of footsteps outside and the clang of metal captured my attention. I stepped out to find six men spread in a half-circle in front of me, all with a menacing look on their unshaven faces. Four of them had swords, and two held small axes. All but one had tattered green pants with holes in them and bare chests, cloaks hanging from their necks by strings made of dark material, possibly leather. The last one had only a brown tunic, long enough to cover his knees. *I really hope he won't lift his leg.*

"Who are you, young man?" asked the man in front of me in a rough voice, like he had a sore throat. Tall, with vicious black eyes, yellow teeth, and a scar on his right cheek, he held a long sword, the tip of the blade pointing in my direction.

"Look, I don't want any trouble," I explained. "I just wanted to see if I could help and ask for some directions. I need to get to Orgetorix's village or town."

"Are you with them?" asked one of the other men.

It took me a moment to realize he meant the soldiers who had attacked Ambenix's town. Probably what was left from their army retreated through these parts on their way back to wherever they came from.

"No, but I need to find them. They've kidnapped a friend of mine. By any chance, have you seen a blond woman?"

The others exchanged a look, and malicious grins spread on their faces.

"If we see her, we'll make sure to have some fun. In the meantime, why don't you give us everything you have, if you want to live," said the one with the rough voice, who appeared to be their leader. "If not..." He made a throat-cutting gesture with his thumb.

I knew I wouldn't get out of there without a conflict. Every fight has a random element in it. No matter how good you are or what weapons you have, there's always the chance you'll get hurt. I couldn't run, and if they got close, I couldn't protect myself from all their swords and axes. But there was no need to run or to wait for them to attack. I had brought a gun to a knife fight. I pulled out the pistol and pointed at the speaker, who I assumed was their leader.

"I would recommend you turn around and leave, and everyone will survive to live another day," I spoke firmly and in a low, menacing tone. I hoped not to burden my conscience even more.

The first who started laughing was the man on my right, one of the ax wielders, and soon, everyone else joined—everyone else but me. I kept my gun pointed at the man in front of me while following all the others in my peripheral vision.

"You have courage, lad, I give you that, but don't think we're stupid. Go get him, boys!" their leader shouted, extending the arm with the blade in my direction.

The first one to fall was the one who laughed first, followed by the two attackers next to him. From the corner of my eye, I saw a blade coming straight for my head. Instinct took over, and it saved my life. I turned my back and started to roll in the opposite direction. I heard the swoosh and felt the blade on my back, but it stopped before touching the skin. My vest had saved me once more. The blow had been powerful enough to send me farther away than expected, and when I turned to look, the attacker was already poised for another strike, a second ax wielder a couple of steps behind him.

My next two shots penetrated my attacker's chest and head, and then I aimed and fired at the second, who had been a tad slower than his colleague. Part of his brain matter was forcefully removed before he had a chance to swing his ax.

Five men were down in that many seconds, and I slowly

stood up and centered my muzzle on the leader's chest. I had plenty of bullets left.

"Drop the weapon," I said, panting. He looked around, disbelief evident on his face, but complied with my request. The sword clattered on the ground at his feet.

"What are you?" he asked, his voice trembling.

"You don't ask the questions here. What can you tell me about Orgetorix and his men?"

He remained quiet, staring at me like I was a rabid dog.

"If you don't tell me, I'll kill you where you stand. If you do, I'll let you live."

My words must have given him hope.

"Look, I only know his men have been attacking everyone in this area in the last few weeks," he answered quickly. "Some of his soldiers were here this morning, and we watched them from the woods where we were hiding. They checked the houses, captured whoever was foolish enough to return, and then left. They had prisoners, but I don't know if they had your woman or not."

"Do you know which direction they took?"

He pointed with his right arm behind me. "Past that hill, there's a valley cut in two by a river. The town you're looking for is beyond that river."

"Thank you for the information. Now I suggest you bury your friends and get out of here. I don't ever want to see you again. If I do, I'll kill you."

He took a few steps back, and when I didn't move, he turned and ran.

I put the weapon away only after I was inside the RV and

had locked the door behind me. My adrenaline levels plummeted, and my knees buckled. I took off my vest with shaking hands and realized my skin was cold and clammy, not entirely from the exertion. When the sword came for my head, I had a moment when I felt sure I was going to die.

Back in high school, my dad had signed me up for some martial arts lessons, and I went to a dojo for a few years, but I was in no form or shape a fighter. Now, those drills saved me from being cut in two.

I don't want to waste another moment in this place. I drove, heading straight through a green turf, in the direction the man had indicated. The farmers probably used the area to plant vegetables, but I doubted anyone was left alive to mind.

The hump of a hill rose in front of me, with a few dark patches made by clumps of trees and lighter tones where bushes and grass prevailed. It wasn't too steep, and the RV had no trouble ascending to the top.

Beneath me lay an enormous valley where a sea of trees sprawled until it reached a river meandering gently along the valley floor. Through my binoculars, I could see the silhouette of a city, surrounded by a stone wall, in the distance across the river. But what unsettled me was the source of that river. It was a place I knew, a place I'd seen many times, a place I'd even swum in.

It was Lake Geneva.

It shook me to the core. The surrounding city, with its buildings, boats, cars, highways, and people, was gone. Like it had disappeared from the face of the earth, and forests and vegetation now filled everything. All my assumptions crumbled, faced with this reality. The civilization I knew, the one I was part of, was no more.

For a while, my brain shut down, refusing to comprehend the gravity of the situation. I don't know how much time passed, but when I was again conscious of my surroundings, I felt thirsty and hungry, and the sun was about to set.

With a sandwich in one hand and a can of sparkling water in the other, I took a seat and looked again through the helicopter-like windshield. In a sci-fi kind of way, the only thing that made sense was that I had traveled back in time. It was possible I had gone forward, but I refused to think humanity would regress so much. I thought again about the grandfather paradox. My knowledge in this area was limited, but I remembered reading about closed time-like curves that were created when an extremely powerful gravitational field warped the space-time and made it bend back on itself. I looked up at the azure sky. *I don't see any black holes, ginormous planets, or another sun.* To my knowledge, those were the only celestial bodies with mass capable of influencing Earth's gravity. The articles mentioned that only fundamental particles could travel back in time, and that when paradoxes were considered in quantum mechanical terms, they went away and were no longer relevant. It wasn't much, but it was something for me to think about.

I took another bite from my sandwich. If this was indeed the past, then I was faced with a huge problem—one with the potential to throw everything into chaos.

Through my actions, I was personally responsible for killing hundreds of people who would otherwise have lived and had children, grandchildren, and so on. The fact that I had also saved the lives of women and children provided small comfort. Even though the people I killed were soldiers, and the ones I saved were innocent, it didn't matter. I had changed the timeline, and when, or rather if I ever returned to my world, I would find something completely different—if I found something at all.

Another theory, the multiverse hypothesis, stated that an infinite number of universes were created based on each decision made. For all I knew, I was in an alternate reality created by my choices. It felt mind-boggling.

I took a sip of water. Assumptions and theories swirled in my head, and I felt lost. I understood Archimedes's pain when he asked for a long enough lever and a fulcrum on which to place it to move the world. I needed something concrete; otherwise, I would drown in the sea of assumptions.

Descartes came to my help. *Cogito ergo sum:* I think; therefore I am. The universe hadn't exploded, and there was still hope left. I didn't know if this was my timeline or not, but I had to be cautious, no matter what. From then on, I had to focus on not causing any more damage to the timeline—no more killings. *But what if saving Alana would cause more damage?* My heart pushed back the idea. If it did, then the universe could burn for all I cared.

To take advantage of the last few rays of reddish sunlight, I took the binoculars and started scanning the area. A triumphant shout resonated in my cabin when I spotted a faint trace of smoke coming from the trees, almost halfway between where I was and the river. I spotted a path that cut through the forest from this side of the valley until it reached the river. With renewed hope, I set a new flight plan for the drone and headed for the road.

It was wider than expected, enough that two RVs could have easily fit side by side. Some time later, the drone reported back. It was already dark, and I couldn't distinguish much from the photos, but I thought I recognized people, horses, and carts. They looked like the soldiers I was following. I stopped the engine not far away from where they were and turned off all the lights.

I had learned my lesson and sent a couple drones in the air. All of them had thermographic cameras capable of finding any hidden sentries. In no more than fifteen minutes, they arrived back, which gave me plenty of time for what I had in mind.

I took apart my hair trimmer; it had a good case for what I needed and made room for a nine-volt rechargeable battery and a step-up converter from one of the drone chargers. With practiced movements, I connected them together, wound the red wires from the converter around two nails (my two metal prongs that would conduct the electricity into the attacker's body), covered the wires in insulating tape, and used some duct tape to put the case and its new contents back together. I pressed on the button and was rewarded by a bright blue arc and a familiar crackling sound. *Bye bye, hair trimmer; welcome stun gun.*

Next, I checked my vest for damage. The sword had left a deep cut on the back, but other than that, it looked ready to serve. I added another small dish and more duct tape to the damaged area, then put it on, along with some black pants and a hoodie, and went to check the data.

The drones had detected four people concealed by the vegetation—guards spread around the camp. They also showed a group of fifteen soldiers and a cart with a large cage filled with people. My hopes swelled. *Maybe Alana is among them.* I took the improvised stun gun along with my Maxim 9 pistol, one of the quietest on the market, and a couple of clips with subsonic rounds for backup. I was sure I had to incapacitate at least one of the four sentries; otherwise, I would leave my back exposed to an unwanted attack.

I studied again the images sent by the drones, noted the positions of the four sentries, and stepped out of the vehicle. From the trees ahead, shouts, voices, and laughter reached my ears.

The first sentry was next to a tree, his head bowed down. I used my night vision binoculars to monitor his breathing for a few seconds, and he seemed asleep. I didn't know if it was a ruse or not, but I had to take my chances. If I ran, I would be at his side in less than twenty seconds.

I spent close to ten minutes cleaning the ground in front of me before each step I took, all the while keeping him under observation. He didn't move. I advanced until I was close enough to touch him. The man must have heard something because his head snapped up, and he turned to look at me, his eyes widening.

I lunged, put a hand over his mouth, and the stun gun to its neck. His body convulsed, and in a few moments, he was out. I put a used pair of socks in his mouth, covered them with duct tape, and quickly bound his hands. I only had a few minutes until he woke up.

When I made my plan of attack, I chose the side closest to the prisoners, so now I had unfettered access to the cage. No one else was guarding them, probably because they thought the metal bars were sufficient. I scanned the area for a few moments to make sure no one else was around, hiding in the dark, and I approached the wagon.

"Hey, is anyone named Alana here with you?"

I was lucky no one shouted, but despite their surprise, the people only started whispering among themselves.

One woman came next to the bars facing the woods and replied in a murmur, "We don't know anyone by that name. Are you here to free us?"

Am I? My goal was to find Alana, not help some prisoners escape. But I couldn't just leave them there, at the mercy of the men around the fire. I wasn't equipped to face those soldiers, so if I had to free these prisoners, I had to do everything quietly.

"Yes, I will help you."

"What do you want us to do?"

That was a good question. I couldn't pick the lock as that would leave me exposed in the fire light. No, I had to remain in the shadows. The cage had metal bars all around, except the roof and the floor. As climbing on the roof increased the chance of being discovered, that left me with only one option.

"I want you all to gather on the side facing the fire. I'll try to make a hole in the floor with my knife."

As they moved, I took out my knife, pushed it between two slats, and started twisting it back and forth.

"Hey, what's that noise?" I heard one of the soldiers shouting. I froze, sweat trickling down my forehead. "I told you people to stay quiet."

He approached with heavy steps, his back to the fire and a sword in hand. I took out my gun and pointed it at his legs. "One more sound and you'll all regret it." The man hit the metallic bars with the blade, making a clanging noise. Above, I heard people shuffling away from him. "Tomorrow, you'll be put in chains and sold in the slave market. If not, you'll be sent to the mines."

A loud, mocking laugh pierced my ears, and I gripped the gun tighter in my hand. I imagined Alana being sold as a slave and rage built up in my chest. I couldn't let that happen. He chortled again, no doubt trying to intimidate the prisoners. *Buddy, if you laugh like this one more time, I'll make sure it's the last thing you do.* I was close to putting a bullet in him when an arrow perforated his neck, dark droplets of blood splattering the grass in front of me.

10

Shouts erupted from the surrounding forest, and a volley of arrows slew half of the soldiers gathered near the fire. The others grabbed their shields and drew their swords or axes, but demonic silhouettes sprang from the trees to meet them. The soldiers were caught by surprise, and the newcomers' ferocious attack must have made them lose whatever courage they had left. A few tried to flee but were cut down like harvest in autumn. In particular, one newcomer moved like a whirlwind, his two blades slashing and stabbing everyone who got in his way. He had a style I'd seen once before.

The fight didn't take long, and when the last soldier died, skewered by two swords, one in his stomach and another one in his throat, I counted seven human shapes, their faces hidden by the shadows, standing in front of the fire.

"Shaman, I know you're there," shouted a familiar voice.

"I'm here to hold the promise I made you. To help you get Alana back."

For a fleeting second, I wondered if it was a ruse to get me to come out and kill me, but I doubted it. His voice had been sincere, and so far, Lann's behavior had been harsh but fair.

From under the wagon, I came into the light. I kept the gun in my hand, patrol style, one finger next to the trigger.

"Why were you hiding there?" he asked in an amused voice.

I didn't answer, just grabbed the cage's metal bars and kicked the wooden floor under them, the slats I loosened earlier. They flew away, leaving enough room for people to get out. Women, children, and two older men stepped out and stood behind me. They didn't run, didn't go to Lann's men, just stood there, and I realized they were looking up to me for protection.

"How did you find me?"

Lann chuckled. "Well, it wasn't too difficult. The tracks left by your carriage were deep. In the nearby village, we found five bodies with small holes in their heads or chests. I've only seen those wounds once before. We followed your tracks until we saw your carriage, abandoned on the road. So here we are."

What he said made sense, but something didn't add up. I couldn't believe I was so important in Ambenix's eyes that he ordered seven men from his already thin army to track me down deep in the enemy's territory so that Lann could help me save Alana. There was something he wasn't telling me.

"There are a few people here who need our help." I motioned for the people behind me to come forth.

"We won't hurt you," said Lann, putting down his swords.

"We are here to protect you by Lord Ambenix's will. No harm will come to you from my men or me."

One of the older men gazed in my direction and smiled, while the others headed to meet their rescuers. "Thank you, young man, for what you did for us. My name is Hadwin. To whom do I have the pleasure to be in debt?"

"Nice to meet you, Hadwin. I'm Duncan. You are safe with these people. I know them. Now I need to get going, to continue my journey until I find Alana, the woman I inquired about."

"I understand. Oh, young love." Hadwin sighed. His words set something alight inside me. Until now I hadn't put a name to what I felt about Alana. I thought it was a feeling of duty because she saved my life, but the old man's words illuminated another reason, one I'd been afraid to admit even to myself.

"Love doesn't know any obstacles," he continued. "If it helps, we saw another group of soldiers carrying a young woman and a man. My eyes are too old to tell you how they looked and the warriors kept them separate from the rest of us." His words were like a shot of adrenaline. I wanted to run, to fly and rescue her. "They traveled with us for a short time, but then the soldiers hurried them to the citadel. I heard one say something about a slave market. Now go and save her, and I hope our paths cross again."

"Thank you for the information, and who knows? Maybe they will. These people," I motioned toward Lann and his men, "will take you home. You can trust them."

I half-turned to leave, but he continued talking.

"Young man, we lost our home and tribe when our chieftain, Helix, was murdered, along with his queen and their daughter. Since then, we have traveled all over this area, trying to find a place to settle, but we never did."

I took another step, but he didn't seem to notice my intention. *Really? This is the moment when he wants to chat?*

"I'm sorry to hear that."

He didn't continue, his gaze on the fire engulfing the bodies of the dead.

"Well, I hope you'll find a new home," I said after a moment of silence. I took another step.

"We will. There is talk among the other tribes of going to Gaul, and I wanted to ask if you and your lady would like to join us?"

I wanted to face-palm myself. Every moment away from Alana meant more danger for her. *Duncan, don't be rude.* During my childhood, my dad taught me to be respectful of older people.

"I'll be sure to ask her when I see her," I said and moved a step farther away, ready to head to my RV.

"I understand. I hope to see you both soon and healthy. May the gods guide your steps to find her." He turned and followed the others toward the fire, where Lann and his people waited.

Finally. I rushed to my RV, but after a few steps, I heard Lann shout. "Shaman, wait."

What's wrong with everyone? Can't they see I'm in a hurry?

"Shaman, you can't do this by yourself. The town's main gate has guards who check everyone. They don't let anyone in at night, and you don't know the layout of the city."

I narrowed my eyes. "And what's your point?"

"You need someone to help get you in, someone who knows

the city. You need my help. My men will escort these people to safety, and I'll come with you."

I wondered why he was so forthcoming with his help. It felt like more than just the need to fulfill a promise.

"Look, I appreciate your willingness to hold your promise and help me, but I have to question if there's something more here."

"What do you mean?" he asked with a frown.

"I mean, you have another reason for helping me get into the city," I pressed.

He didn't reply, just stared at me. After a few seconds of silence, he continued. "Look, on this, our missions have a common goal, to get us inside the city. That's all you need to know, and I can't say more at the moment."

It was my turn to stare. From the little I knew about him, Lann seemed to be a man of his word—a man of honor. I didn't trust him—his allegiance was to Ambenix first and foremost, but his apparent knowledge of the city might come in handy. And if he had a way that didn't involve sniping all the guards, his help could be useful.

"Very well, we'll meet at the bridge."

"Shaman, you can't pass with your carriage on the other side. I suggest leaving it somewhere close to it, hidden by the trees."

Is he trying to set a trap to steal it from me? Yeah, good luck getting past the locked door.

"And how do we get from there to the city?" To say I wasn't comfortable leaving my one and only safe place was an understatement.

"We walk, as I assume your riding skills haven't improved overnight," Lann said in a condescending tone. "It's not a short walk, though."

I wanted to punch his face, but it was only my hurt ego. He was right; I didn't know how to ride, and if I didn't have to, I didn't want to do it. Ever again.

"Fine, we'll do as you suggested, and I'll see you at dawn, near the bridge." I turned on my heels and left, pushing away a branch that almost took my eye out.

The dashboard clock displayed 00:06 when I saw the bridge and the black river in front of me, courtesy of the moon shining above. I found a place through the trees wide enough to fit my RV and camped there for the night. My sleep was agitated, and I woke up several times, drenched in sweat. Nightmares of finding Alana too late stretched my nerves to the maximum.

The alarm woke me up—my ringtone, the William Tell overture, inundating the quiet in my bedroom. The clock showed 5:00.

I remained in bed, thinking of the events of the last few days. I was far away from home, by several hundred years, if not more, with no idea how I got there or how to get back. And something nagged me.

One implication of time travel was the grandfather paradox. Chances were low, but if this truly were my past and not some alternate universe's history, then any action here would have repercussions in the future. In my future. If I, or through my actions, killed one of my ancestors, what would happen to me? Would I disappear? Or maybe the universe had a fail-safe and blocked my attempt? I needed time to consider the implications, but dawn was upon me.

I added a few more items to my backpack, trying to prepare for any eventuality, put on my makeshift vest, a black hoodie over it, and stepped into the weak light of the foggy morning. All around me, the forest was clouded by a milky white mist undulating gently through the trees.

When I arrived at the bridge, Lann was already waiting for me. He wore a large gray cloak with sweeping folds and a deep hood. Here and there were a few patches of faded brown and green. It looked like a cloak well worn. He threw a bundle of cloth in my direction.

"You need to put that on; otherwise, you won't pass the guards." It was a similar cloth, maybe with a few more threads sticking out. The cloak was made for someone a head taller than me, but it fit well enough after putting it over the backpack. "You look good as a hunchback," he said, not without a smirk. Before I had time to come up with a reply, he continued. "We should arrive there when the food vendors are coming into the city. With some luck, we'll get through without anyone questioning us. Let's make haste."

Ten minutes later, I was panting and wished I didn't have the backpack with me. I had a hard time keeping up with him. My pride stopped me from asking Lann to wait for me to catch my breath, so I thought about asking questions, with the hope he would slow the pace to hear me out.

"Hey, can I ask you something?"

"You just did," Lann replied, keeping the same speed.

This guy is really annoying.

I had to run a couple of steps to get next to him. "Fine, another one then. Why does Ambenix want me dead?"

My plan worked better than expected. Lann stopped and turned to face me, a surprised expression on his face.

"He doesn't."

"Then why is he always threatening me with death?"

"Because that's how he rules. The more people are afraid of you, the harder they'll work to fulfill the commands." Lann shrugged. "Plus, he doesn't really think you're a shaman, and neither do I."

Besides Alana and possibly her father, until now, everyone had thought I was one.

"Then why do you call me a shaman?"

"The lack of a better name, I guess." He started walking, this time at a slower pace.

"And how do you know I'm not one?"

"All the things I've heard about them don't match with how you behave or the things you do. Of course, you have powers I cannot understand, but at the end of the day, you're just a man."

Lann's words upset me. *Maybe I got used to everyone seeing me as a mystical being.*

"Well, I never said I was one," I said, annoyed.

He shrugged and picked up the pace.

There was another thing on my mind, something that had bugged me since I escaped from Ambenix's clutches.

"One other thing. It's about that boy, Madoc. Do you know what happened to him?"

"Why would anything happen to him?" he asked in a disinterested voice.

"Well, it's just you left me with him, and now I'm here. I hope he didn't get into trouble because I got away."

"Ah, I see. To ease your concerns, my nephew is fine."

"Your nephew?" His words took me by surprise.

"Yes, his mother is my sister. From what I understood, everyone went to sleep, and in the morning, when the guards came to get you, you were gone. Strangely enough, you left some drawings that Ambenix threw into the fire. Also, in case you didn't know, Noland, Gwenn's husband and my brother-in-law, had a miraculous recovery and was already feeling better when I left to find you. I don't know how you did it, and I don't want to know, but I respect that you didn't break your word and tried to help us."

His words filled me with joy, but also with a glimmer of suspicion. *Did he orchestrate all this so I could heal Madoc's father?*

A group of half a dozen people surrounding a cart approached from an adjacent road, their silhouettes barely visible through the fog.

"Let's see if we can mingle with them. From now on, until we pass the gates, you don't utter a sound. You have a habit of using words I've never heard. If anyone asks you something, you'll play a mute and point in my direction. I'll handle all the questions."

Lann and I swiftly approached the group. The cart, pulled by a small gray donkey, was filled with all sorts of vegetables and fruits: green apples, yellow pears, red berries, and lots of leafy greens that I didn't recognize.

"Morning, good people. Looks like you had a good harvest there," Lann said in a cheerful tone.

"Morning to you, traveler. Yes, gods were kind enough to give us these things. Are you a merchant too?" asked one of the men, whose burly figure sported a battered old gray cloak.

I remained quiet and let Lann answer the man's question.

"Yes, but two days ago, a group of marauders attacked us, and they stole everything we had. We were lucky to escape with our lives."

"I'm sorry to hear that," the merchant said earnestly. "Since the wars started, the roads aren't safe anymore. Most of the army is away, and there aren't that many people left to patrol and protect us." He pointedly looked over Lann's shoulder at me. "What about your friend over there? Is he shy?"

My heart quickened its pace, but I remained quiet.

"Oh no, he's mute, and he is my servant," said Lann with a laugh.

Servant? I had to bite my tongue not to give Lann a piece of my mind.

"He works hard and doesn't ask for much," Lann continued. That drew chuckles from the merchants. Lann made similar jokes at my expense, but the fog had dissipated, and my attention shifted to the approaching gate. The queue of people waiting to get in wasn't too long, but it advanced slowly, and it gave me time to study the stone fortress lying ahead.

Unlike Ambenix's village, here a stone wall encircled the city, and a grand arch, with two open doors, was the only way inside. Five guards wearing metal armor stood in front of it, seemingly questioning people at random. A dozen archers lined the walls above the gate, bows at the ready. I could feel my heart beating faster and sweat pouring out from my skin, even though it was early, and the air was chilly.

It must have been more than half an hour before I arrived in front of the gate. I risked a glance above and wished I hadn't. If one of those archers aimed for my head, I was a dead man. My gaze fell upon Lann, who talked animatedly with the other merchants like he didn't have a care in the world. My hand moved to my holster, but Lann must have seen the movement, and for a second, our eyes met. I didn't know what he saw there, but he shook his head, almost imperceptibly, and his attention moved back to the people he was talking to. I took his advice.

When I approached the guards, my knees almost buckled, but a few deep breaths gave me enough strength to remain upright.

"Hey, Roy, good to see you this morning," said one guard to the merchant who appeared to be in charge of our group.

"Good to see you too," replied Roy and passed him a small sack. It made a clinking noise when the guard grabbed it.

Without another word, the guard waved the merchant and his entire group, including Lann and me, through.

I kept my eyes forward, but I watched them from the corner of my eye. No one gave me a second look, and I soon turned around a corner and out of their sight. I let out a deep breath.

"We'll stop here," Lann told the burly merchant and put a hand on my shoulder.

"Very nice to meet you, Lann." He waved and continued following the cart. Suddenly, Lann pushed me inside a narrow alley, between two buildings.

"Listen here, you do exactly as I say," he ordered. "Otherwise, we'll both be dead. We'll go to an inn where I know some people. You don't talk to anyone unless I tell you to. After, I'll lead you to wherever you need to go. Do you know where she is?"

"I think she'll be at a slave market," I said, remembering Hadwin's words. I hoped that Lann would show me where the slave market was and help me rescue her. For a brief second, I wondered if I could simply bid for her rather than resorting to violence. *They probably don't accept credit cards.*

Lann pursed his lips. "It won't be easy, but I'm sure you'll come up with something."

"You're not staying?" My hopes of having Lann at my side fell like a house of cards blown by the wind.

"I have other things I need to do, but we'll meet here before sundown. If you do not show up, I'll leave. You do the same; otherwise, you won't get out of the city until morning, and chances are you'll be discovered by one of the patrols."

His knowledge of this place amazed me.

"How come you know so much?"

"Didn't I tell you? I was born here." A mischievous grin stretched across Lann's face. Then he turned and began walking toward the inn, leaving me with my mouth agape.

Compared to Ambenix's village, this was luxurious. Instead of the disgusting slime, here the roads were made of cobblestone. Instead of the ramshackle houses made of wood or mud, here the houses were made of stone and were in much better condition. It had the feeling of one of those old castles I'd visited in the UK, the main difference being it was filled with people who lived here instead of tourists.

The inn resembled one of the old pubs I'd visited in London, just without decorations, TVs, or paintings on the walls. And, of course, without any taps. The place smelled like my grandfather's house—old, dusty, and with a hint of alcohol. It had a bar on the right and a group of tables with chairs and benches on the left. They looked like they'd seen better days: dirty, scratched, some even with wood chunks missing.

"It's closed," said a deep voice behind the counter. The bartender had his back to me, arranging some jars. He had black curly hair, broad shoulders, and wore a brown leather tunic.

"Not even for old friends?" replied Lann in a jovial tone.

"Kierann," shouted the bartender and turned to face us. His square jaw and dark, bushy eyebrows placed him in late thirties, or early forties.

"Farrin, my old friend. It is good to see you." Lann approached the bar and they clasped hands.

"And who is your friend?" asked Farrin, gazing at me.

"He's one of my men," replied Lann, without giving any other details. "Look, I need your help." Farrin frowned but nodded. "Is there someplace where we can talk?"

"Yeah, in the back," the bartender replied and motioned for Lann to follow. I started after them, but Lann turned and said, "Wait here, and clap your hands if anyone enters." They both disappeared through a side door.

I would have appreciated it more if he'd just asked me to stay here without any kind of pretense, but maybe he had his reasons. I took a seat at one of the empty tables. Even though they were dirty, sticky, and smelled of alcohol, at least the chairs and tables were made from solid oak. My cloak had more stains than the chair, so I didn't worry I'd ruin it. I took the phone out of my pocket and checked, just for the fun of it, if there was a WiFi signal. *Of course, there isn't one, duh.* I opened a game on my phone and started playing. It felt so good and normal that for a moment I forgot where I was.

"Thank you, Farrin," I heard Lann say and hurried to put the phone back.

"Anytime, Kierann. You know that."

Lann walked past me, toward the exit. "Let's go," he said over his shoulder.

I stood, nodded in Farrin's direction, and followed Lann outside. He walked in silence until I reached a large plaza filled with people. Ahead, across the square, close to the wall, was an empty wooden platform with guards posted at both ends. From an adjacent alley, a group of people emerged. At the front was a short man with long, black, wavy hair and an imposing belly, wearing a red and green robe. Men and women in chains, framed by soldiers, followed him. My heart skipped a beat. *Is she among them?* I gazed at the prisoners, studied their clothes—or better said, the few remaining strips of clothes they had—their hair, their faces, searching for Alana, but she wasn't there.

"Looks like you arrived just in time," whispered Lann in my ear. I kept my gaze on the prisoners and the soldiers.

The short guy with the belly and the robes climbed onto the platform and raised his hands, and everyone fell silent.

"By the grace of our chieftain Orgetorix, today, we have a new stock among us," he shouted.

The place's acoustics must have been exceptional, because I could clearly hear him above the crowd's whispers.

"Captured from the great battles won by our armies, in front of you," he said and gestured to the people in chains, who were pushed on the stage alongside him, "you have five who stood against us. They, and those that will follow, are now ready to serve you. The rules are the same as before. You bid for what you see. The payment must be received in full before you leave with your choice. If you win and do not pay, you will be lashed and imprisoned," he said and pointed to the building behind him.

Yeah, they definitely don't take credit cards.

He approached one of the prisoners, put a hand on his bare shoulder, and continued. "With that said, the market is open for bids. Let's see how much this magnificent body is worth."

"I need to go now, but I'll meet you near the gates when the sun sets," Lan murmured beside me. "Remember, leave the city before nightfall. Otherwise, the patrols will find you. If I'm not there, leave without me." Before I could say anything, Lann mingled through the people filling the square and disappeared.

For the next few hours, people shouted amounts, paid sacks of coins, and leered at the humiliated beings who just stood there on the podium. The prisoners all wore scanty clothes to allow the buyers to see their physical qualities. Some of them shook, either from the cold or from fear, and my thoughts grew darker with each new person being sold.

After many hours, five new people were brought, and among them was a black girl, no more than twelve years old. She was scared; her body trembled, and tears rolled down her cheeks. An older man, somewhere around fifty years old, dressed in a dark red robe and surrounded by a couple of armed bodyguards, bid heavily for her. He outbid everyone else, and when he turned to say something to one of his companions, I noticed his face. His greedy expression and the lustful look in his eyes told me everything I needed to know.

He approached and started touching the girl, assessing her, like someone looking at a piece of meat. She shied away from his repulsive touch, but he continued more forcefully. At that moment, my hand, by its own accord, grabbed the gun. I knew what his look meant, what he wanted with the girl, and I swore to myself I wouldn't let him do it. I didn't care about what consequences it brought, but the man would die before he had a chance to defile her.

I focused on him, trying to find a way to rescue the girl, and I didn't realize the market had closed. People started pouring out of the square, and with all the commotion, I lost sight of my target. Frantically, I looked around, scanning the crowd and the now-empty platform, until I spotted him holding the girl by the arm and dragging her after him, followed by his men. I launched myself after them.

11

The streets were narrow and packed with people. Beggars in rags asked passers-by for food and coins. Carts pulled by donkeys, filled with large amphoras, vegetables, and fruits, made their way through the muddy streets, and young boys dashed from alleys to grab whatever they could and run before they were whipped by the cartman or caught by the soldiers passing through.

With all the commotion, no one spared a glance in my direction, and that made it easier to follow without being seen, but it hindered my movements. I had to hurry and find my way through the crowd every time the man and his entourage rounded a corner.

Before long, they stopped in front of a one-story house with a small wall surrounding a garden in front. The house had a wooden door and square holes on the sides covered by shutters, similar to those I'd seen all over the city. The door opened when they entered the garden, an elderly servant kowtowing to them. None of the three men even looked at the old man, who bowed deeply.

I glanced around me. The area looked deserted compared to the slave market. Two people dressed in skintight green pants and brown tunics stood with their backs against a house wall at one end of the street, talking animatedly. Above me, the sun looked like it was preparing to depart, leaving me much less time than I wanted to get back and meet with Lann. Assuming I could find the way back to the gate.

On the west-facing side of the building, the windows were open to let some light in. I sneaked around the garden walls, ran through the garden until I reached one of the lateral square holes, and peeked inside. The room was empty, small, and looked like a vestibule, with only a long, dark wooden bench. A closed door led the way inside the house. I continued past the few open windows until I reached one next to the end of the dwelling. Voices emanated from inside, so I crouched under the sill to hear them better.

"Don't just stand there," came a woman's voice. "I need to make sure you're all clean for tonight. He'll want you with only a robe and nothing else. Do you understand what I'm saying? Are you mute?" A second later, I heard a slap and then the unmistakable sobs of a child. "Why he had to bring one like you, I don't know. Now stop crying and come here."

I heard enough to know that even a second more in that house was nothing a child should have to endure. Like a spring, I stood up, and with one look, I noted what lay in front of me. With her back to me was a woman, wearing a yellowish bonnet and a long brown dress. For a second, I was frozen in place, unsure of what to do. I couldn't outright shoot her, and I didn't want to harm her physically. Fortunately, she took the decision from my hands because she turned, took one look at me, and ran screaming.

"I'm here to help you," I said to the frightened-looking girl.

"You...you speak my language?" she asked, surprised.

"Yes." *Odd. I just talked to her in English.* "Now, let's run before someone comes and sees us."

With a leap, she was on the windowsill, and then on the ground, next to me. She started running toward the front garden.

She's agile. I bolted after her.

There were shouts and then a heavy thud. One guard jumped over the sill and came after me at a dead sprint. I was carrying a backpack and had a little girl with me, so I couldn't run at full speed. But even if I could, I wasn't a runner, and he was fast like a gazelle. *That guy needs an incentive to stop following me.* I turned, raised my gun, and shot him in the left leg. His face contorted in pain, and then he stumbled and fell, sprawled forward, his chin hitting the dirt. *Good night and sleep tight. Don't let the garden bugs bite.* I reached the garden's entrance, where the girl waited, her eyes wide, focused beyond me on the man I'd just wounded. People were shouting from inside the building, so I took the girl by the arm, crossed the street, and entered a deserted alley.

"Call the guards!" someone shouted behind me. I glanced back to see the two people in brown tunics and green leggings running after me. They were catching up. I turned left and entered a crowded square.

It was packed with street vendors, all yelling, selling, and buying food. The smell of baked potatoes and roasted meat assaulted my nostrils. My mouth watered instantly, and I felt a deep, almost painful rumble in my stomach. I had eaten nothing since this morning, and the thought made my stomach clench. A glance at the girl told me she was in the same boat.

A water seller passed by me, his voice loud enough to cover the busy noise of the street.

"Cold, fresh water, cold water!" He was dressed in shabby clothes, and on his back he carried a giant ceramic carafe.

At the other end of the street, a group of soldiers carrying spears came my way. I stopped, unsure of what to do. Ahead, I would face the warriors, if I turned back, it would be me against the two people in brown tunics.

The water seller's eyes met mine. "Go there. When they reach me, I'll tell them you went some other way." He pointed to a narrow road between two buildings.

"Thanks." I pulled the girl into the alley.

The racket died down, and the street led to a patch of green grass, surrounded by a tall white wall. I motioned for her to go inside. On my left was a gray stone bench under a walnut tree.

I peered around the wall and saw the soldiers talking to the water seller. The two pursuers in brown tunics joined them.

Did the water seller send me here so he could tell the soldiers where I was? Maybe he wants to make some money selling the information. I gripped the gun tighter.

The soldiers looked around, and I retreated for a couple of

seconds, afraid they would see me. When I peered again, they had left. I let out a deep breath.

"Let's stop there for a moment," I said and took a seat on the bench, panting. "Are you hungry?" I asked once I got my breathing under control, even though I was quite sure of her answer. She just nodded, and her gaze moved down like she was afraid she had said something bad.

"Don't worry, I have food for both of us. Would you like a sandwich?" I asked and took the backpack off, reaching inside.

"What is a san...wich?"

"Here you go," I said and handed her one wrapped in aluminum foil. I took one as well and unwrapped it slowly to give her time to follow my movements. Both were pastrami, spread cheese, and lettuce. I took a hearty bite, and she soon followed my example. She was starving, given how she finished it in record time. With the sandwich gone, I took out a couple of bottles of water and handed her one. With deliberate movements, I showed her how to unscrew the cap and open it. Carefully, she took a sip, tasted it, closed her eyes, and drank the rest of the water without a pause.

"You have to slow down when you drink," I said and showed her by taking a few swigs, with a slight pause in between.

She gazed at her empty bottle, then at mine, and finally, she lifted her gaze to watch me. I capitulated and gave her my container.

"What do you say about some dessert? I have a chocolate bar if you want. It has a lot of proteins." She nodded again without saying a word. I took out two Snickers bars and handed her one. The expression on her face when she tasted it made my day. Her face radiated joy and pleasure, like, well, like a kid when she tastes chocolate for the first time. She ate the first half before I had the chance to even take a bite. Then, realizing she didn't have much left, she covered it the best she could with the wrapping and made a tiny first around it. My eyes misted as I realized that the piece of chocolate, for her, was a prized possession, the only thing she had.

"If you want, you can finish it," I said and handed her mine. She gazed at me with sparkling eyes, as though she couldn't believe it was true. "Yes, it's all yours."

"May I ask a question?" she asked in a tiny voice.

I had a feeling the poor girl had been instructed to speak only when she was given permission.

"Sure. What do you want to know?"

"Why are you so good to me?" She finished her chocolate and handed me the wrapping.

It was a simple question, a natural question, to which I had no immediate answer. I took a few moments to think it through and discover the real reason behind my actions.

"Because no one, especially a child, should have to go through what you did and what would have happened if you had remained there." For a few seconds, she didn't say anything else. She just watched me.

"Thank you. I'm glad you helped me."

My heart melted at her words. This world was a cruel one for children.

"No problem. By the way, what's your name?"

"I'm Nabil."

"Nice to meet you, Nabil, I'm Duncan. What do you say we

find a place to lie low for a while? I'm sure those people won't give up so easily."

A frightened look flashed across her eyes.

"Don't worry, they won't find us, but it's better not to tempt fate," I hurried to assure her.

She nodded and took my hand in hers, or more accurately, only half of my fingers, as her hands were small. She didn't have the soft skin most kids had. She had been put to hard work.

I glanced at the other end of the alley where the street vendors were, but no one looked in my direction. I headed the opposite way, and after a few crossroads, I realized I was lost. My plan was to bring her to Farrin's tavern and ask him if he could watch her until I could find Alana. If Lann trusted him, I assumed I could too. But first, I needed to see where the gate was.

"Nabil, do you know how we can get out of town by any chance?"

"No. They kept me in a cage, alone, until last night, when another woman was brought in. She was kind to me, not like the others."

"How long were you imprisoned?" I looked around, trying to find something familiar. People were already staring at Nabil.

"For many days. They brought me in at night and put me in a metal cage. A few days later, they took me out during the day for people to see me. I was so scared. The first day, an old lady with no teeth came and started poking me. I don't know what she said, but she seemed very angry and left."

"Where are your parents?" I asked, my eyes darting left and

right, trying to find some landmark. When I spotted the square I'd spent most of my day in, I let out a breath of relief.

"The bad men killed them, then they took me to a boat. It was the first time I saw so much water, but they kept me inside for many days. Then they gave me to an old woman. She was very mean, and if I didn't do what she said, she didn't give me any food. That's how I learned their language."

Fresh tears dripped from her eyelashes. My desire to protect Nabil intensified tenfold.

"I've been in other places, but all of them were cruel to me. I thought I wouldn't find anyone else like my parents until the woman with the hair the color of wheat grain. And you. You were both nice to me. I'm sorry for her. I heard the guards talk about her, and they said awful things. I didn't understand everything, but they were terrible. The old man who took me said he would do similar things to me." A flood of tears flowed down her face. She bowed her head, staring at my feet. Her shoulders shook.

"Don't worry, I won't let anything bad happen to you." I put a gentle arm on her shoulder for comfort. *No one will hurt you again.*

"Can you save her too?" she asked, wiping the tears with her palm.

What can I say to her? Should I lie and give her false hopes? Maybe after I save Alana, I could look into helping whoever Nabil wanted me to get out of jail.

"I don't know. I have to find someone, and I also need to keep you safe."

"She was very kind to me, and she is beautiful. I haven't

seen hair as golden as hers. And she had similar shoes to yours."

My breath caught in my throat.

"Say that again?" I was afraid I misunderstood her words.

"Both of you have these strings on your shoes. I haven't seen anyone else with shoes like that."

I gazed down at the laces, then knelt and took one in my hand. "You mean these?"

"Yes."

Ice ran up my spine. *Could that woman be Alana?*

"And do you know where she's kept?" My heart skipped a beat, and all the tiredness disappeared, washed away by a feeling of anticipation, a desire to find and protect Alana.

"Yes, she was in the same place where I was."

"And you know how to get there?"

People pointed in my direction, but I didn't care. I was getting close to finding out where Alana was.

She nodded. "It's close to the market where they sold me today."

I gestured toward the square I'd seen earlier. I really hated that she used the *market*. People aren't goods to be traded and sold to whoever bid more.

"Yes, that's the one," she exclaimed.

"Keep your voice down." People were now openly staring at me, kneeling in front of a little girl. *Huh, maybe they're not used to seeing children treated as...well, children.* "Can you give me some directions on how to get to her?"

She crossed her arms. "I want to come with you."

What? Why would she wanna do that?

"It's dangerous." A prison was no place for a child. Plus, everyone in this world seemed more determined to stab you and ask questions later.

I looked around and was welcomed by a lot of suspicious stares. *Better to leave this place.*

I took her hand and headed toward the square.

"Not for you. You are the shaman from the story," she said in a determined tone.

"What?" I asked, surprised.

"Last night, when I couldn't sleep, she told me a story about a shaman who would come and save us. You are the shaman. You won't let anyone harm me, I'm sure of it. And I feel safe with you. Please don't leave me."

What could I say to this little girl? She seemed committed to believing I was the hero in whatever story Alana told her. Whatever arguments I had against her coming with me melted at the sound of her pleading voice.

"Very well. Against my better judgment, I'll let you come with me, under one condition. You do exactly as I say. Understood?"

She nodded, happiness painted on her face. "Yes," she said at last. I shook my head. She was too eager to put herself in danger.

"Okay. Now I have to plan and see when's the best time to sneak in."

She took one look at the sky and said, "Many will soon leave for supper. Later, new people will come. If we go now, there will be fewer bad people there."

"But won't they see us?"

"No," she said and shook her head. "When they first brought me, I was near a door used by the servants. I didn't see any soldiers there. Maybe one."

I took a deep breath, and adrenaline plunged into my veins. *That's why I came here. It's time to rock and roll.*

"Show me the way."

I crossed the square and entered a narrow, dark alley on the other side of the building where the podium was.

"Stay behind me," I instructed Nabil and took out my gun. I pushed on the doorknob, but the door didn't budge. It was locked.

I took my Mastercard from my wallet, pulled the door toward me, inserted it at an angle between the door and the jamb, just above the doorknob's latch. With some downward and inward pressure, after some wiggling, I felt it clunk when the card separated the bolt from the strike face. The door opened with a squeak. I murmured thanks to Martin, my CERN team's mechanical engineer, who, among other things, taught me how to shim a lock.

Inside it was dark, and I took a moment to let my eyes adjust. It was a small empty room, devoid of furniture, with only one wooden door. I pressed gently on it. It wasn't locked, and it opened to reveal a long empty corridor. A pale flickering torch posted on the wall halfway through the shadowy hall was the only light source. "Follow me," I whispered to Nabil.

"Turn there," she said after half a dozen steps.

In the shadows, another door made of metal bars blocked my way. Through the bars, stairs led down into a semi-darkness. I felt a chill air caressing my face, filled with the pungent smell of urine and other, more unpleasant things. The bars were cold to the touch, but they opened with a barely audible clink when I pushed them. Ahead, at the other end, coming from under the door, light and voices reached me. I counted ten steps.

"This way, my lord," I heard a man's voice say on the other side of the door. I listened to the sound of steps, then a clang and a screech, probably made by an opening door, receding footsteps, then silence.

I peeked through the keyhole but couldn't see anything. It was blocked. Someone had forgotten to take the key out of the hole. I tried the handle. Locked. I had a moment of panic because I didn't know how to get in, then an idea flashed through my mind, and I reached in my backpack for my paper map. There was more than enough space under the wooden frame for what I had in mind. I unfolded the map and slid the paper under the door to where I approximated the key would land, then used the tip of my knife to push the key out of the keyhole. It fell with a dull thud. I slid the map back to me, with the key on it. I tightened my grip on the gun, pointed it ahead of me, and unlocked and opened the door.

The room was small, illuminated by a torch positioned next to the entrance. There was a table, an empty chair next to it, and a cloak on the backrest. On the right-hand side, through metal bars, I saw a long passageway and two men turning around a corner. On both sides of the corridor were empty cells.

"The others were here," Nabil said and pointed to one of the cells.

"Who?"

"The ones who were sold with me today. Yesterday they moved me to a cage beyond that corner. That's where she is."

I gently pushed the metal bars and the door opened without a noise. *I wonder what they use, as I very much doubt WD40 was invented yet.* Careful not to make any noise, I followed the two men, Nabil keeping close to me. I stopped before a rounding corner. The voices were clear now.

"My spies told me you were the one who helped the shaman. I want to know what he did and how he was able to defeat our army." The man's voice was pitched high, like he was missing a couple of important things near his crotch.

"I won't tell you anything," Alana's voice answered, and my heart leaped, thumping loudly in my ears. *I hope they don't hear me.*

"Oh, you will talk. The only question is how much you will scream before you tell us what we want. I'll make sure to keep that beautiful face intact, but I can't promise the same about the rest of your body. When I'm done with you, you will crawl at my feet, eager to fulfill my every wish. If you don't want to tell me now, that's fine. You will squeal later when my blade is around your breasts."

I heard the sound of keys jingling, and then a metal door open. *Time's up.*

"Stay here," I whispered to Nabil. I couldn't wait and stepped around the corner, gun in hand, ready to shoot. I was dimly aware of the potential impact each kill could have over the future, but I couldn't let anything happen to Alana.

The fist caught me in my jaw and sent me on the opposite side, where I collapsed at the base of the wall, my gun slipping out of my hand. For a second, my vision blurred, and everything spun around me. The guard kicked me hard in the stomach, and I had the impression he cracked one of my ceramic plates.

"Who are you?" he asked.

I tried to talk, but it hurt. *His fist must have dislodged a tooth.*

"Kill him," came the cold high-pitched voice of the other man.

In a flash, his sword cleared the scabbard, the gleaming blade heading in a downward arc for my head.

I would have died right then and there if Nabil hadn't jumped on his back. It only took a moment for him to shove her away, but it was enough for me to dive for the gun. He raised his sword once more, and I fired. Twice. First in the belly, and the second on his knee. I didn't want to kill him unless I absolutely had to. *Yeah, talk about calm during a highly stressful situation.* For a moment, his body remained on his feet, like a puppet on strings, and then he collapsed to the floor with a heavy thud, the sword hitting the cold stone with a clank.

I rose and focused on the second man, who wore a bronze breastplate. He already had a long sword in hand and stepped out of the cell to meet me. I was glad he did. I didn't want him anywhere near Alana. For a brief second, my attention was distracted by the sight of her in chains. The black pants I'd given her were dirty, and her shirt was in tatters. Most of it was torn, exposing her delicate skin. Her brown eyes glinted in recognition when they met mine and hope brightened her face. It almost cost me my life.

My attacker made a thrusting motion with the sword, and I

felt its tip in my stomach. If he had gone for my neck or head, I would have died, but one of the plates in my makeshift vest stopped the blade. Unfortunately, it didn't stop the force behind it, and it pushed me back a few steps until I hit the wall again, knocking the wind out of me. He raised the sword for the killing stroke.

Suddenly, the tip of a sword protruded from his neck, and dark red blood gushed out, splattering the breastplate with crimson spots. He sank to his knees and dropped face-first to the ground. Behind him, Nabil stared at the body, her eyes wide. *She had killed a man to save me.*

"Duncan," cried Alana. "Is it really you?" Her face was pale, and her voice betrayed concern and hope.

"It's me." I stepped inside her cell. Shackles covered her wrists, and she was tied to the wall facing the entrance. "Are you hurt?"

"No. See if you can get the key from him." She motioned with her head behind me.

I hurried back and checked the body of the guard.

"Here they are." Nabil handed me a large ring with several keys.

"Are you hurt?" I asked gently, studying her. There was no blood on her.

Nabil shook her head.

"Thank you for saving me. Without you, I would have died." I watched her for another moment, just to make sure she was really fine. "Now stay here and tell me if you hear anyone else coming."

She nodded, her eyes shining brightly.

I went back to Alana and, after a couple of tries, found the right key and freed her.

"Let's go." I offered my hand to help her up. She took it and rose, but after a couple of steps, she staggered and almost fell. I caught her just in time. "Are you injured?"

"No. Do you have some water?"

I rummaged through my backpack and handed her a bottle of water.

She took a few swigs and handed it back. "I think I can walk on my own now."

I didn't want to argue with her and let go, keeping my arms close to her body.

Alana took a few steps, then knelt to take the sword of the man with the bronze plate. My gaze shifted to the backpack, and I put the bottle of water inside when I heard the scrape of metal on stone, followed by a whoosh. The head of the man with the bronze breastplate rolled past me, empty eyes staring at the ceiling. Alana swiftly moved to the next target and planted the blade in the guard's belly, where I shot him. The man grunted in pain. *Hmm, I thought he lost consciousness.* She lifted the sword, and it came crashing down in an arc, beheading him. *Alana really is a woman men lose their heads for.*

She staggered on her feet and placed a hand on the wall to support herself.

"Alana?" came Nabil's concerned voice.

"Oh, child, I'm so happy to see you. I thought they sold you when you didn't come back." She extended a hand and Nabil came to hug Alana.

"They did, but he saved me."

Both of them gazed at me, their eyes filled with gratitude. It made me uncomfortable. Maybe in a different setting, not surrounded by two decapitated lifeless bodies with blood pouring out from them like a river, things would have been different.

"I think we should get out of here," I said and took the lead. One moment longer and everything I'd eaten in the last few days would color the floor.

When I arrived in the small antechamber leading to the cells, Alana took the cloak left by the guard on his chair and hid the blade in it.

Outside, the sun was already set behind the horizon. *I hope it's not past closing time.*

"Let's head to the gates. We have little time," I said, remembering Lann's words.

"No. I need to save my father." Alana's tone was resolute, and I knew there was no point fighting against her decision.

"Do you know where he is?"

She shook her head. *Well, that doesn't help.*

"Is he here, in this prison?" *That would make things so much easier.*

"No, they took him somewhere else."

But of course. Why would the universe make things easy for me?

"Look, Lann is in the city as well. He said he'll be at the gates when the sun sets." She didn't seem convinced by my words. "Lann knows the city better than I do," I insisted. "We'll ask for his help to rescue your father, and he'll do it. He owes me one. Otherwise, we can spend a great deal of time searching for Tyrenn, and we'll get caught, which won't help your father at all."

She reluctantly agreed with a slow nod.

We spent the journey back to the gate in a state of heightened alert. I half expected to hear an alarm, but nothing like that happened. Farmers and merchants with empty carts, weary expressions, and tired movements clustered around the exit. I looked for Lann but couldn't see him. *Did he leave without me?* Nabil took my hand and stuck close to me. She had a frightened look on her face.

"Everything will be all right," I whispered in her ear. "See, they don't check anyone, and we'll soon be outside the gates."

Compared to earlier, when everyone was scrutinized, the guards were now talking among themselves without even a glance at the people passing through. Up on the walls, I counted half a dozen archers, but they looked bored and weren't paying attention either.

We weren't even twenty paces from the gate when the bells started ringing.

12

I heard the sound of hooves on the rocky street before I saw the rider. He had a golden crest on his fluttering green cloak, and he headed straight for the gate. People moved away from him, and I followed suit. I thought he would continue past the guards, but the rider stopped at the last second and turned the horse.

"A young woman escaped, and we believe she had help. One, maybe two others are with her. Stop all young women and their escorts and send them to me. Also, there was a report of a young slave running away. Stop any children and interrogate them. Is that understood?" thundered the rider.

"Yes, sir," replied the guards in unison. He took one look around him, then started galloping back.

The universe must love me. Not.

I desperately checked around, trying to find another way

out, but there was none. The guards already started checking everyone, and the archers had the bows at the ready.

"We can't go this way," I whispered. "Let's go back."

I took advantage of the crowd of people, and found a way to a back alley, hidden from the guard's scrutinizing eyes.

"What shall we do?" asked Alana. "We don't know anyone here to help us."

Her words gave me an idea. "Actually, that's not entirely accurate. Let me check first if Lann is here. I think he came with a mission, but he helped me get inside the city and said he'd meet me here when they close the gate."

Around the corner, I spent a few more minutes looking for him, but when it became clear he wasn't there, I decided not to wait any longer.

"This morning, we visited an inn, and he knew the innkeeper," I explained. "Maybe he can help us. If not to get out, at least to find Lann."

Alana put an arm around Nabil. "They'll recognize her if we go out like this."

I scratched my head thinking how to have Nabil look less conspicuous. Alana and I had cloaks to blend in, but Nabil had only the clothes that woman had prepared for her. She really looked like a fugitive. Something behind Nabil attracted my attention.

"You're right, but I have an idea." On the alley, along with trash, was a dirty rag, which once must have been a large potato bag. I took it and used my knife to cut a few holes in it. When I finished, it looked like a miserable old cloak, which I put over her head and shoulders. It worked beautifully; she looked like a beggar.

Both Alana and I put our hoods up, and I guided them to where the tavern was. It took me a couple of tries, going back and forth a few times until I found it. From inside the tavern came voices of people shouting, and I didn't want to attract more attention, so I continued past it and turned to a side alley, where I hoped to find another entrance.

I was mistaken. A tall wooden wall separated the street from the inn's backyard. I could hear chickens and pigs on the other side of the fence. There didn't seem to be a door, so I had to create one. I unsheathed my knife and used it to dislodge a few boards, enough for me to go through. Inside was a small courtyard filled with chickens, and one rooster. He had bright red feathers with a few black specs and a large comb on top. *He looks cute.* The bird lowered his head and started jumping from one foot to another, like he was dancing. That's when I realized my mistake. You never stare at a rooster.

He stretched his wings and tried to attack me, so I hurriedly followed Alana and Nabil, who had already located the back entrance. I didn't squeal. Honestly. The door was unlocked, so we sneaked inside, right into a dark closet that smelled of old, rancid cheese. I closed the door right into the rooster's nose. *Ha, take that you kamikaze bird.*

There were several jars around me, their silhouettes visible in the light coming from under the door leading inside the tavern. The room was filled with the aroma of different types of smoked meat, and my stomach growled. From behind the door came the unmistakable sound of pots, pans, and customers' voices shouting, laughing, and the clinking sound of people toasting and drinking. I grabbed a piece of sausage hanging on the wall. *Oh, this smells so good. Maybe I should take a bite.*

"Shall we go in?" asked Alana, her voice pitched low.

Before I had the chance to answer, the innkeeper's voice came from the other side of the door. "Make sure that chicken is roasted properly. I'll go and grab some more onions."

I let go of the sausage, quickly pulled everyone behind the door, and waited for Farrin. He pushed it open, and I heard the gnashing of a wooden crate dragged to create a doorstop.

"Now, where did I put those," I heard him mutter to himself.

"Farrin," I said in a low voice.

"Who's there?" He turned, a butcher's knife in his hand.

I hoped he would remember me from our short meeting this morning.

"It's me, Kierann's friend. We met this morning." I stepped out of the shadows.

"What do you want?" he asked, his tone rough. He hadn't put the knife away.

"Your help."

His eyes widened in surprise. "I can't help you."

"But you don't even know what I need."

Farrin shook his head. "Whatever it is, it's not my problem."

I didn't have too much experience in negotiations, and I couldn't think of a way to make him help me, other than threatening him. Then I remembered his behavior when he saw Lann.

"Look, Kierann was supposed to meet me at the gates, but he didn't arrive. Do you at least know where he is?"

His gaze remained hard, and for a few seconds, I thought he'd drive me off, but then the man lowered the knife and let out a breath.

"That boy always gets into trouble."

He seems to have a soft spot for Lann.

"You know where he is?" I insisted.

"I have my suspicions. He asked me how to get into Orgetorix's house."

"He's where?" I heard Alana splutter from behind me.

"Who's she?" asked Farrin, his eyes narrowing suspiciously. "Is she your woman?"

I didn't know what to say, so I nodded. "Do you know why he went there?"

"Because he's a fool, that's why," replied Farrin forcefully.

"I don't understand." There was something here I was missing.

He stopped and gazed at me for a few seconds, assessing me. "Because many people come to my inn, and after a few drinks, secrets get spilled, boy."

"Do you know how many prisons are in this city?" asked Alana.

Ah, she thinks Lann was arrested.

Farrin seemed taken aback by her question and replied after a few moments.

"Only one. It's up next to the slave market."

Alana bit her lower lip in frustration.

"What if someone is taken from prison to somewhere else? Any idea where they would go?" I didn't understand the reason behind Alana's question. From what I'd seen, the only other place a prisoner is sent to is either the slave market or where the guillotine is. *If they even have a guillotine in this world.*

"Well," Farrin started, scratching his chin, "the only other place would be to Orgetorix's house. There are rumors he has dungeons underneath, where he brings people to...well, you can imagine why."

"Can you tell us where it is and how to get in?" I asked.

He nodded, giving me a thoughtful look. "Only because Kierann saved my life when I was younger. When you see him, tell him we're even. I'll give you directions."

I used an app on my phone to draw a rough sketch of the town's layout, according to Farrin's instructions. It took me longer to convince him my phone wasn't a magical item that would suck his soul than to get the details from him. At least I was reasonably sure he wouldn't tell anyone, afraid of what the scary shaman would do to him. I hadn't actually threatened him at all. Everything was in his head. Promise.

According to Farrin, Orgetorix's house was the biggest and most beautiful of all the city buildings, and I couldn't miss it. The biggest problem was the guards. No one could enter without invitation, but I wasn't deeply concerned about that. I still had my credit card.

After slipping back out past the evil rooster, I walked behind Alana, who held Nabil's hand, keeping an eye out for any soldiers.

"Do you think both my father and Lann are kept there?" Alana asked, over her shoulder.

"I think so. If what Farrin said is true, and Lann went to Orgetorix, then I assume he was caught."

"Why would he go there?"

"To kill him?" I could think of no other reason Lann would have.

He didn't strike me as the man who would betray his leader. *Otherwise why fight at Ambenix's side where he could easily have been killed?*

"Maybe. Or maybe he's secretly working for Orgetorix?"

"I don't think so. He doesn't strike me as someone who would break his word. During the battle, he had ample opportunities to kill Ambenix or to escape. He didn't. And if he worked for Orgetorix, then he wouldn't need to know how to enter his house unseen."

"That's true," Alana agreed.

"Also, when we came here, I had the impression he had a purpose. He didn't tell me what kind of mission, but if I had to guess, I think he wanted to assassinate Orgetorix. That's the reason he wanted to get inside Orgetorix's house without anyone else knowing."

"Do you think he succeeded?" There was an ounce of hope in Alana's voice.

"I don't think so. Otherwise, he would have met us back at the gates."

Alana let out a sigh. "I thought so as well, but I hoped that maybe I was missing something."

I had just stepped onto a well-lit street when a door opened and three soldiers came out, singing. Alana turned, pushed Nabil in my arms, and I staggered back until I hit the wall. Alana pressed into me, letting her cloak fall around my body to hide Nabil from sight, and kissed me softly. Her lips were moist, and I fought to keep my desire down. The sound of boots faded away, and Alana stepped back. There was a hint of red in her cheeks. Alana took Nabil's hand and continued forward without saying a word.

The kiss swayed me on my feet. I shook my head to clear it and followed them.

A few minutes later, I understood why Farrin had said I couldn't miss it. The house was big enough to occupy an entire block. The line of parked chaises gathered in front was even longer. It had a mix of litters, which looked like portable beds, and coaches with four wheels and wooden arched rooftops.

Compared to the other houses I'd seen, this one looked like a palace, with a luxurious square garden in front, painted by the colors of hundreds of flowers, and over a dozen columns surrounding it. All the columns had torches attached; these cast enough light to shower everything in a golden-yellow. A row of soldiers protected the garden's entrance, each wearing armor, shield, and spear. In front of them stood an older man dressed in a white robe, with red markings at its edges, holding a scroll. He seemed to be the one in charge of welcoming the guests. Each group stopped in front of him, and after a few words, he looked them up on the scroll. I assumed it was the guest list. Some people had similar white robes, but others wore animal skins or dark dresses with golden threads that sparkled in the moonlight.

I kept in the shadows until I passed the main entrance, my view now obstructed by the lined-up carriages and the men surrounding them. They were either the drivers or the litter bearers. Very few stood next to their assigned vehicles. Most gathered in small groups, drinking and talking loudly.

I was near the back of the house, where a multitude of servants went in and out like bees in a hive. They unloaded fruits, bread, cheese, and amphoras filled with the sweet, alcoholic smell of crushed grapes. This was the entrance Farrin told us about, except it had two soldiers who closely watched all the people coming and going.

I had an idea and approached one of the deserted litters. On one of the four posts, I saw the cloaks left there by the litter bearers, and without any hesitation, I snatched two of them. They were damp and stank of sweat.

I handed the first to Alana. She scoffed at the sight of it but put it on.

"Here, put this over you," I said to Nabil. "Hopefully, they'll think you're servants." Nabil obeyed without a word. It was too long for her, so Alana shortened it with her sword. *She's so much better than I am with sharp objects.*

"And what about you?" asked Nabil. "I can go and steal another one."

"Well, my cloak is in similar shape to these, so it shouldn't get much attention. Look, I think it's safer if you remain here."

If even Lann had been caught, then chances were this house was much better guarded than the town's jail.

She grabbed my cloak with her small hands. "Please don't leave me."

My conviction started melting at her plea. I tried again, even though in my heart, I already made the decision. "It's dangerous there, and if something happens, I'm not sure I can protect you. We could all get killed."

"You saved me from something worse than death," Nabil said. "Where I come from, death is just another part of a soul's journey. I'm not scared of it."

I was surprised by how mature her words were. *Maybe her parents taught her that.*

"You should be. Life is precious."

I glanced at Alana who had an amused expression on her face. *She probably knows the result of this debate.*

"And I feel safe when I'm around you," Nabil said, her voice full of conviction.

With no arguments left, I relented. "You can come, but please do exactly what I say." She nodded, her eyes sparkling.

I approached one of the carts, nothing more than a wooden board with four iron-shod wheels, used to hold the perishables. On one side was a stack of wooden plates I'd seen people use to bring the food inside the building. I picked up one and put a pile of grape clusters on it, enough to hide my face if I carried the plate on one of my shoulders. I kept my right hand free, holding the handgun up my sleeve, its muzzle in my bent palm.

I picked a moment when a group of servants, some dressed in tunics, some with tattered cloaks, approached the entrance and quickly joined them, making a sign for Alana and Nabil to follow me. When I was only ten feet away from the entrance, one soldier stopped a servant and took some bread from the plate he was carrying.

"Let's see what else we have here," said his companion in a gruff voice. He stopped the next one and picked an apple, then signaled for the servant to pass.

Beads of sweat accumulated on my forehead. When the two people in front of us, carrying a large amphora, arrived in front of the guards, an idea came to me.

I hastily let the pistol drop in my palm, pointed the barrel in front, and shot. The popping sound, no louder than the release of a cork from a wine bottle, was instantly followed by a crack in the ceramic container, and wine started leaking, inundating the soldiers' sandals.

"Hey, what are you doing?" shouted the soldier, his attention directed at the red liquid at its feet.

"You'll be whipped for this," said his colleague, catching the arm of one of the two servants.

I took advantage of their distraction and continued past them and inside the house. The two guards started shouting at and blaming the two servants for their mistake. A pang of guilt speared my heart, but I forced myself to ignore it. I had people to save.

"Where to?" asked Alana, her voice low.

"Farrin said the main entrance is next to Orgetorix's study room, on the other side of the house. We have to go past the area where the slaves and animals live and reach Orgetorix's quarters. He said we'll recognize it by the paintings on the walls."

"Let's follow the others," Alana suggested. "They're bound to bring the food to where the crowd is, and we'll see from there."

I nodded and started after one servant, who had a plate full of apples, pears, cherries, and plums. The hallway was poorly lit, with only enough lamps hanging on the walls to give an idea of where to go. The sides were packed with storerooms. These were small and dark, filled with ceramic and terracotta jars. Some even had hay spread on the floor and looked like animals or people slept there. I turned around a corner, and it was like I had stepped into a different world. The number of lamps doubled, illuminating the painted walls. Figures of all shapes and sizes—male and female, most scantily dressed—painted over a red background helped open and lighten the space. From up ahead, I heard the gentle tones of a string instrument.

"This way," whispered Alana. I entered another room, which led to a different hallway, filled with paintings of buildings, all over a blue setting. She left her plate in a corner and instructed Nabil to do the same.

"How do you know where to go?" I asked Alana, my voice pitched low. *No reason to risk someone hearing me.*

"Because I've been in a Roman house before, and they all look the same."

"Roman?" I asked, surprised. *I can't possibly be in Italy.*

"Yes. Only the very wealthy can afford them."

Ah, Roman architecture, got it.

"I think I hear someone," whispered Nabil and hid behind me.

"Let's step in here," I heard a man with a honeyed voice say. Afraid they would walk into the room where I was, I pointed the gun toward the entrance. But the steps stopped, and the conversation continued in an adjacent room.

"I spoke to Casticus, and he is waiting to join us," continued the man with the honeyed voice. "We'll cross the river and march toward the winter sunset, to Santones. The crops are ready, and I have enough oxen to carry everything we need. When spring arrives, we'll move."

"My people will go, but have you talked with the other chieftains? Do they want to come so soon?" replied another, with a nasal voice.

"I showed them how we're prisoners if we remain here, and we'll surely die. The northerners' incursions are becoming more aggressive, and surrounded as we are by mountains and water, we can't take much more. We need to go, and we need to do it now."

"That's a good discourse, Orgetorix. How did they respond?"

I felt Alana's body tense and I gently grabbed her hand, shaking my head when she looked in my direction. This wasn't the moment to attack, not with Nabil here. I had no idea if Orgetorix had any other guards with him, and if Alana killed him now, there was a chance his body would be discovered before she could free her father, which would jeopardize the entire operation.

Alana's hard eyes searched my face, and she must have followed my train of thought, as her expression softened, and she gave me a quick nod.

"As we expected, most agreed. The others...won't be a problem for long. Everyone will take what they can carry. We'll burn the homes and start marching. And then, with our three armies combined, we'll take control of the other tribes. They won't be able to hide behind their puny walls. I'm telling you, Dumnorix, no one will stand in our way to become kings of the entire Gaul."

This sounded like an interesting plot for someone else more interested in the affairs of this world. Me, I just wanted to get Alana out of here so she could help me find my way back to civilization. My gut feeling told me Alana was my one and only hope. It sounded crazy, but I'd learnt never to ignore my instincts. When reason fails, they're the only things you can rely upon.

"What about the Romans? Do you think they'll just let us cross Gallia Narbonensis? We can't march and fight them at the same time," asked Dumnorix.

"That's why we have Casticus. His father, Catamantaledes, is considered a friend of the Roman senate. They won't attack." Orgetorix's voice was full of confidence.

"Speaking of attacks, what happened with Ambenix? I thought it was supposed to be an easy victory?"

My ears perked up at Ambenix's name. Now I had confirmation who was behind the assault.

"That's what I'll find out. My men brought two prisoners, and I had one of them transferred here." I felt Alana stiffen next to me. Orgetorix was talking about her father. "I had the prisoner questioned, but my men only got one thing out of him—some ramblings about a shaman. Then earlier today, my guards caught an assassin. He's down below, sharing the dungeons with the prisoner, or what is left of him."

Alana took a step forward, but I caught her arm. She shot me a look that made me flinch, but I kept my hand on her biceps. "Not now," I whispered, hoping she would see reason. I know in her place, I would have shot Orgetorix dead.

"Well, I wouldn't want anything to happen to the father of my future queen," laughed Dumnorix. "And speaking of her, where is your lovely daughter?"

"She must still be in her rooms, getting ready. You know how women are."

"That, my dear Orgetorix, I do." I heard both of them laugh stupidly.

The sound of running steps and the clanking of metal made me tense. The noise stopped somewhere nearby, and I heard a third man's voice.

"My chieftain Orgetorix, you have a messenger sent by the council of magistrates. They request your presence at a hearing, which will be held in three days, and they need your answer."

"Tell the messenger to wait," said Orgetorix, all the sweetness gone from his voice.

"Yes, my chieftain." The heavy steps and the clank of metal resonated through the corridor.

"Do you think they found out? Do they want to put us on trial? What other reason can it be for them to summon you for a hearing?" asked Dumnorix once silence settled again. His voice betrayed his nervousness and an ounce of panic.

"Impossible," came Orgetorix's immediate answer. "But even if they did, there's nothing they can do."

"Well, they could ask you, Casticus, and me to face the council. And there, the magistrates have the power. As rulers of their own clans, they would be happy to kill us and split our lands among themselves."

"We'll see about that. No single chieftain will dare move against us. I need to talk to my captains. If they want me there, I'll go, but I won't be alone."

"But you can't go to war against them. The other clans will—"

"Don't worry, I'm not planning to attack them," interrupted Orgetorix. "Once they see my army, there won't be any real trial."

I heard steps coming out of the room, and then moving away from us, their voices becoming less clear.

"If they think they can order me around, they are wrong. My spies..." The voices moved farther away, and whatever else they said wasn't clear enough to understand.

"Let's go," said Alana, sneaking around the corner in the opposite direction of the voices. Nabil and I followed her into the corridor. She turned right, took a few wrong turns, and had to backtrack until she arrived in front of a wooden door. From behind it came a breeze of cold air that raised goosebumps on my skin.

"This must be it," whispered Alana, and she pulled the door open. It wasn't locked.

Orgetorix must be confident no one will escape from his dungeon. Well, he'll have quite a surprise.

It was dark and musty, much like the prison I'd been to earlier. More than ten meters away from me, a single torch provided a dim light, enough to illuminate a set of stairs going down and stopping in front of another, similar door.

Nabil and I followed Alana into the semi-darkness.

"It's locked," came Alana's frustrated voice when the door in front of her wouldn't budge.

"Let me try it." I did my trick with the credit card again and gently pushed the door open for her.

"A shaman with a thief's skills," she murmured and passed by me, followed closely by Nabil. I continued after them and let the door close.

"Don't close it. There's no light," Alana whispered.

Oops. Too late.

I took an electric torch from my backpack, and a moment later, ninety thousand lumens illuminated a small hallway, enough to say it was daytime. On my right was nothing but a granite wall. Opposite, I counted two metal cages, each holding a prisoner: Tyrenn and Lann.

"Tyrenn!" shouted Alana, worry evident in her voice. Calling him by his first name struck me as odd, but I blamed it on her agitated state. She reached for the prison door and tried to pull it open. It didn't budge. "Can you open this one the same way?" she asked, her gaze fixed on her father.

Tyrenn wasn't in good shape. He was tied to a chair next to the wall opposite his prison door. His clothes were torn, exposing bleeding cuts all over his body. His face was almost twice its size, swollen and filled with purple bruises. On the next cell, tied to a chair, was Lann, but compared with Tyrenn, he only looked like he'd had a tough day at the gym.

"Let me try," I suggested and approached the metal bars. The lock was similar, and it took me even less time to shim it.

"Get your dad," I said and headed for Lann's door, while Nabil followed Alana. I repeated the process, and ten seconds later, I cut the ropes binding him to the chair.

"I thought I told you to wait for me at the gate," said Lann in a half accusatory tone, massaging his wrists. Before I had time to reply, he continued, "I'm glad you didn't."

"Let's get out of here first," I suggested, staring at his swollen face. "Do you need any help getting up?"

"I can manage. It probably looks worse than it is," Lann said, noticing my stare. He stood, pushed the chair back and broke one of its legs with a swift kick. Lann bent and picked it up, holding the sharp end in front of him. "Can't leave without a souvenir, and this may come in handy." *Yeah, in his hands this timber is as deadly as a sword.* "Shall we?"

His words made me realize I had made no plans about how to get out. In my rush to help Alana's father, and to a lesser degree, Lann, I'd never considered what would happen once I found them.

"Duncan!" shouted Alana, her voice full of worry.

I turned, expecting company, but there was no one else around, only the five of us. Alana was next to her father, who lay on the floor. Nabil was next to her, a scared look on her face. I rushed to Alana's side, the backpack already in my hands, my fingers searching frantically for a medkit. Tyrenn had dozens of cuts on his face, hands, and chest, and blood poured out from them like water from a watering can.

"Let's stop the bleeding," I suggested, giving Alana several clotting sponges used by military medics on the battlefield. "Place them over the wounds and apply pressure while I wrap a bandage over them."

"Duncan, I'm sorry for not trusting you," said Tyrenn, his bright eyes focused on me. "Promise me you'll protect her. "

"I will do everything in my power to make sure she's safe," I promised.

He held my eyes for a few seconds, then turned his gaze to meet Alana's.

"Alana," her father said in a barely audible voice. "My time is near. I can feel it coming."

"Don't talk like this." Tears ran down on Alana's cheeks.

"Listen to me. You have to avenge your mother and father. You have to find our people and bring them back together. You have to take back what is rightfully yours. Helix would have wanted that, no matter what."

Say what? Why does the name sound familiar?

Alana stopped bandaging Tyrenn's arm and looked at him, a pained expression on her face.

"As captain of the guards, it was my duty to defend my chief and his noble family, so when Ellana, your mother, entrusted me with you, she made me swear I'd protect you no matter what. She said you had a much better chance of survival with me than with her." Tyrenn took a breath and winced, pain written on his face.

"I would have fought and died for Helix, for Ellana, and for you, but your father ordered me to remain next to you and your mother, and if something happened to him, to save you both. But Ellana had the soul of a warrior, and when Helix fell in battle at the hand of Orgetorix's men, she went to avenge her chieftain, her husband, and save you." Tyrenn closed his eyes, and for a moment I thought he'd taken his last breath, but he continued. "She fought well, but an arrow found her, giving her a fatal wound. She crawled back, kissed you one last time with her bloodied lips, handed me your father's dagger and ring as proof of your lineage, and with her dying breath ordered me to run and guard you." He started coughing violently, pink foam dripping on his chin.

"I never knew why she didn't come with me." Alana's voice was barely audible.

"Since then, I've always been afraid you'd hate me for not trying to help."

"You would have died there too, Tyrenn, as would I. And you will always be my father, no matter what, and I will always love you." Alana took Tyrenn's hand in hers.

"I love you too," came Tyrenn's murmur as he closed his eyes and went to sleep, one last time.

She didn't say anything, didn't shout, didn't even sob. She remained there, holding Tyrenn's dead hand in hers, her eyes glistening in the empty white light.

During the past few days, I had seen death enough to last me a thousand lifetimes, but they'd all been people I didn't really know. Tyrenn's passing was different. I knew him, and his death hit me hard. I could barely imagine how Alana felt.

"We have to leave," came Lann's voice, filled with urgency. "Someone may come, and if they see us, they'll raise the alarm." I wanted to shout at him, to unleash my fury, but he wasn't the one to blame. Orgetorix was. I glanced at Alana. Her mind was lost somewhere far away, looking at the dead sword master she held in her arms.

Lann tried to say something else, but I raised a palm to stop him.

"I'll talk to her. You check to see if anyone is coming." He gave me a short nod. I put an arm over Alana's shoulders and said, in a low tone, "I hate to say it, but he's right. There is nothing else we can do here."

"You're wrong!" she shouted, her gaze fixed on Tyrenn's immovable face. "There is something I can do. I can avenge him."

In her state, she would face an entire army. And die.

"I agree with you, but now is not the time."

"I don't care." Her gaze bored into mine, and her eyes were filled with murderous rage. "I will kill Orgetorix, even if it kills me."

"I don't want anything to happen to you," I pleaded. "I will help you kill him, but we can't do it now. We're not prepared for something like this."

"I am," she said, and with one last look at Tyrenn's corpse, she stood and raised her sword. "You'd better not stand in my way. I don't want to hurt you."

I took a step back and spread my arms in a nonaggressive gesture as she marched by me, heading to the door.

Lann was a smart man; he opened it for her. I took the flashlight back from Nabil, and, holding her hand, I followed in Alana's wake.

"Wait," whispered Lann once Alana reached the outer door of the dungeons. He put his head next to the door and closed his eyes. A few seconds passed, and just as I was preparing to ask, he opened the door and leaped out in one fluid motion. I spotted another person's shadow, but it disappeared behind the door. I swiftly pushed Nabil behind me and tightened the grip on my gun. I followed Alana outside as she watched the empty hallway to her right, her back to Lann.

Pinned to the wall, with the chair's wooden leg close to her throat, stood a woman, not older than thirty years, with ginger hair, deep brown eyes, and fair skin. Her dark cloak was open in front to reveal a long brown skirt, a thin leather belt with an empty sheath, and a white blouse stretched over a well-developed chest.

"Tarrah, what are you doing here?" asked Lann, surprise evident in his voice.

"I could ask you the same, Kierann. I almost didn't recognize you," answered the woman in an amused tone. "You're the one who wanted to kill my father," she continued, her eyes narrowing.

"And what if I did?" Lann challenged.

"If I'd known, I would have helped you."

That was apparently not what Lann had been prepared to hear. He paused a beat. "Against your father?"

"He deserves it." Her tone reflected the truth behind her words.

Lann seemed to consider what she said, then he took a step back, lowering the wooden stick.

"You know, I could have killed you."

"Not before I killed you," Tarrah replied. The glint of the steel blade disappeared in the folds of her cloak.

"Same as when we were young," Lann conceded in an amused tone.

"From what I remember, you always lost." A small smile crossed Tarrah's face.

Alana took a step forward, her eyes burning fiercely. *Her patience must be growing thin.*

Lann cleared his throat and asked, "So, what are you doing here?"

"I came to ask and offer help."

"What?" Lann asked before I could.

"I have everything prepared to run away, as far as possible from where my father is, but I don't have anywhere to go where his power won't reach me. I wanted to know who was brave enough to send an assassin to kill my father and ask for their protection in exchange for information."

Lann narrowed his eyes. "What information?"

"That my father received a message from the magistrates and left."

Ah, she must be referring to the conversion I heard earlier.

Alana spun around and asked, her voice almost a shout, "Orgetorix left?"

Tarrah's gaze fell on Alana and then moved to Nabil and me before returning to Lann.

"Who are they?" Her voice was now cold and distant.

"They came to save me."

Well, I'd actually come to save Tyrenn, but I didn't want to contradict Lann. This way, he now owed me twice. *Or is that three times if you count the war? Anyway, he owes me big time.*

"Do you know where he went?" intervened Alana. "I need to find and kill him."

Tarrah moved her gaze to Alana, took in her clothes and the sword in her hands, and raised an eyebrow. "You won't be able to. Not tonight."

"Why?" asked Lann, his voice less passionate than Alana's.

"Because he left to meet with the captains of his army. They march in the morning."

Army? Well, that news blows whatever chances Alana had.

"Where?" There was a hint of despair in Alana's voice.

"Toward Lacus Lausonius. Vercingetorix's citadel isn't far from the great lake. Lucterius, his war chief, told Vercingetorix about my father's plan. Vercingetorix must have invoked the leader's council to hold a trial against my father's actions." At Lann's confused expression, she continued. "My father, along with Dumnorix and Casticus, are planning for all our tribes to move to Gaul and in the process to kill the other leaders and become kings. He also wants to give me to Dumnorix as his wife."

I noticed Lann's expression harden, and his hands closed into fists.

Nabil tugged at my cloak, and I motioned for her to wait, wanting to follow the discussion.

"But I took care of that," Tarrah continued. "I secretly informed Lucterius and a few others about my father's plans, and now that he's not here, I can get away from his grasp and watch his demise."

"Who is Vercingetorix?" I asked, barely able to follow this torrent of information.

"He's the Arverni's chieftain," replied Tarrah, giving me a curious look, probably asking herself if I'd lived under a rock until now. *Little does she know.*

"What about your brother?" Lann asked.

"Varik doesn't hold any power over me," Tarrah said stubbornly. "He can't force me to do anything. Without my father here, he cannot command me." She sniffed in disdain. "He's also too drunk right now to care about anything else."

"Why does Orgetorix need an army?" asked Alana, looking over her shoulder at Tarrah.

"To intimidate the magistrates and have them vote in his favor."

"But the other leaders won't stand for it," said Lann with conviction. "This will result in a war."

"My father's men won't enter the city. They'll just camp around it, creating a blockade. My father hopes with his men there, he'll sway enough of the leaders to vote against any punishments before the others have the time to summon their armies."

"It's a daring plan." I detected a hint of admiration in Lann's voice.

"Then we have to get inside the city before he does," said Alana, her gaze focused on Tarrah. "That's where he'll be unprotected."

Nabil tugged again at my cloak. I put a hand over her head but kept my gaze on Tarrah.

"But we can't leave the city. The guards have closed the gates," I said, wanting to insert myself into the discussion.

Tarrah waved a hand. "I know of a way out."

"Near the main gate?" Lann raised his eyebrows in disbelief.

"Not that one, it's guarded," Tarrah dismissed. "It's on the opposite side. Remember the woods where we used to play when we were little?" Lann nodded, and a tiny smile stretched his lips. "We'll camp outside and continue tomorrow morning."

"Can't we go around the city and back to the bridge?" I asked, hoping to have them guide me back to my RV. Tarrah looked at me, a puzzled expression on her face. "My...carriage is there," I said with a shrug.

"From what I heard, the army stationed here will camp in front of the city tonight. To try to go through them is foolish, and my authority doesn't extend beyond this house. Why do you think there were no guards here?"

"Will we still be able to catch Orgetorix if he left already?" Alana asked, ignoring Tarrah's question.

Tarrah nodded. "They'll start marching tomorrow, and it will take significantly longer for them to reach Lausonius before you do."

"You're not coming?" There was something in Lann's voice. *Sadness? Longing? Disappointment?*

"No," she answered sharply. "I don't want to be anywhere near him."

"But what about the magistrates?" he pressed. "Won't they need to hear from you?"

"I already said what I had to. There's nothing I can do anymore. And if my father isn't found guilty, he'll kill me. So, no, I'm not going there."

"Then where are you going?" Lann wasn't a man to give up easily.

"I was hoping you could tell me," Tarrah said with a smirk.

Lann took a few moments, but just when I thought he wouldn't reply, he said, "Ambenix."

"Oh," said Tarrah, and I thought I detected a hint of disappointment. "I thought it was one of the others."

"Others?" I asked.

"One of the other leaders, with more power and influence. Ambenix has, what, a few hundred men?"

"That's not important," Lann said. "What is, is that you'll find protection there; I'll make sure of it."

"If my father survives and finds out I was the one who betrayed him, he'll wipe out the whole town to get to me."

"He already tried and failed. Most of his army of one thousand men was defeated by us," Lann said, lifting his chin.

"That was you? So that's why he was so furious," said Tarrah, pure amazement in her voice.

I cleared my throat.

"Actually, they helped too," declared Lann, pointing at Alana.

Nabil tugged again at my cloak and this time I focused on her.

"Why are they wasting so much time?" Nabil asked.

Hmm, the little girl is right. Should have realized it sooner. What if someone comes and finds us here?

"Wouldn't it be better if we continued this discussion somewhere else?" I asked, letting some annoyance trickle in my voice.

"No one comes here besides my father and his butchers.

And since my father isn't here, you don't need to worry. I am in charge."

"The boy is right, though. We had better leave," suggested Lann.

Boy? I just saved your life twice in the past few days.

"Oh, very well, if you insist. Put your weapons away and follow me." She gave Lann a flirtatious grin. "You'll be my servants until we get out."

13

I marched through the same hallways and passed the two guards waiting at the servant's entrance, the pungent smell of wine still strong. Besides a regal nod to both soldiers, Tarrah said nothing else, and she continued unimpeded out of the estate.

Lann swiftly moved next to Tarrah, leaving me, along with Alana and Nabil, behind them. Nabil started dragging her feet, exhaustion evident on her face. I couldn't blame her. I was getting tired as well. Alana became quiet, and when she thought I wasn't looking, her eyes glistened, no doubt from the loss she'd suffered.

Outside the estate, the streets were mostly empty, and Tarrah took a narrow alley, barely lit by the milky moonlight. *I miss streetlamps.* The lane was surrounded on both sides by the tall walls of the wooden houses.

"We have company," came Lann's whisper. "Two at the back and three in front."

I tensed and made a movement to grab my gun, but Alana put a hand over mine to stop me and shook her head.

I frowned, not understanding why, but did as she instructed.

"You two. Give us your coin, and leave the girls with us," came a man's voice from up ahead. Three tall silhouettes stepped forward, their faces hidden by the shadows. Two had clubs in their hand, and the third one, a knife, its blade catching the pale light for an instant.

I heard steps from behind, and I turned to see two more figures waiting in the shadows.

"Leave us alone, and you'll live." Tarrah's voice was sharp like an ice pick, and with a practiced movement, she pulled out a knife.

"Look at that, boys," said the same man. "The kitten has claws. You know, sweetheart, I like it when my women are feisty. It makes it so much better when I'm going to—"

He didn't get to finish his sentence. Tarrah lunged, the tip of her blade pointing straight to the man's heart. I didn't see what happened because I heard noises behind me and saw two more men attacking from the opposite side. Nabil hid behind me, and I put a protecting hand over her head. *No one would get to her.* Alana positioned herself in front of me. The first to reach her received an ugly cut across his bearded face. The second man swung the club at my head, but Alana's sword parried the strike, pushing the weapon down, and lifted the pointy blade to my attacker's throat. He took a few steps back, then fled.

I turned to see three people, including the one who spoke to

Tarrah, lying on the ground, unmoving. Everything happened so fast, I didn't even have a chance to draw my gun.

"Let's move. More people may come," came Tarrah's voice as she stepped over the dead bodies like they were just trash.

Several minutes later, Tarrah stopped in front of a quiet, dark house with bricked windows at the city's edge, next to the surrounding wall. She pulled out a key, and with some effort, she opened the door.

"Come in quickly," Tarrah said from inside the darkness of the house.

I was the last to get inside and closed the door after me. Everything was pitch-black and the house had a musty, damp smell.

"You shouldn't have closed the door," came Tarrah's voice. "Kierann, to your right, there should be a lamp nailed to the wall. Could you find it and give it to me?"

If they want light, then let there be light. A second later, my flashlight illuminated the small room, no larger than a walk-in closet.

"A rat," I cried in surprise when my gaze automatically moved to something moving between my legs. I hopped on one foot until the little monster disappeared from sight. A giggle came from behind me, either Nabil or Alana, and I felt my cheeks grow warm with embarrassment. Tarrah had her mouth open in surprise and an astonished look on her face. Next to her, Lann's lips curved into a small smile.

"I think I forgot to mention he's a shaman," said Lann in an amused voice.

"Yes, you did," Tarrah replied, giving me a look reserved for giant rats. She then shook her head and continued addressing me. "I'll have to ask you later how you can make light without a fire. Now we must hurry."

She moved next to the wall in front of me, where a large piece of yellow cloth hid what lay behind. Tarrah swiftly pushed it aside to reveal a hole in the wall.

"I convinced my brother to buy this house as storage for grains and oil because it's joined to the city wall. Then I hired a couple of workers to make this." Tarrah indicated the dark tunnel in front of me. "It will bring us past the wall, and we can escape into the surrounding forest from there."

She ducked and entered the dark tunnel. I kept the light on until everyone was inside, then turned the flashlight off, to avoid being detected from the exit, and followed through. Thanks to the little monster from earlier, I imagined rats at my feet with every footstep, climbing on my pants, over my cloak, hoping to bite me with their sharp teeth.

After what felt like a never-ending journey, I finally saw a touch of silver-white light, and it took all I had not to rush outside.

Tarrah and Lann went first, cautiously peering around and listening for noises. Then Lann made a gesture to join him, his finger over his lips.

I felt like a prisoner seeing the light of day after a long time. Anything was better than the dark, creepy tunnel behind me. Bathed in the moon's luminescence was a patch of trees and high bushes that created a tunnel to the nearby forest. I moved my gaze up to see the might of the brick wall standing tall and ominous. The wind carried word fragments and the clank of metal, and I realized guards were up there, watching.

Tarrah crouched and started moving slowly through the high grass, followed at a close distance by Lann.

"Nabil is exhausted," Alana whispered in my ear. "I think she'll fall asleep standing if we let her. She can't keep on for long. We'll stop once we reach the forest. I'll go with Nabil, and you take the rear." I nodded. I could imagine how she felt because I did too. Now that I had Alana with me, the only other thing I wanted was to get her and Nabil somewhere safe and then go to sleep.

She motioned for Nabil to follow her, took the sword in one hand, ducked, and went after Tarrah and Lann.

I sucked in a deep breath and let the chilly night's air give me a boost of energy. *This should be easy, keep low and out of sight.*

Sometimes the universe hates me. I took my first step, when I heard the crackle of a branch under my foot.

"Who's there?" came a voice from atop the wall. I stopped, counted to three, and took another step. Another branch snapped. *Oh, come on.*

"You. Stop." This time, I kept on going. A moment later, an arrow whizzed past me.

"Run," hissed Alana, who already reached the tree line. I stood, and something slammed into my right shoulder, propelling me forward. I stumbled but kept running. Another arrow flew millimeters past my ear and stuck in a tree to my left. I threw in all the energy reserves I had and sprinted. With only a couple of meters left, my foot must have caught a root or something, and I sprawled forward onto my palms and face. I heard the whooshing sound of another arrow, and then I felt the wind knocked out of me as my chest hit the ground.

"I got him," a boisterous voice came from atop the walls.

I remained there on the ground, groggy from the fall.

"Duncan?" Alana whispered.

"Yes. Still here," I groaned. My palms felt like they had grabbed a hot iron. I must have scraped them when I planted my face in the ground.

"Can you move?"

I wiggled my toes. "I think so."

"Crawl slowly. Do not stand. Do you understand me? They think you're dead."

Some of the best news I've heard today.

I did as she said, putting pressure on my palms' edges and the backs of my hands until I reached the relative safety of the forest.

"You're safe now." I felt Alana's soft hand touching my cheek and then my shoulder.

"Ouch." I winced.

"Stand. I need to see where you're hurt."

I pushed the earth down so I could get up. It felt like a herculean effort. I staggered and leaned on a nearby tree, closing my eyes, trying to catch my breath.

"We can't remain here," came Tarrah's voice.

"Give him a moment. He just had an arrow hit him," said Alana.

"Speaking of which, why is there no wound? I don't see any blood."

I turned to inspect the wound, but Tarra was right, there was none. Only the torn cloak. One of the plates must have kept the arrow from going through my body.

"That's because—" Alana started, but I interrupted her.

"I think I can walk now. How far do we have to go?"

"Not far," Tarrah answered. "Follow me."

"I'll help you." Alana put my arm around her shoulder and her hand around my waist.

I was too tired and battered; otherwise, I would have enjoyed the experience and the close proximity to her body. With Alana's help, I limped after them. I didn't even care about the darkness or what animals might have lurked in the shadows. My only desire was to stop somewhere, anywhere, and sleep. After a few steps, Nabil, as tired as she was, came to help too, and my eyes moistened, but luckily it was too dark for anyone to see.

To my relief, soon Tarrah stopped in a small clearing, bathed in silver light.

"We can stop here for a few hours. If they do come after us, they won't send anyone until the morning. But chances are, they won't, as the army is leaving, and they don't have people to spare." Tarrah's tone didn't seem concerned, and I was too tired to think, so I took her words at face value.

I struggled to take my cloak and backpack off. Pain seared through my right shoulder when I tried to move it, and it must have shown on my face, as at my third attempt, Alana came and helped take the weight off.

"I'll set up a tent, and we can sleep there," I announced, but was welcomed by curious looks. Too tired to care what everyone thought, I unzipped my backpack.

"What's that?" asked Nabil, when she saw me getting a bag out and unfolding it on the ground.

"It's a tent. Think of it as a portable room with thin walls and a roof." After I bought it, I checked the instructions it came with and had to throw away the booklet. It was that bad. In the end, I ended up watching the "How to assemble a tent for dummies" video clip I'd previously downloaded from YouTube. It was perfect for me.

"But it's so small. I've never seen one like this," Nabil commented. "Is it big enough for all of us to sleep inside?"

"We'll see. Now, can you hold this for me?" I handed her one corner of the tent while I planted one of the stakes in the ground. "Give me that corner, so I can tie it to this." I was impressed by her curiosity, even though I knew she was dead tired, probably more than me.

With her help, I was able to have the tent up in only a few minutes. It was one of those light tents, advertised for three people but comfortable only for two.

"I guess we can have three people sleep here," I said, gazing at the others.

Tarrah's eyes were wide, and Lann looked bored, but something told me he was surprised as well. He tried too much to appear uninterested. Nabil was fascinated, though, and her eyes were sparkling with curiosity.

"We'll need someone to keep watch," said Lann. "I can be first."

"I'll join you," Tarrah said quickly. "All three of you look like something a cat dragged in. Better get some rest, and we'll wake the two of you later." I guessed she meant Alana and me.

I didn't argue and crawled inside, followed by Nabil and then Alana. I took out two thermal blankets, each big enough to comfortably fit in my palm, and handed one to Alana.

"These two should be large enough to cover all three of us." Alana studied it curiously, then followed my lead and unfurled it.

"It's thin," Nabil said, rubbing the aluminum foil between her fingers.

"It's better than it looks. Just handle it with care so you won't rip it apart. And trust me, it will keep you warm at night."

I took my cloak out and folded it to resemble a pillow. Alana did the same thing, but she made it longer to reach Nabil too. I followed her example, and soon, all three of us lay down—Alana and me on each side of the tent, and Nabil between us.

I closed my eyes, and sleep responded to my calling.

14

I woke up sharply, surrounded by darkness. My palms were on fire, like I had kept them on burning hot coals. For a second, I thought I'd had a nightmare and I was back in my apartment. The gentle breathing of the bodies next to me said otherwise.

"It will take me some time to get used to your new name," I heard Tarrah's voice from outside the tent.

"I had to. Back then I was young, and it was easy to change it." Lann's voice had a trace of regret.

Listening to other people talking without them knowing isn't polite, but my curiosity helped me ignore the heat emanating from my palms. It gave me something else to focus on. *It's all for a good cause.*

"But why did you leave? When you didn't come to my house anymore, I asked the servants where you lived, but no one knew. I've even asked my father if he knew where you were, and he told me you and your parents had left town."

"Is that what he said?" Lann scoffed. "No, that's not what happened. He sent someone to kill my family and me. Do you remember that day we came back from the forest, holding hands and dancing?"

"I remember," Tarrah said wistfully.

"Well, that night, while eating supper, I heard a knock at the door and went to open it. Someone planted a fist in my nose that sent me to the ground in a daze. My father came to see what happened, but the man pulled a sword and stabbed him in the chest."

I could barely imagine what Lann felt seeing his father murdered in front of him. I'd been at the hospital next to my mother's bed when she died, and without anyone to blame, I got angry with the entire world. I'll be forever grateful to my dad for helping me overcome those terrible months.

"He fell right next to me," Lann continued. "My brain refused to process what I was seeing, and I felt like I couldn't move. My mother started crying when she saw my father on the ground, his chest all bloody. She screamed and jumped on him. The assassin must have cut her throat, and she landed on top of my father, blood gushing from a wound around her neck. I watched my sister hurling herself toward the man who murdered our parents. He planted a kick in her chest, sending her flying into the back wall, where she dropped to the ground."

I clenched my fists, wanting to kill whoever had done that. *What is wrong with this world? Why is it so brutal?*

"How did you survive?" Tarrah exclaimed, shock clear in her voice.

"I heard neighbors shouting outside. The assassin must have heard them too, because he smashed the oil lamp to the floor and fled, leaving us there to burn. Embers started flying, and one must have jumped on my skin. The burn shook me from my stupor. My parents were dead. I checked on my sister, and she was still breathing, so I pulled her from the house and ran outside the city. I was afraid the assassin would come to finish the job if he found out we were alive, so when we encountered a group of merchants, I gave them a different name. An older couple took pity on us and took my sister and me into their care. That's how we got to Ambenix's town."

There was some shuffling, but I couldn't see through the tent's flap. *She probably hugged him. If I were there, I would have hugged him too.*

"I'm sorry. I wish I'd known your parents. They must have been some amazing people."

"Yes, they were," replied Lann, his voice filled with sadness.

"There's one thing I don't understand. How do you know it was my father who sent the assassin? Couldn't—"

"Because I recognized him. I've seen him before at your house."

The heat enveloping my palms subsided and felt itchy, but I tried to ignore it. Lann had just given me another reason to help Alana kill Orgetorix. Such a man couldn't be left alive. *How could Tarrah be so nice compared to her murderous father? Well, she did kill three people in that dark alley earlier—maybe she took the niceness from her mother?*

Tarrah sighed. "I didn't know. I wish I could say I'm surprised my father would do such a thing, but I can't. What you said adds to my conviction of wanting to see him dead."

"Over the years, I've been back a couple of times, for this same reason: to kill him. But each time, he wasn't in the city. Nor were you."

"Until today."

"Yes, but his guards caught me before I could reach him."

"Well, hopefully, the magistrates will give my father the punishment he deserves."

The fragment of conversation I'd caught between Orgetorix and Dumnorix made me realize chances were, she wouldn't have her wish fulfilled. Not if Orgetorix showed up for trial in front of an entire army.

"I hope so too, even though I would like to stare him in the eyes and ask why he killed my parents while my blade cuts deep in his chest."

"It's my only chance," Tarrah said absently. "Otherwise, he'll send soldiers after me to bring me back, under his control. Or have me killed."

Would Orgetorix murder his own daughter? Based on the things I've seen so far, I had little doubt. I let out a quiet breath. *I really wish I had a sniper rifle with me. It would make things so easy.*

"I know we'll have a much better chance if you're there," suggested Lann.

"But I already told you why I can't. If he sees me, he'll kill me. It's better to be far away, where his schemes can't reach me."

"And you think Ambenix's town is safe for you?" he asked.

"It certainly is far from his power, and you said Ambenix survived my father's attack already."

"About that. We only did it because of him."

"The shaman? You can't tell me he had such a big role to play," said Tarrah, her tone incredulous.

I felt a smile creeping over my face, curious to hear what Lann thought about me and what I'd done.

"He saved us all."

You got that right. I hadn't expected him to say it, but it felt good to receive his acknowledgement. He had been so aloof despite all the things I'd done to help the village.

"I don't know if he's a shaman or something else, from different plains, but he has knowledge of things I've never even heard of. He has something that can kill people just by pointing it at them. He killed dozens with it during the fight. And you saw earlier how the arrows bounced off him. I'm telling you, the safest place to be is around him. This is the second time he saved my life. Well, the third if you count that he saved the whole town."

So he did keep track too. Well, good to have confirmation.

"But we've both heard the stories. They're pure evil. And now you're telling me he's not like all the others?" asked Tarrah, disbelief evident in her voice.

This talk about evil shamans was starting to get on my nerves. *Why am I labeled based on what other people have done?*

"There are things I've seen him do, things my eyes couldn't believe were possible. I don't know why the gods bestowed him with so much power, but I think..." Lann stopped, and I was afraid he wouldn't continue.

"What?" Tarrah asked, most probably as curious as me to find out what Lann thought.

"I think he could help you bring your father down."

I coughed in surprise, but they mustn't have heard me because they continued without skipping a beat.

"You think I should ask him for help? You know very well what happens when you ask their kind for favors. What price would I have to pay? My life? Or worse?"

Why did Lann see me as a killer? Well, I did shoot a lot of people, but that was different. It was during a war. I wouldn't murder someone in cold blood.

"I don't know, but you've seen how the boy looks at Alana and how she looks at him. I'm quite sure for her, he could destroy your father's entire army. Then even if your brother succeeded Orgetorix, he wouldn't have power over you."

I knew I should be upset about his intention to manipulate me, but my mind remained stuck at what he'd said about Alana and me. *Does she have feelings for me too?* Every time we kissed was because of an upcoming danger.

"Ah, I see. You think the shaman will kill him or help Alana do it. Why does she want my father dead?"

I glanced in Alana's direction, but she had her eyes closed and seemed like she was sleeping, though I wasn't sure. *Hmm, maybe she's listening like I am?*

"It's not my story to tell." For a few seconds, there was silence, then Lann sighed and continued. "Well, if you look at me with those eyes, who can resist you."

Tarrah giggled.

"I don't know much, but I have a feeling what I know is crucial to what could happen in the next few days, and I would like your opinion on this as well."

"Now I'm curious."

Me too.

"I'll start from the beginning, so you'll know everything. A day before Orgetorix's army attacked, Alana and Tyrenn, a man who said he was her father, came to our town, bringing news their village had been invaded. With them was Duncan, who they claimed helped them defeat some of Orgetorix's scouts. Long story short, Duncan started talking with strange words, like a mad man, and Ambenix gave me the order to kill him; however, Alana jumped in his defense and took him as her varlet. I didn't think much of it, but later, they both came to me and said they could help us fight your father's army. I convinced Ambenix to let them try; after all, what harm could they do?"

"And what did he do?" asked Tarrah, her voice barely audible.

"He did something that made the ground shake, and dirt flew in the air, leaving behind a large hole, as if an unseen giant had stepped there. When the army came, hundreds of men and horses were torn apart, as if ghostly hands had ripped them to pieces."

I had been too preoccupied at that time to notice all that, but I'd seen the corpses when they piled them into huge mounds. The memory made me shudder. I had been responsible for a genocide and, sooner or later, I would pay for what I did. The town had been saved, but at what price?

"During the fight, we lost some of our food, so a few parties were sent to hunt and make sure our attackers ran and wouldn't come back. Alana and Tyrenn joined my group and went hunting. Unfortunately, we stumbled upon some of the retreating troops, who had prepared an ambush. Out of almost a dozen people, only the three of us were left. Their commander decided to send Alana and Tyrenn ahead to be questioned."

"How did you escape?" asked Tarrah.

"Later, while I remained their prisoner, Duncan saved me, and then he ran after Alana and Tyrenn. When I came back to the town, Ambenix ordered me to take a group of men and bring back the boy. I did, but he escaped, so I went again after him. It didn't take long to follow his movements. I saw him in the woods across the bridge, trying to save a group of prisoners, part of Helix's tribe. After I gave him a hand, I decided to accompany him to the city."

I was grateful for his words; he and his men did more than give me a hand in helping the prisoners. Interestingly, Lann didn't mention Madoc's involvement. *Maybe he doesn't want anyone to know the boy orchestrated my escape.*

"I showed Duncan the slave market and then went after your father to pay my blood debt. I wasn't careful enough, and his guards found me and threw me into the dungeon."

"I heard my father say the guards found an assassin, but I had no idea it was you."

"I don't know how much time had passed when a bright light inundated the dungeon, and then Duncan, Alana, and the little girl appeared, as would gods appear to a mortal man. A ball of fire, brighter than anything I've seen, made me close my eyes in pain, and when I opened them, Duncan was next to me, untying my hands. We rushed to Tyrenn, the man I knew as Alana's father, but Morrigan was clinging to him, dragging him with her to the underworld. With his dying breath, he revealed who she was. Helix's daughter."

I heard a gasp escaping Tarrah's lips. "She is Helix's daughter?"

Why does Tarrah sound so surprised? Was Helix someone important?

"That's what Tyrenn said. The rest, you know."

"I overheard my father once saying Helix was the only chieftain he believed had guessed what they planned. Helix was his most fierce opponent against the resettlement. I think that's why my father had him killed."

Things were finally falling into place, like pieces of a puzzle. So Orgetorix killed Alana's real father, and he probably wanted to kill her too. *In that case, it means Alana wants revenge.*

"Hmm. I wonder if the only reason Orgetorix's men attacked was because he knew where Alana was," Lann mused.

"No, I don't think so. If my father knew she was there, or that she was alive, he would have tried to get her out first before the attack."

"Why?"

"Because he wouldn't pass up an opportunity to gather more power. He most likely would have married her with my brother. That way, he would control her tribe as well."

Tarrah's words bothered me. Just the thought of having Alana married to someone made me sick. *If that was what she* wanted, I would stay out of her way—but before then, I must tell her how I feel.

"My father has this vision of becoming king and ruling everyone," Tarrah continued. "That's why he attacked all the villages and towns that opposed the resettling. He wants everyone to start moving as soon as spring is here."

"I understand," said Lann, and I heard him yawn.

Sleep had left me. Now my thoughts swirled around Alana being forcefully married to someone and how I could prevent that.

"It's late, and we've talked for hours," Lann said. "What you've said changes things, but I have to think about them when my head is clear. I'll go wake those two up so we can get some rest."

I let out a gentle snore as I heard someone open the tent's door. I felt a hand shake my leg and opened my eyes to see Tarrah with a finger over her lips. She nodded toward Nabil, still asleep with a peaceful expression on her face. Alana silently moved past Tarrah, and I followed her outside the tent. *Was Alana awake the whole time too? Did she hear the conversation?*

"Keep an eye out and make sure you don't fall asleep," Lann told me and followed Tarrah inside the tent.

I took a seat on the damp grassy ground next to Alana. The pale moon illuminated a small area around me, enough to fill it with countless shadows. I shivered. The itchiness refused to be ignored anymore, and I used the black jeans as a scratcher. It didn't seem to help much.

Alana was quiet, lost in her own thoughts. Moment passed,

and I grew uncomfortable. I needed to talk to her, to see what she was thinking of.

"It's eerie, isn't it," I started.

"What is?" she asked in a flat voice.

"Here, with all the rustling and shadows."

She shrugged but kept quiet. Her eyes glistened and a tear rolled down her cheek and dropped to the ground.

My heart broke with her pain. I understood what she was going through. When my mother died, I was furious about everything and everyone around me. I didn't understand why she was taken away when I needed her. "I'm sorry about Tyrenn."

She turned to face me, her eyes searching my face.

"And I'm sorry I had to lie to you," she answered. "I wanted to tell you, but Tyrenn forbade me. He was afraid you'd betray us and tell Orgetorix where we were. After Orgetorix killed my parents, the man I was supposed to marry, my friends, and everyone I knew, Tyrenn and I ran and hid from his spies. Tyrenn protected me. He was my uncle. My mother's brother. Since I was little, he watched over me, taught me how to fight and ride a horse. And after my parents were murdered, he was my only family."

I didn't say anything; there was nothing to say. Instead, I put an arm around her shoulders. Human beings need to talk about the dramatic events that happened in their life. It helps them process and move on. *Or that's what I read in a book.*

"How did it happen?" I asked in a low voice.

She stared into the darkness, her eyes shining in the moonlight.

"My father had arranged for me to marry someone from our tribe. On the evening I was supposed to meet him, everyone had gathered for the feast when I heard shouts from all around the town. People started running, screaming, as riders swept over in a dark wave, killing everything in their path. A group of them headed straight for us with spears in their hands. My father and his guards went to meet them, along with Ronan, my betrothed. My mother kissed me and went to help my father. I hid until Tyrenn found me and we fled."

She wiped a tear from her eyes. I wished there was something I could do to alleviate her pain, erase those dreadful events, but it was beyond my power.

"We ran until we couldn't hear the screams anymore. We came back the next day, but they had burned the corpses. There was no one left."

She kept quiet for a long time and stared ahead, not meeting my eyes. I could barely imagine searching through mounds of corpses, looking for your parents. The image made me want to throw up.

Alana turned to face me, a resolute expression on her face. "I want to kill Orgetorix for what he did, and I need to do it while he's on his way to the trial, when he least expects it." Her voice had a tone of finality. She didn't ask for my opinion; she made a statement, a prediction. Like something she knew would happen.

I was at a crossroads. I had saved Alana. I'd repaid my debt to her, and I could leave. She would follow her path of revenge, and I would follow mine. But I had nowhere to go. The thought should have scared me, but it didn't. My subconscious must have prepared me for the possibility that I would remain in this era forever. It wasn't something I wanted, but if it was my only option, I had to make the best of it. If this was indeed my past, I would focus on minimizing the impact my actions had. But I couldn't just sit there while Alana needed my help. She was going to face an entire army, outmanned and outgunned. She was a formidable fighter, but I doubted even she could win. I took a deep breath to let the night's cold air illuminate my thoughts and guide my decision.

"I'll help you." I was surprised by the conviction in my voice.

Her glistening eyes met mine, and I saw the pain and the desire for revenge, unshakable as a mountain.

"Thank you," she whispered, her voice like the passing wind. "Now, let me see what's wrong with your hands."

Helped by the diffuse silver light, she found some dark fruits and squeezed their juice over my itchy palms. It felt like an icy bath on a torrid day, and moments later, the itchiness died down. It soon went away entirely.

The night was chilly, but having her body close made it bearable, and the first light of day found the two of us hugging a thermal blanket.

The distant sound of horns stirred me from my drowsiness.

"That's the signal to announce the army's departure," Alana said, her first words in hours.

"Shall we wake the others?"

"No need," Alana turned to face the tent just as a sleepy Tarrah emerged, rubbing her eyes.

"We should leave soon," she said, stifling a yawn.

"What smells so good?" asked Nabil, her head peering out.

I pointed to a hole in the ground Alana had made. Inside, with the flame hidden by the dirt walls, on a frame made of sticks, was a camping pot I had in my backpack, filled with boiling water and the contents of a couple of freeze-dried beef stroganoff pouches. I had laid several containers on the ground, a foldable pan, two bowls, and a cup.

"I didn't have enough bowls, but I think these should be fine."

"It smells too good to complain," said Lann, his half-swollen face a shade of deep purple.

Everybody kept quiet during the meal. It wasn't enough to fill all our bellies, judging by the longing looks to the empty bowl, but it provided the strength needed for a new day.

"So, where to?" I asked after I finished packing the tent.

"We'll head north." Tarrah jerked her thumb behind her. "There's another bridge, with an inn near it. From there, we can buy horses and food—or at least that was my plan. We can then ride to Ambenix's town, and if we keep a good pace, we should arrive by lunchtime."

"We'll go with you until we reach the bridge, but then we'll go after Orgetorix," said Alana. "Duncan and I will try to reach him before he gets to the trial. If we do, I'll sneak inside the camp and kill him."

It sounded easy, but I had my doubts that Alana could sneak in and out of a military camp unnoticed.

Silence fell, but no one objected. *I guess everyone here is okay with killing Orgetorix, one way or another.*

Tarrah found a path through the forest, and by noon, the

branches and leaves gave way to a green valley, its high grass gently swaying in the wind. A large wooden building rose in front of us, positioned between the forest and the river, whose sinuous body cut the land in two irregular shapes. Near the house was a stable with more than a dozen stalls, though half were empty. Surrounding the structures was a wall made of wooden spikes with an open gate in the middle.

"We'll need to go in and buy some horses and a few other things," announced Tarrah.

"I don't think we have any money," said Alana, looking questioningly at me. I shook my head. I doubted they'd accept my credit card, either. *In several hundred years, maybe, but not now.*

"Here," said Tarrah and handed Alana several silver-like coins. "Use these to buy some food, and I'll take care of the horses."

"Actually," I intervened, "how far is the other bridge? I have my carriage there."

Tarrah looked out, gauging the distance. "It's not far, maybe half the time it took us to get here if you follow the river."

"Then I don't think we need any horses." I didn't want to repeat my one and only horse-riding experience.

Alana shrugged, then nodded.

"Very well, I'll buy only two," Tarrah said with a wave of her hand.

"One other thing." I faced Nabil. "Do you know how to ride?"

"Why?" she asked, her brows furrowed.

"Because I think it's better if you go with them."

"No, I want to remain with you," Nabil protested, clinging to Alana's hand.

"I know, but we're going to face an army, and I don't know what will happen. It will be safer if you go with them."

"I'm safe with you."

I sighed. "No, you're not. Where we're going, it could be much worse than all that happened yesterday. We'll face an entire army." As I was saying the words, I realized how true they were. I hadn't spent any time thinking about how I would help Alana have her revenge against Orgetorix, but saying these words to Nabil made me realize it wouldn't be easy. It would be difficult and dangerous. Maybe even lethal.

"Duncan is right," intervened Lann. "You'll be safer with us. I have a nephew who's the same age as you. His name is Madoc. He'll be delighted to meet you, and his mother, my sister, is a welcoming woman."

"Look," I said to Nabil, who still looked uncertain. "I promise after all this is over, I'll come to visit you. If you don't like it there, then we can leave together."

"Will she come too?" Nabil said, her gaze on Alana.

"I will. I promise," Alana replied and caressed Nabil's cheek. Nabil hugged her and Alana put her arms around the little girl.

"Let's go and buy what we need," said Tarrah, her tone impatient.

I entered the house to see a large room filled with tables, half of them empty. On one side was a small podium where a man played a string instrument, similar to a small harp. Two women swayed between tables, holding plates filled with roasted meat and drinks.

Tarrah gestured toward the bar, where a man in his late thirties with a dirty gray apron poured drinks into clay cups.

"You two," she said, looking at Lann and me, "stay here while Alana and I go and talk to him. From what I heard, he's more inclined to negotiate with us than with you."

Lann shrugged and headed toward one of the empty tables.

I hadn't realized how much I needed to rest until I took a seat. *This feels so good.* I let out a deep breath and closed my eyes, letting my shoulders sag.

"Do you think we can get something to drink?" asked Nabil, a short time later, her tone cautious.

"Sure, let me see what I have." I opened the backpack and started to take out a bottle of water.

"Not here," said Lann forcefully, putting a firm hand over mine, his gaze circling around the room. "Put that thing away unless you want to have all of us killed."

"Why?" I asked, but put the bottle back.

"First, because people don't take kindly to shamans, and even if they do, you'll quickly become the target for the things you have in your bag. Better not to attract attention. We'll drink when we're back on the road."

I looked around the room and saw a bald man with a shaggy brown beard and a black patch over his left eye looking straight at me. He was sitting at the table with three others, drinking. I continued my scan of the room but kept him in my peripheral vision. Eventually, he stopped staring and started drinking.

"Here you go," said Alana and placed two small but heavy-looking sacks on the table in front of Lann. "Tarrah went outside to get the horses."

Lann took the two bags with food and headed outside, after Alana. Nabil followed him, but I put a hand on her shoulder to stop her before she got outside and gave Nabil the bottle with water. She drank it fully.

Tarrah stood at the front of the gate, holding the reins of three brown horses. Two were taller than I was, but the third looked like a pony, a head shorter than the other two.

"Nabil, this one's for you." She handed Nabil the reins of the pony. The little girl's face brightened.

"I've never had one just for me." She took the reins in her little hands, approached, and patted the horse on its neck, her fingers brushing the black mane. "It's beautiful and soft."

"Let's head to the bridge. We'll walk until we reach the other side," suggested Lann.

This bridge was narrower and shorter than the one near where I'd left the RV, and in no time, we traversed the stream.

"Follow it and you'll soon reach the other bridge, next to the city. I don't think there will be any soldiers patrolling the area, but be careful," Tarrah told Alana and me. "For what it's worth, I'm sorry for what my father did to you. I hope you'll get what you want. For all our sake."

Alana gave Tarrah a quick hug. "I'm glad I've met you."

"This is where our paths diverge," said Lann as he helped Nabil get on the horse. "I know these lands well, and by sunrise, we'll reach Ambenix's town. If all goes well, we'll see you in three days' time for the trial. If Orgetorix reaches that far." He winked at me. "May the gods be with you both." Lann lifted himself up in the saddle and followed Tarrah and Nabil, who kept looking back, her eyes sparkling in the sunlight.

"We'll see you soon, Nabil," I shouted and waved. She waved back until the trees hid her from sight.

The high grass had already made way for trees, but the forest wasn't thick, and there was plenty of space, making it easy to follow the river. I had been walking for almost an hour when a sudden sharp pain made my right calf hard like a stone.

"Let's stop for a moment, shall we?"

I chose one of the trees nearby and sat on the damp ground. My leg hurt, and I began massaging and flexing the muscle. Alana sat next to me, placed a hand on my calf and squeezed. The pain retracted like it hadn't been there a second ago.

"Thank you." I let out a deep breath and closed my eyes for a second, leaning against the solid bark. The water's murmur, the gentle sound of the swaying leaves had a calming effect.

"Duncan, we can rest here for a moment, but after that we need to go. Do you have one of those things that have water inside and a drawing of a mountain?"

"Sure." I unzipped the backpack. *Only two left.* "So, do you have a plan for killing Orgetorix?" I asked as I split my last two bottles of water with Alana. For a moment I thought of refilling the bottles in the river, but decided against it. *It's too muddy.*

"Yes. If we catch up with him tomorrow, I'll wait until it's night, then sneak into his tent and kill him."

"Easier said than done. I assume he'll have guards posted around the camp."

"That's where I hope you'll help me with your bird. What did you call it?"

I knew what she was referring to and chuckled.

"A drone. But what if he has guards at the entrance?"

"Then I'll cut a hole where they won't see me." A small smile appeared on her face.

"What if he has guards around the tent?"

"Then I'll find another way," her smile disappeared, and a note of irritation crept into her voice.

Maybe I should stop asking her questions.

An urge I couldn't ignore anymore made me sit up.

"I need a bio break."

"What?"

"I...I need to find a tree."

Alana glanced at the leaves swaying over us.

"A different one."

She smiled but didn't say anything else, just leaned against the tree and closed her eyes.

Hopping from one foot to the other, I found a wide enough trunk to hide me from her sight.

I had just finished when I heard a woman's scream. *Alana.* I peered around the tree. Two people were holding her, while a third had a sword pressed to her chest. A fourth bandit had my backpack in one hand and was examining it with interest. He was bald, with a shaggy brown beard, broad shoulders, and a black eye patch. He was the man from the inn who kept staring at me.

Anger and fear swept over me. *I have to do something.*

"Where is your man?" asked the bald one, still studying my backpack.

I wanted to slap myself. Both my gun and knife were there,

and I had no weapon with me. I looked around and picked up a stick, as long as a baseball bat but not as wide.

"What is this?" asked the man with the eye patch, holding one of the empty water bottles. He had approached Alana, and the man holding the sword moved out of the way. She didn't reply but spat on his face. I winced. *Why is she provoking them?*

"Look at that." The man wiped his face with his forearm. "We have a feisty one here." He dropped the backpack and pulled out a knife he kept in a sheath at his belt. I felt my blood begin to boil. I gripped my stick and moved to another tree, closer to them.

"Until he's back, we can have some fun, isn't that right, boys?" Snickers and laughs resonated from the other three. I moved closer, behind the tree where he had dropped my opened backpack.

With a swift movement, the bald man cut through her shirt, then put a hand on her exposed chest. Alana struggled, but he grabbed her throat, his massive fingers wrapping around her neck.

"I'll enjoy having you. Tell me, have you had a real man before?"

I couldn't wait any longer, and I sneaked behind the tree, going straight for my backpack.

"Hey," shouted one of the men holding Alana. I reached for my bag and put my hand inside it, looking for my weapon.

The man holding the sword spun and raised the blade, ready to chop my head off. I rolled out of the way, still grabbing the backpack with one hand, and felt the blow like a hammer over my back. The ceramic and aluminum plates must have protected me from its cut. I turned to see him take another step and raise the sword one more time, aiming for my head. My left hand grabbed the gun, but the sword was coming down faster than I could have pulled it out. At the last moment, I used the stick to deviate its trajectory, but the force behind it was too great, and the blade sank deep into the ground, next to my left ear, cutting a few strands of hair.

That was close.

I planted a kick with my right foot in his stomach, and the attacker staggered back a few steps. It was the respite I needed. One of the men holding Alana came to help him, but it was too late. I took out the gun, aimed, and shot twice, each one accompanied by the familiar popping sound. While I wasn't as accurate with my left hand, the men were close enough I couldn't miss. They both crumpled down to the ground, one with a perforated stomach and the other one with a wound in his chest. Right where his black heart was.

I pointed my gun toward the bald man, but there was no need. He was on the ground, gurgling and bleeding profusely from a cut on his throat. The last of them, his nose bleeding, turned to run. He only managed a couple of steps before a spinning blade sank deep into his back. He dropped like a tree trunk and remained there, unmoving.

"Are you hurt?" I asked, panting from the effort.

Alana didn't reply. Instead, she retrieved the knife from the man's back, then approached the two I'd shot and, with swift movements, cut their throats.

"We need to go," she said in an ice-cold tone, a muted rage filling her words.

15

For the next two hours, Alana ignored me. She talked sparingly and spent much of the hike in silence. I knew she was full of rage over what had happened, and I didn't blame her even one bit. They deserved to die for what they tried to do. I just wished she would talk to me. It was always better to speak to someone than to let it fester inside.

"Do you know where it is?" Alana pointed in the distance, at the familiar bridge.

My heartbeat quickened. I was getting close to the RV.

"Let me see. It was still dark when I joined Lann, but I don't remember it being far from the main road. Let's go this way," I said and pointed to my two o'clock.

I had only taken a few steps when she put an arm on my shoulder and a finger over her lips.

"I hear something," she said quietly. She dragged me behind a large tree trunk, and I looked around but couldn't hear or see anyone. "There," she pointed ahead. At first, I didn't see it, but the swaying leaves uncovered the silhouettes of two people, each with their backs toward me. They were both leaning against a tree, axes at their belts and shields at their backs.

"Do you think there are more?"

Alana nodded.

"What should we do?" Besides shooting them, I was out of ideas. An open attack was something to be avoided, not knowing exactly how many enemies were here and where they were positioned.

"We can try to go around them, but we have to be very quiet. You must do exactly what I say. Step where I step, stop when I stop, and whisper only if you must. Better if you don't talk at all."

"I will," I said and was met by her raised eyebrows. "Sorry. I'll be quiet." I mimicked closing a zipper over my mouth, but her questioning expression told me she didn't get the reference.

She continued even deeper into the woods, in a broad arc around the two sentinels. Alana stopped from time to time to listen. I could only hear the birds and the rustle of leaves.

Ten minutes later, I spotted my RV's familiar white shape through the trees. My heart swelled at the familiar sight until I observed the armed men surrounding it. My hopes sank. *I don't have enough bullets.*

"Should we try to sneak past the guards?" I suggested. "If we get inside, then they won't be able to do anything to us."

"Yes, but we'll have to wait for the cover of darkness," Alana murmured.

I clenched my fists in frustration. Again, I was so close to safety, but it was still out of reach.

"What about if we try to get closer? I can open it from here, and then we can make a run for it," I insisted. My mind had only one goal. Get inside.

"It's too dangerous. They have guards all around it, and we won't reach even half the distance before they kill us."

"If we run, I can take care of the ones that stand in our way. We can then climb the ladder and reach the roof. Then—"

"I'm sure there are others we can't see from here," Alana interrupted, "and on the roof, the archers will skewer us, as there's no shelter. Be patient. We don't have to wait too much. Darkness is coming soon." Alana pointed at the sky, the dark clouds clumping together, forming a veritable apparition of a bad omen.

I retreated to a safe distance, careful not to step on any dead branches on the forest's floor.

"So, what now? We wait for the storm to come?" I asked. Alana stopped next to a tree with branches going every which way, like a tall, leafy octopus.

"There won't be any storm," she told me. "At least not now. Maybe later, during the night. But the clouds will cover the sun. Now, give me one of those things you had put water into."

"A bottle?" I asked, surprised by her request. "Here you go, but what do you need it for?"

"Wait here," she commanded and disappeared into the surrounding forest. Alana returned a quarter hour later, and I noticed she had cut the water bottle in two and filled one with red berry-looking fruits and the other with green leaves, with a red tint at their edges.

"Those look delicious," I said admiringly and extended my arm to grab one of the berries.

"They're poisonous," she said matter-of-factly. My hand stopped centimeters away from grabbing one.

"Then why did you get them?"

"You'll see. Now grab me some branches, both from the trees and from the ground."

I did as she requested and brought back almost two dozen sticks. The berries were now on the ground, and she had a piece of tree bark in front of her. As I approached, she carefully sliced one of the red berries and squeezed the seeds out over one of the red-tinted leaves. She crushed them to paste with a rock, their content blending with the berry juice, and poured the mixture into the lower half of the water bottle.

"Don't come any closer. I don't want you to touch any of it. See if you can remove the bark from the wood sticks."

I took a seat on the ground, several meters away from her, and started peeling them off, as she instructed. I watched her work, amazed by how sure and precise her movements were, her fingers never touching the seeds or leaves.

"We can eat them once I'm done," she said, motioning to the growing mound of eviscerated berries next to her.

"I think I'm good. I'll wait until I'm back inside the RV."

"Suit yourself." To prove her point, she took one and put it in her mouth, nodding appreciatively. "Mmmm...they're very sweet."

My mouth instantly watered, and I took my eyes away from

her. "I'm almost done with these," I said to distract myself. "What do you need them for?"

"I'll make needles from them, which we'll throw at the guards."

"And what good will that do?"

"Well, if you dip them in this"—She pointed to the container holding the berry mix.—"then they won't be able to fight. If the tip gets in their blood, they'll start to feel confused and have trouble breathing. Next, their bodies will feel weak and start shaking, like they are possessed by Balor himself."

"Balor?" I asked.

"One of the monsters that live under the earth," she explained. "I've seen people possessed by him..." She didn't continue, her gaze lost somewhere in the past.

"And how long will that take?" I asked, pointing to the dark sludge.

"It's fast. A matter of seconds."

I looked at her, stunned. I'd never heard of a toxin that acts that fast.

"How do you know all this?" My knowledge of wild plants and fruits was limited at best.

"A woman must have her secrets," she said, showing her first grin in hours. I was happy to see her lighthearted. "Now give me your cloak, so I can make a few spikes we can throw."

She worked quickly with her knife, much faster than it took me to peel the branches, and with threads ripped from my cloak, she tied them to one end and made a couple dozen rudimentary darts, which she placed in the container where the leaves had been.

"Do you think they're sharp enough to go through the skin?"

"Do you want to try it?" she challenged, picking one.

"No need," I said, raising my arms in front of me, palms facing her in a placating gesture.

"Hold on to this and follow me. It's time," Alana said and gave me the container with the darts.

I hadn't realized, but all around us, darkness had fallen, enough to make it difficult to see through the trees.

"And how will we see them?"

"Most will have torches. The rest, leave them to me," Alana replied mysteriously.

"Oh. Right." From what I'd seen so far, the forest seemed like her home. I imagined her presenting the woods like the owner of a new house: *And here you have the kitchen, with these wonderful berries and tea leaves, and next to it is the kitchen sink, right near this stream...*

Alana stopped at a place that gave me a good view of the RV and the area around it. A feeling of dread washed over me when I realized they had brought a couple of oxen to move my vehicle. *If they take it, I'm finished.*

"We have to act fast. Otherwise, they'll take it with them." I didn't even want to think what would happen if I lost the RV.

"This is good," she assured me. "See, most of the guards are away from the door, helping with the oxen. Be prepared to run when I give you the signal." She took the darts from me and took a step forward.

"Wait, what are you going to do?"

"I'll poison the sentinels on the side with the door."

"But I can shoot them," I suggested and nodded to the gun I held in my hand.

"It will make too much noise. My way is better. Once you see me, start running. We won't have much time."

Like a wraith, she disappeared in the shadows ahead, her steps soundless on the forest's mossy carpet.

Minutes passed, and nothing happened. The guards were posted at each end of the RV and along the trees. Their scrutinizing gazes moved left to right, like radar searching for incoming objects.

Then one of them put a hand over his neck, took something, and looked at it. From where I was, I couldn't see what, but he started staggering. Before he collapsed to the ground, two hands appeared behind him, and his body disappeared into the shadows. My heart started thumping, and I looked around, afraid someone would hear it, but no one noticed.

A few more minutes passed, then the process repeated, and another guard was swallowed by the dark forest. However, something must have happened because one of the two guards near the RV's door abruptly turned his head and started toward the place where his comrade had been.

A second later, a dark silhouette emerged from the trees. The guard's hand moved to the side, where he kept his sword, but Alana was faster. Two darts flew from her hand, and by the time the warrior had pulled half of his sword from its scabbard, the poisonous bolt struck him. The sword cleared its sheath, and he took a couple more steps, then fell to his knees, hands clutching his throat. His body leaned on the side, hitting the ground hard, and started convulsing.

I pressed the unlock button and bolted, heading straight for the door. I jumped over the body of the other guard, who was slumped to the ground next to my back wheel, and arrived half a second before Alana did.

People started shouting, and I saw archers aiming for me. I pulled the door open, and several clinking sounds announced the moment the arrows met the RV's armor. Alana rushed in, and I locked the door behind me.

"That was close," I said, still breathing hard. "Now, let's get out of here."

I hurried to the front, and I took the wheel while Alana sat next to me. When I turned on the engine, a sense of panic swept over me. The battery was almost depleted. With these roads, I was lucky to have five, maybe ten kilometers, until the battery died out. *Why there's no gas station when you need one?*

The sound of arrows scratching the windshield brought me back to the situation at hand. They had no chance of getting through, but what worried me were the people carrying torches. If any of them decided to incinerate the vehicle, the situation would complicate immensely. They already had the oxen blocking my way, and people were trying to force their way in through the locked door.

"Hold on," I said and honked twice, then pressed hard on the acceleration. The effect would have been comic if the situation weren't so dire. Fear must have entered the two oxen's hearts, because they decided to run, trampling down whoever was in front of them. It resulted in a veritable stampede, with men running for their lives to get out of the way of the two scared beasts. I took advantage of the distraction and accelerated, getting out of the clearing and onto the main road. One side was blocked by several fallen tree trunks, so I turned left on the road leading to the stone bridge. In the side mirrors, I saw several soldiers hurrying after the RV, swords in hands. I pulled down the side window, raised a fist and extended a finger. The gesture was lost on them.

I kept an eye on the battery level; it was diminishing rapidly.

"I'll turn right once we exit the bridge and follow Orgetorix's army." I hoped the road they'd taken would be better and put less stress on the battery.

In the left side mirror, I noticed someone hanging from the rear ladder, sword in hand. I slammed the brakes and turned the wheel, and both the man and the sword went flying through the air. *Didn't you know it's never a good idea to hang on the back of a moving vehicle?*

The road the army had taken was easily recognizable, being close to the river. I rechecked the mirrors and saw a few stragglers still trying to catch up, the distance growing with each passing second. Soon, even they stopped. It was futile; they couldn't catch the RV. Unless the battery died on me.

"Alana, do you think they'll follow us on horses?" If they did, I couldn't outrun them, not until I recharged.

"Even if they do, it will take a while, and there's not much light left."

Alana was right; I could barely see the road ahead. The dark clouds stopped any celestial light from reaching the ground, making the road more difficult to navigate.

"I can't turn on the lights because they will see us." *And rapidly consume whatever power the RV has left.* "I'll find a place to stop to launch one of the drones with a night vision camera. I don't want to stumble upon Orgetorix's army."

I drove until I found a spot near the surrounding forest, partially hidden between the trees. It was too dark to drive any longer and I doubted the RV had enough energy for one more mile.

"I'll go on the roof and launch the drone. Do you want to come with me?"

"Where do you want me to put these?" asked Alana. She still had the poison and the darts with her.

"Somewhere far away from me, please," I raised my hands and pulled back, creating some distance between us.

I pulled down the ladder and stepped on the roof, drone in hand, when something slammed into my back, sending me sprawling on the cold metal, my head hitting the L-shaped couch. A moment later, I felt someone jumping on my back, then a strong arm passing under my neck, around my throat. Terror swept over me, and I tried to inhale, but my head jerked back, and all airflow stopped. I used both my hands to pull at the snake-like arm, but I couldn't do anything about it; I had no leverage. It was like trying to pull against a rock. White spots danced in front of me, like stars on a black sky. My lungs were burning, and my head felt like a boiler under extreme pressure, ready to explode. I tried to call for help but only managed a croak. Every cell in my body screamed for air, and I used the last strength I had to dig my nails into the arm to pry it loose and give me a moment to breathe. To no avail. My vision darkened, and I felt my energy leaking away, leaving my body all at once, as a desire to sleep made its presence known, like a train hurrying in a tunnel. Maybe it was time to rest...

Fresh air inundated my nostrils and spread into the burning lungs. It felt like cold water on a stifling summer day, and I wanted more. The weight on my back leaned to one side, and then the arm around my throat was gone. I started coughing violently. It felt like something was stuck in my throat. Like a wounded animal, I looked around, dreading another attack, but I only saw Alana kicking a man's body over the edge. She had a knife in her hand, and it was stained with blood.

I turned on my back, closed my eyes, and inhaled—as deeply as I could—the fresh, crisp night air. There was a hint of a darker scent, carrying the notes of tree trunks, moss, and wild jasmine. I was exhausted, and my only wish was to remain there and rest.

"Duncan, can you hear me?" Alana's tone of voice fit perfectly with the scents dancing in my head. I didn't even have the energy to move my lips and reply to her question. "Duncan, can you hear me?" she asked again, her voice betraying concern.

I opened my eyes to see her face a few centimeters away from me. She looked like an angel in the light coming from inside the RV, and something inside me erupted. Relief, gratitude, elation, and a strange desire, one I had never felt before. I wanted to remain there, in her life. Forever.

"Can you get up? Let's get inside."

"Water," I said, my voice unrecognizable, like someone had used a saw to cut it to shreds.

"Stay here. Don't move. I'll be right back."

I blinked, and she was gone. My eyelids felt heavy, and I closed them. My mind drifted in a sea of blackness. I was glad to be alive. Until now, I hadn't realized how many fragrances floated around me, carried through the air. *You never realize how precious something is until you lose it.*

"Here." I heard Alana's voice and felt her hand behind my neck, lifting me gently. I kept my eyes closed and felt the cold, tasteless, magnificent liquid that is water dripping through my parted lips. It was like everything it touched came back to life, like flowers waking up when the spring arrives.

"Thank you." With her help, I stood and staggered on to my feet. "Who was it?" I asked, my voice better but still like the hinges of an old door. I tried to peer over the edge, but it was too dark to see anything.

"One of the soldiers who followed us. He must have remained on the ladder and then climbed when we stopped."

"Is he…"

"Yes."

Her confirmation made me feel better. *He almost killed me.*

"What shall we do with the body? It's fairly close to the road, and he may be found." The sounds coming from my mouth were strange, alien to me. My voice was unrecognizable, even though I spoke slowly to avoid straining my neck muscles.

"And? I see no reason not to leave it where it is."

If Alana didn't think there was an issue, then I wouldn't worry. *She has more experience with dead bodies than I do.*

"Duncan, we should leave. By morning, vultures and crows will circle this place. The soldiers will spend some time looking to see why, and we can use that to distance ourselves even farther."

That makes sense. Use the dead body as a distraction. I found nothing wrong with her logic, so I went back to my original plan. After a quick search, I located the drone at the opposite edge of the roof. I used my phone to send the command, and with a barely audible buzz, it disappeared into the night.

Alana remained staring into the darkness, and anger flashed across her face, replaced by a mask of grim determination. Whatever she had decided, I was sure nothing could stop her.

16

"Come here," shouted Alana from the kitchen. For the past few minutes, she had been rummaging through her bag for reasons known only to her.

"Yes?" I asked, my voice croaky.

"I have prepared something for your throat. Sit." *She's the sort of person born to command. When Alana gives an order, she expects to be obeyed. Must be because her father was a chieftain.*

She dipped two fingers into a cup and extracted a dark, slimy substance.

"What is that?" It looked repulsive.

"It will heal your skin. Now lift your chin up."

With precise movements, she began applying the disgusting-looking thing over my throat. A pungent onion smell assaulted my nostrils, and I lifted my chin even farther, trying to get away from it.

"I'm so glad I found it. I thought I lost it."

"Mmm?" I didn't want to speak and taste that foul smell.

"My bag. I forgot I left it here when we went hunting for food."

"Mmm."

"By morning, you should feel much better."

I shrugged, not wanting to disagree with her, but I doubted. It would take several days to recover.

The next morning, I found out she was right. Only a dull pain registered when the transient light preceding the rising sun arrived; my neck felt stiff, but the bruises were gone. I looked from the bathroom's mirror, through the open door, at Alana's face. She slept on the couch, her face partially covered by shadows but peaceful, and her breathing steady. It was the first night we'd slept near each other without anyone else around, and a warm sensation enveloped me at the thought.

I closed the door to reduce the noise and turned on the shower. With the battery almost drained, I didn't even try to turn on the hot water. At first, it felt like I'd entered a blizzard, naked, but I steeled myself to endure it. Slowly the ice-cold sensation moved to the back of my mind, and I closed my hands into fists of rage, frustration, and shame, as the images from the last couple of days replayed in my mind, forever engraved into memory. I let the water wash everything away, burying the horrific memories deep inside, and prepared myself for what had to come next. My skin turned a shade of blue, and my stomach growled, reminding me I hadn't had a proper meal in forever.

I draped a towel over my waist and opened the door to see

Alana already up, hunting through the fridge, the light showing her silhouette.

"What is this?" she asked, lifting a plastic bag, not looking at me.

"Salami."

"What is salami?"

"Meat."

She placed it on the counter, next to a bag of sliced bread, several tomatoes, and one cucumber. It didn't look like much, but to me, it was a real feast.

In no time, I threw on a T-shirt and sweatpants, found some clothes for her, and came back to see slices of tomato, salami, cucumber, and bread neatly arranged on a plate.

"Leave some for me," Alana said, taking the clothes I'd prepared for her and closing the door to the bathroom.

"Don't use the hot water," I shouted after her. If she did, the RV battery would be fully depleted.

I fished for some cream cheese from the fridge, and two sandwiches disappeared before I had time to draw a breath. With the worst of my hunger abated, I slowed down to a normal pace of eating. My eyes fell on my vest lying next to the door; it looked like swiss cheese, with holes and tears everywhere.

From the corner of my eye, I caught a glimpse of a shadow gliding past the windshield. My heartbeat accelerated and, with half of a sandwich in hand, I hurried to my office, where I turned on the display showing views from all the security cameras surrounding the vehicle. *They found us.*

I wanted to slap myself for being so forgetful. I thought I would be gone by the time the pursuers arrived, but there was nothing I could do now. Near the vehicle, were three armed men, one next to the door, one on the opposite side, under the tinted kitchen window, and the third one at the rear ladder. Farther away, in the pre-dawn the cameras showed another attacker with a bow. Behind him, blocking the exit, was the trunk of a fallen tree. *How did they drag it over here?*

I grabbed the gun from my backpack and knocked on the bathroom door.

"What?" Alana's sharp voice came from the other side.

"We have visitors."

A fraction of a second later, her slender body—a towel covering her chest and long enough to reach her knees—appeared through the cracked door.

"How many?"

"I counted four, but there could be more."

"Show me." I did. *She got used to the technology, way better than I've gotten used to this world.*

"I think we need a distraction. If you exit like this..." I started, but she threw me an icy look, enough to stop me in my tracks. "Sorry. I can honk again."

"They've heard it once and will expect it."

"I can go on the roof..."

"They'll hear and see when the bench with the torches appears."

"You mean the Sky Lounge with the couch and lights? I can select for them to remain where they are. I'll open the access door and crawl along the roof. There are enough leaves so they won't see me, and I have enough bullets to injure them. We can then tie them up and leave them there."

She looked questioningly at me, like I wasn't in my right mind.

"Very good. Start with the archer first. He's the only one that has a chance to see you."

"Will do. Stay here."

By the time I got into position, I already planned my next moves. The air was cold and damp, like after the autumn rain. I knew where to look, and I spotted the archer's silhouette hidden behind a bush. He must have thought it would protect him. He was wrong. I took a deep breath, set my sights on the unmoving shadow, exhaled, and pulled the trigger. The man wasn't far, and my shot went straight into his right bicep. His body fell backward over the tree trunk, causing a loud creak. The game was afoot.

The noise made by my gun and the dead body meant the attackers knew they'd been spotted. I crawled to face the attacker on my right, next to the door, and he received a shot straight into his right kneecap, dropping to the ground like he'd been struck by lightning.

Before I had time to align another shot, the door opened and Alana emerged, wearing black tights and a black Linux penguin T-shirt, brandishing her sword. *Why did I ever think she would listen to me?* Her body was illuminated by the light coming from inside the vehicle. The man hiding behind the RV rushed her, and she met him head-on. Even though I'd seen her fight before, it wasn't this close, and hundreds of other warriors had surrounded her. I remained there, on the roof, stunned, admiring her figure and how nonchalantly she moved, avoiding the slashes and thrusts until she found the opening she needed.

The warrior's body dropped to the ground, blood pouring out from his chest. She wore a small smile and was in complete control.

I almost missed the other two attackers circling her. One came from the front of the RV, sneaking behind her, and another from the trees nearby, to her left.

The one behind her was the closest and most dangerous, so I pulled the trigger without even aiming properly. I must have hit him in the shoulder because he reeled back a few steps, but it gave Alana the time she needed to turn and lunge, sword aiming for his heart. Her graceful movement continued and slashed the throat of the other man, the one I shot in the knee earlier.

I looked up to see the last attacker poised to throw an ax, its polished metal glinting in the dawn light coming through the trees. I shot two times in rapid succession, aiming for his throwing arm, and saw the body fall, but the blade had already started spinning through the air, straight for Alana's head. I watched in horror as it came closer and closer, the malevolent steel hungry to cut through flesh.

At the last moment, Alana sidestepped, and in a blur, her blade deflected the ax, which hit the metallic frame of the RV with a loud clank.

"Wait here," she shouted, and like a deer, she disappeared through the trees in the dim light.

Several minutes later, she came back, sword held loosely to one side.

"I missed them," Alana said, panting. At my inquisitive look, she continued. "I heard the horses, but it took me longer than expected to reach them. They took off the moment they saw me, dragging the other beasts with them. And it's not the worst part." She inhaled, then blurted out, "They galloped toward Orgetorix's army. Now he'll know we're after him and will be prepared."

"You think so?"

"You can be sure of it," she said, her voice full of conviction and annoyance.

"But it doesn't mean he'll know our plan. He'll think we're just running away, not coming after him. I mean, he's surrounded by an entire army. What reason does he have to be afraid?"

"He heard what happened to his men when they attacked Ambenix's town," she reminded me. "He knows a shaman is coming after him. You. I'm sure rumors about your carriage have reached him by now."

"But he doesn't believe it," I insisted. "And he wasn't there, so anything he heard will be dismissed as an exaggeration."

"Maybe." She didn't sound convinced. "Nevertheless, we must leave this place."

"About that," I said, scratching the back of my head. "We can't. We have to wait for the sun to clear the tree line so it can charge the solar panels. The sun will give power to this carriage," I clarified. Dressed like she was, I had moments when I forgot who I was talking to.

"So, you want us to stay here?"

"Well, we need to get out of these woods, but there's a big log blocking our way."

"We have some work to do then," she said and grabbed the last two sandwiches from the plate.

The growing rays of the morning sun caught Alana and I on the roof, on the Sky Lounge couch, checking the nearby area. I had a splendid view, a couple of miles, and everything looked peaceful. The firmament was again azure blue, with only a few white streaks painted on it. The fully extended solar panels soaked in the morning light, charging the depleted batteries, making the entire RV look like a giant butterfly.

Alana had been different since Tyrenn died. Her words were sharper, and I had the impression she mostly kept thinking of revenge. It was understandable, but it felt like there was something more directed at me.

"Can we talk?"

She turned and faced me, her expression hard to read.

"Since we left Orgetorix's city, you seem different. Did I upset you? "

Alana let out a sigh, and her shoulders sagged. "I'm sorry, Duncan. I tried not to, but my thoughts go back to when Tyrenn died. I told myself there was nothing anyone could do, but a part of me wonders—could you have saved him?"

I started to say something, but she lifted her palm to silence me.

"I've seen you do powerful magic. Your carriage is like nothing I ever dreamed of. You've shown me amazing things, and I can't stop thinking that you could have saved him."

"Oh, Alana," I said and cupped her hands in mine. "Please believe me, there was nothing I could do. You may think I have this great power, but I don't. I possess some advanced tools, but I have nothing that can stop death. No one has."

"But you did so many things. You saved so many people. You saved me," she said in a low voice, tears flowing freely down her cheeks. "Why couldn't you save him?" She rested her head on my chest and started crying, sobs shaking her body.

I put an arm around her shoulders and started caressing her wheat-like hair.

"When I was young, my mother was diagnosed with cancer, a terrible disease," I told her. "My father had the best doctors at her side, the latest technology a military hospital could offer, but in the end, no one could save her. It's not always up to us to decide who lives and who dies. Sometimes not even the greatest magic in the world can cheat death."

I remained quiet for a long time until she lifted her head and wiped away the wetness on her cheeks.

"Thank you," she said and caressed my cheek. "I needed to hear that."

I put a hand over hers and kissed her palm. She smiled, and it filled my heart with joy.

I took a deep breath and straightened my back.

"Let's get inside. I'll fix you a hot beverage. It does wonders for the soul."

A tea, hot chocolate, or any other hot drink was my grandma's answer to all her friends visiting her, looking for healing words for a broken heart. She had a knack for knowing what to say and do for people who needed an ear and shoulder to cry on.

I rummaged through a tin box in the kitchen, produced two

tea bags of chamomile, and started the kettle. I made a mental note to keep that box supplied with a larger variety of teas. *If I ever get back home.*

"So, what's the plan once we reach Orgetorix?" I reached for two cups on an upper shelf.

"I was thinking I'd wait until night arrives, then find the tent where he's sleeping and kill him."

"And how do you plan to get past the guards?"

"If I see Orgetorix, I can plant an arrow in his chest even if he's surrounded by soldiers. If not, I'll find another way. They're not in a state of war, so there will be a minimum of guards around the camp."

"One of the men who attacked us had a bow."

"Yes, but you didn't kill him, and he got away."

I winced at her reproach.

"About that..." I started, but she put a finger over my lips.

"I understand. You blame yourself for what happened in Ambenix's town. It's my fault. I pushed you to do something you didn't want to."

While I felt guilty for what happened, the real reason was that I was afraid of what would happen if I continued killing people. I had no idea if or how it might affect the timeline, and even though the chances of going back were close to none, I still had a shred of hope. I just didn't know how to explain it, so I nodded. The kettle beeped, notifying me it had reached the desired temperature.

"How will you send an arrow without a bow?" I asked, trying to detour the conversation, and poured the steaming liquid into the cups over the chamomile bags.

"That's easy. I'll make one," she replied, and her lips curled into a smirk. I hadn't expected her answer.

"And what do you need me to do? How can I help?"

"Rescue me if I get captured," she said with a laugh. "No, I need you to get me there. The rest I can take care of all by myself."

For the first time since I arrived, I spent the day exactly how I imagined my vacation would be—on the roof, sipping drinks, and watching the nature around me. I also checked the level of the water tank. It had a quarter left, and I hoped it would rain soon. The water collectors and filters I had installed on the RV would help fill the tank even if I couldn't find a good water source nearby. I was especially pleased with my decision to buy a state-of-the-art system to help filter and dispose of most of the things that would typically go into the sewer tank. It occupied much less space, and I didn't have to waste any time dumping the black tank.

Alana had gone to collect some sticks and other fruits and leaves I didn't recognize, and then she joined me in the Sky Lounge. She shared some of the red fruits with me. They were sweet but with a sharp, bitter flavor. I thanked her and got a can of Coke to wash away the astringent taste.

It wasn't until the afternoon that my powerful binoculars spotted a group of riders coming from the direction where Orgetorix's army was located.

I had already scouted the best course to take through the trees, and in a few minutes, I was following a parallel but hidden road.

If those riders were indeed coming from Orgetorix's camp, I calculated the RV would reach the site before midnight.

When night fell, I decided to get outside the forest to take advantage of the moonlight. It was too difficult to drive through the trees holding the night vision binoculars.

I had two drones in the air, scouting ahead and behind, to make sure I didn't stumble upon the camp and to see if anyone followed us. My calculations had been correct, and when the clock blinked 11:00, I stopped behind a cluster of trees, the campsite less than a kilometer ahead of me. I set the drones to circle the area from above and create a map.

Based on Alana's description, I used imaging processing software to create a path to the middle of the camp, where Orgetorix's tent was. From the data collected by the drones, it had the least chance of being detected.

"You stay here and be ready to go when I return," Alana said.

"But—"

"We've talked about this, Duncan. Please. This will be dangerous, and while you have many wonderful qualities, you don't have the skills to remain undetected. I don't want to lose anyone else I care about."

I was prepared to protest more, but she closed the distance, and her sultry lips touched mine. A jolt ran through me, but before I could react, she retreated, her breathing heavy. "Please," she said. "Do this for me."

Her glistening eyes met mine, and I caught a glimpse of sadness behind them. Alana strapped the makeshift bow to her back, grabbed the arrows she had made, and headed to the exit. After a couple of steps, she turned, closed the distance, and planted another kiss on my hungry lips. Then she was gone, like the wind.

"Don't go." My words were lost in the empty room. *She doesn't believe she'll survive.* A shudder ran through me, and pain clenched my heart. *No, I can't let her die.*

I closed the door and rushed inside my command center. I had all three drones aloft, two for surveillance and one in tracking mode. I wanted to be with her every step of the way.

The camp was immense, with hundreds of fires illuminating thousands of tents. *That might pose a problem for my drones.* It was arranged in a large square in a valley with tall grass, next to the river.

When I asked Alana how she would find Orgetorix's tent, she said it would be in the center, guarded by soldiers. She mentioned other things, like sentinels guarding supplies, and night patrols walking around the camp to keep it in order. They and the sentries posted around the encampment had the night's password, set by Orgetorix himself, to identify friend from foe. She planned to capture one of them, get the password, silence him, steal his clothes, and walk straight to Orgetorix's shelter, keeping in the shadows.

My drones were high enough not to be spotted, but I had zoomed in to track Alana's movements. She walked fast, hiding behind the trees, and then ducked through the tall grass until she reached one isolated sentry. He went down quickly, and a minute later, he got back up. Except it wasn't him; Alana was wearing his clothes, a dark cloak, and a helmet. She dragged the body several meters away, then walked straight into the camp.

My night vision camera had trouble with the light blazing from the fires spread throughout, so I switched to a regular view to make sure Alana's planned route was clear. People were still outside, near the fires, talking and drinking, the drones capturing the cheer clearly through their microphones. Patrols in formations of five people walked through the camp, breaking up fights and sending people inside their tents.

Like a shadow, Alana moved through the tents, keeping out of sight, until she was more than halfway through. That's when it happened.

She walked past a tent when a man got out and bumped into her. Alana recovered quickly, and I held my breath, expecting the fight followed by the general alarm. I grabbed my gun, even though I couldn't do anything about it. The man staggered on his feet, saluted, then continued to a wooden box, which I guessed was their latrine. Judging by the way he couldn't walk straight, he was drunk.

Alana continued until she reached the vicinity of the commander's tent, which sat right in the middle of the camp, where four soldiers holding spears guarded its entrance.

She waited until the patrol passed, then sneaked behind the tent. The angle made it impossible to see her through the tent, so despite the campfire interference, I switched over to thermal imaging. I bit back a scream, wishing I could warn her to stop. But it was too late; she had already cut a hole and was inside.

I watched in desperation as multiple bright orange dots encircled her. After what must have been a struggle, I observed through the drone's camera how two people holding Alana's limp body exited the tent, followed by three more. Another man appeared from a nearby tent, and the four guards from earlier joined him. I had a flash of insight and realized it must be Orgetorix. He had guessed someone might come after him, switched tents, and left a bunch of soldiers in his place. I wanted to scream in frustration.

My first thought was to put my vest on, go there, and shoot everyone who stood in my way, but there was a minor impediment. I only had thirty bullets left, and based on a rough estimate from what I'd seen, there were close to ten thousand people in the camp.

If I forced my way through with the RV, I would be killed the moment I stepped out. No, I needed something else. I recalled the other two drones, leaving only the one tracking Alana in place, and started my preparations.

Once I was ready, I left the safety of the RV, looking everywhere around me as I neared the camp. I crawled, waited, ran over small distances when no one was looking until I arrived close to her tent. It was guarded on all sides—but I knew that already. I took my phone out, held my black jacket around it to block any light from escaping, and studied the thermal image sent by the drone floating above. The four orange dots of the guards were posted at the corners, and inside were two other forms. One wasn't moving, probably Alana, but the other one appeared to be pacing back and forth.

With a glance at my phone, I confirmed the position of the other two drones and sent the command. From the remaining thirty rounds, I'd tied a bag with ten bullets bathed in a small quantity of petrol from my tank to each of the two drones. I had them hover over the nearest campfires and then plunge straight down. They crash-landed, scattering the embers at the soldiers gathered, some sparks even reaching the nearby tents. Soon, like fireworks, loud cracks emanated from the campfires, and blazes whooshed in the air, aided by the gunpowder and gases liberated from the bullet casings. People came out to see what was going on, bewildered looks on their faces. I hoped two guards at the rear of the tent would join them, and I would slide by unnoticed. *The universe doesn't seem to like me.* Only one of them did. The second guard remained put, looking in the direction of the exploding sounds.

My improvised stun gun was ready, and I sprinted toward him, hoping no one would see me. Only when the electrodes touched his neck did he turn and raise his arms to push me away, but it was too late, and he dropped to the ground, his body convulsing. He should be out for a few minutes. *If I'm not out by then...it won't matter anymore.*

I took out the knife, and with a swift slash, I was inside the tent.

Alana was tied to a pole, her head leaning to one side like she was asleep. Or unconscious. Next to me, on a wooden table, were her weapons, the bow, arrows, and a knife with traces of blood on it. Next to them, on each side of the table, were two oil lamps, the only light sources. At the mouth of the tent was a tall man, bald, with his back to me. He was shouting at the guards to see what the commotion was.

I was at Alana's side in a flash and sliced through the rope tying her hands behind her back. She slumped in my arms, groggy, and I saw a bruise under her temple. She barely registered my presence. I put an arm around her waist and guided her to the exit I'd made.

"You!" I heard a shout and turned to see the bald man with a long, dark beard unsheathing a sword. His face was full of gleeful hatred. A tight gray shirt highlighted his beefy frame and broad chest. He took a step forward and brandished the sword, poised to strike.

I had no hope of matching him in strength, and with one arm around Alana, I couldn't do anything but stare at his malevolent face. He took one more step, and his muscles contracted, ready for the mortal blow. My stun gun was discharged, my gun was in my jacket, I only had the knife in my right hand, but with my left arm supporting Alana, I had no chance.

Instinct took over, and I dropped the knife to the ground, grabbed one of the oil lamps, and launched it at his head. His blade stopped it easily, but the fiery liquid continued its movement and hit him in his head, causing him to scream in pain. He dropped the sword and put his hands over his face.

He staggered forward and fell on the table, scattering everything on the floor. The other lamp rolled to the edge of the tent, and the fabric ignited.

The place was quickly becoming a furnace, and I put the knife in its sheath, took out my gun, and carried Alana in my arms through the makeshift hole. I was ready to put her on the ground and shoot everything around me, but no one paid any attention to me. People were shouting, gesticulating, running. I saw buckets of water being carried to several nearby tents engulfed in roaring fires. *Hmm, maybe the universe gave me a break. Yeah, I'll probably pay for this later.*

In the general commotion, I slipped into the darkness and followed the same route until Alana and I reached the safety of the RV. I gently set Alana on my bed, then hurried to the driver's seat and accelerated into the night.

17

Hours later, when I finally had a chance to check on her, Alana was conscious enough to ask questions. "What happened?" Alana raised on her elbows to look at me. "Where are my weapons?"

"You're safe," I replied and placed a bottle of water on the nightstand next to her. "What do you remember?"

"I entered the tent, and then people jumped on me, and…I don't know. I remember you, then fire all around, and not much else."

"Orgetorix had people waiting for you in his tent," I confirmed. "I wish we'd realized it sooner. They must have knocked you unconscious, then dragged you somewhere else."

She placed a hand over her temple and grimaced in pain.

"Yeah," I said, "the blow must have been pretty hard. When I saw what happened, I came and got you out."

"Just like that?" she asked incredulously.

"Well, people were busy putting out some fires in the process." I couldn't hold it any longer. "Look, I know what you wanted to do. I was a fool not to realize it sooner."

"What—"

"You had no intention of coming back, did you? In fact, you knew once you killed Orgetorix, you wouldn't escape." I was furious, but I kept my voice down. "You should have told me."

Her eyes widened in surprise, then I read her shame. "How did you know?"

"The kiss. It had a sense of finality to it."

Her shoulders sagged. "I'm sorry, Duncan. Orgetorix had taken away from me everyone I cared about. I didn't want to lose you too."

"So that's why you left all alone with no thoughts of coming back? Because you wanted to keep me safe?" I wanted to laugh.

She nodded, and tears began slipping down her cheeks, dropping onto the white bedsheet.

"I can take care of myself," I said, unable to conceal my frustration, but my heart began to melt.

"Because of me, you almost died."

I shook my head. "I could have died when Ambenix's camp was attacked. I could have died when I came to save you from prison. We don't know how much time we have left. Next time let me choose. How do you think I would have felt if you had died there?"

She lowered her gaze and started sobbing.

I let out a deep breath, and along with it, my accumulated frustration.

"I'm sorry, but please know I care about you. A lot. Don't do this to me again. Please."

Her gaze met mine, and I saw the surprised look on her blotched face.

"I've never met anyone like you," she said in a low voice. "I care about you too. More than I'm supposed to."

"What do you mean by you're not supposed to?"

"In my tribe, if a woman's husband is killed, she needs to avenge him. The night when my parents died, I was supposed to be married."

A sharp pain stabbed my heart.

"Did you love him?"

Her head bowed slightly. "I'd only met him that day, remember? But he seemed to be a good man."

Oddly enough, her words filled me with cheer. I knew it wasn't nice to be happy with the news of her fiancé being killed, but I couldn't help it. My right hand cupped her cheek. She leaned on it and closed her eyes.

"Thank you for coming after me."

"Anytime." My words surprised even myself.

She smiled and kissed my palm. Then she straightened her body. "And where are we now?"

"After I brought you here, I wanted to put some distance between them and us..."

"And I lost my best chance to kill him..." she said bitterly, her shoulders sagging.

"...And I realized they were too distracted, so I circled around the camp, keeping near the woods, then drove for half the night and then again this morning. I only stopped when we reached this." I pointed to the hallway.

She slowly got up and headed toward the front of the vehicle. Through the windshield, in the distance, the imposing silhouette of a castle watched over its surroundings.

"Is this where we need to be?" I hoped I'd correctly guessed Orgetorix's destination.

"Yes. My father, my real father, brought me here once when I was younger, and we stayed for several days while he attended a tribal meeting." Her voice was full of emotion, triggered most likely by fond memories she had of her parents. "Everything is how I remembered."

"I'm sorry," I said and put an arm around her shoulders.

"I miss them, all of them. My father, my mother, Tyrenn, and everyone from the town. I knew most of them."

"Did they kill everyone?"

She nodded. "Everyone in our settlement and the ones nearby. There might be others who escaped, but I never heard anything about them."

"I might have stumbled upon someone from your tribe." I described my meeting with Hadwin, the old man Lann and I had saved from Orgetorix's men. I told her how Hadwin had mentioned Helix, who I now knew was her father, and about Hadwin's invitation to join them in the south.

Her eyes were sparkling when I finished, and her face radiated with joy.

"I never met anyone else who survived. Maybe when all this is over..." She didn't continue, instead turned to face the castle. "So, what are we going to do now?"

"Well, we need to attend the trial. If I can't kill Orgetorix myself, at the least I can make sure he will be punished for the things he did." She said his name with disdain.

"Will he be imprisoned?" After what I'd seen, decapitation was the only sentence they had here.

"For what he's accused of? No. He will most likely be burned alive," she replied. "Unless he's not found guilty, and then he'll get to walk free."

Well, decapitation sounds better than being burned alive.

"But they have Tarrah's testimony." I didn't know their laws, but I assumed a witness's testimony was important.

"Duncan, what matters is what the kings decide. They are appointed by the tribal councils, much like my father, Helix, was appointed by our council of elders. The most powerful of them are elected into the council of magistrates."

"Is Ambenix one of them?"

She shook her head. "To be king, you need to have more than one town. You need thousands of people on your domains, and most importantly, a large enough army to keep from being easily conquered. While there are many tens of tribes, only a handful are that strong: the Aedui, Aquitani, Arverni, Remi, Sequani, and Helvetii."

I vaguely recognized some of those names from my history classes.

"Is Orgetorix one of them?"

"Yes. He's part of the Helvetii, but unlike the other tribes, they don't have kings, just noblemen. Dumnorix is the chieftain of the Aedui tribe, and Casticus leads the Sequani."

The names flew over my head. Politics had never been my

strong suit. But I could do the math. "That means that out of seven powerful tribes, they control three of them?"

"Yes, and while they cannot vote, whoever they choose will."

"But that means out of seven votes, they already have almost half."

Alana ran a thumb over her bottom lip, calculating. "Not exactly. The Helvetii have two other noblemen who will attend the trial, and from what I've heard from Tarrah, there is no love lost between them. But I don't know how others will vote. Well, besides Vercingetorix."

I think I heard that name before.

"Who's he again? I know Tarrah said something about him, but I don't remember."

"He's the king of the Arverni. If he sees me, he'll recognize who I am." There was a note of certainty in her voice.

I guess that's a good thing. Okay, so we have to find this guy.

"So, how do we get to him? Can we ask at the gate to show us the way?"

Alana laughed. "No. Other times, I might have tried, but not now." Her tone became serious. "I'm sure it's full of spies there, and chances are we'll have our throats slit before we take two steps inside."

My muscles stiffened at her words. *No one will harm Alana. Not while I'm around.*

"Is there another way then? Another gate?"

She shook her head. "I don't know."

"Well, I don't think we have much time left until Orgetorix and his army will be here."

Alana bit her lip in frustration, and then her eyes brightened.

"We must disguise ourselves. When they see the army, many people from the farms surrounding the castle will flee inside, looking for shelter and protection. That's our only chance of getting in, undetected."

"Let me park this somewhere out of sight, then. I'll put some things in a bag, and we can go."

I left the RV behind a mass of trees, the vehicle hidden by the thick vegetation.

Alana's cloak had remained in the camp the previous night and most likely caught fire, and mine was riddled with holes and tears, so Alana and I swung by the impromptu village near the castle to see if I could "borrow" some clothes to disguise my appearance and hers; otherwise, our out-of-time clothes would have attracted a lot of undesired attention.

The way the houses were built had no logic. Some were scattered, and many more were packed tightly together, their rundown appearance giving the impression of a slum. I approached a building at the edge of the village, wary of any prying eyes, but everything looked deserted, the only noise was the bark of a dog in the distance.

The first few houses proved to be empty. The doors were wide open, tables and chairs were either turned or broken, and the pots and jugs were smashed to pieces. *It's like a band of thugs trashed this place already.*

I was halfway through the village when Alana pointed to a house with its door closed. I sneaked around the walls, the castle's profile hidden by the ramshackle cottage, and peered through the side window. Everything looked dark and abandoned, but a sliver of light illuminated an open wooden chest, with garments spread all around it like someone had searched through it in a hurry.

Like two shadows, Alana and I slid around the wall and entered the house, the door's scratchy creak making me hold my breath. I'd seen too many horror movies to keep my cool.

I let Alana pick through clothes while I looked around. *No ax wielders, check. No psychopaths with knives, check.* There were no beds, only a large patch of hay covered with wide cloth sheets, giving the impression of a mattress laid on the floor. On the other side of the room was a fireplace, and next to it, a wooden table with four plates resting on it. They were empty except for the few traces of food still left on them.

"Try this," Alana said, and I spun to see her holding what looked like a bedsheet.

"It doesn't have any holes where I can put my hands through," I said, still studying it.

"Just put it over your shoulders and tie a knot at your neck," she suggested and did the same with a similar one she found. "Good, now bring the sides together, like you're doing with a cloak when it's cold outside."

The improvised coat was large enough to go over my backpack and cover my entire body, except it wasn't long enough, and it reached only to my knees, leaving my boots exposed. Hers fit her better, covering her shoes.

"It will have to do," said Alana, then turned and started toward the door. She took only a couple of steps, then stopped abruptly, and I bumped into her.

"What's wrong?"

"Do you hear anything?" she whispered.

"No," I said after a few seconds. It was as quiet as a graveyard.

"Exactly. The dog's bark is gone. Keep your eyes open." She unsheathed her sword, and, with careful, silent movements, peered outside through the open door. "I have a feeling someone is watching us."

"Where?" I asked and gripped my gun tighter. She shrugged.

"Follow me. We can't stay here."

I exited the house, my eyes darting right to left, but there was only the empty road before me. Everything was quiet and still, like the calm before the storm. I kept near the wall and turned around the corner.

At that moment Alana gave a warning, and she raised her sword, but a white powder struck her eyes. She stepped back, bumping into me, and dropped the steel blade. A log came toward her, but she ducked.

I remained there, like a deer in the headlights, and it hit me in the stomach. I landed on my backside just as two bearded men with blond hair and torn brown tunics approached Alana, one holding a thick stick, a tad larger than a baseball bat.

Alana started rubbing her eyes when the second man grabbed her arm. She kicked him in the groin and followed up with an elbow to his face, and I heard the satisfying crunch of a broken nose. Crimson blood poured freely over his mouth, chin, and clothes.

But the second attacker didn't waste any time and struck her arm, making her cry out in pain, then punched her in the stomach. He then grabbed a lock of hair and spun Alana around, pressing his body to her back. His meaty fingers grabbed Alana's throat, ready to squeeze the life out of her. The second man lifted the fallen sword and pointed its tip at me. Drops of blood from his broken nose fell down on its hilt.

"What do we have here?" asked a third man coming from behind the other two. He had a rough voice, one that sounded familiar, even though I couldn't place it. He wasn't as tall as the other two but was well built, and I saw a scar on his right cheek. His black eyes were fixed on Alana, and he licked his lips as if looking at a delicious meal.

"Oh, we're going to have so much fun with you," he said and caressed her cheek with one finger. He then turned to face me. I lifted my gun.

The transformation happened in an instant. One moment he radiated confidence and malice. The next, he grew pale and his knees started shaking. He dropped the knife he was holding and started asking for forgiveness.

For a second, I remained stunned, and then I realized I had met him before, in another village, burned to the ground by Orgetorix's men. He was the only one I had left alive after I killed his companions, who tried to attack me.

I rose, pointed the gun at the man holding Alana, and said with as much conviction as I could muster, "Let her go."

For a second, I thought I could resolve all this without bloodshed. I was naïve. Instead, Alana's captor looked at me, at the black piece of metal I was holding, at the man who still shook like he had chills, then at his colleague holding the sword, and started laughing.

I took a deep breath, exhaled, letting all the air out, and pressed the trigger. The missile hit the man holding the sword in the left foot, making him shout in agony. I had eight bullets left.

"I'm a shaman, and if you don't let her go, I'll call thunder and lightning and burn you to the ground. Then I'll drink your souls and bathe in your ashes."

His eyes widened, and a split second later, he let Alana go and ran. I let the injured man limp away as well, but aimed the gun at the scarred man, who froze.

"Are you hurt?" I asked Alana.

"No," she said, rubbing her eyes. "They threw sand in my face and blinded me. I'll be fine."

"You," I said, my voice firm, looking at the last attacker. He lifted his gaze, his face pale and his eyes terrified. "What's your name?"

"Ferris," he replied, his voice trembling.

"So, Ferris, do you remember what I've told you?" He didn't answer, just bowed his head and started sobbing.

"You know him?" asked Alana in a surprised tone.

I nodded. "Ferris and his men attacked me a few days ago. I left him alive and told him...what did I tell you, Ferris?"

"That you'll kill me," he squeaked, not raising his head.

"Exactly, and I hate not keeping my word," I said and gave Alana a wink. I had no intention of killing an unarmed man.

"Wait, don't kill him just yet," Alana insisted, immediately catching on to both my signal and my desire not to kill him.

"Ferris, do you know how we can get inside the city without being seen?" she asked.

"Yes, yes, I do," said Ferris, nodding furiously, like his life depended on it.

"Well, Ferris, if you help us, then I'll try to convince the shaman to let you live," said Alana, tipping her head in my direction.

"Thank you, oh, thank you. I will help you, shaman. I will do as you ask," Ferris said, gazing at me without meeting my eyes. "There is a passage used by...the thieves in the area. I'm not one of them, I swear. They just took me through it once or twice."

"I don't care if you're a thief or not. I only need you to tell us where it is," I said, my voice sharp.

"It's in one of the houses closer to the wall. I'll show you."

I asked him to go in front, and both Alana and I followed him through the empty streets. I kept my gun trained on him the whole way, and Alana kept an eye out to make sure no one attacked us from behind.

The town wasn't big, and we soon arrived in front of the door of a rundown house, tucked inside an alley filled with trash and what smelled like human waste.

Ferris took out a key and opened the door, the movement accompanied by an ominous creaking sound.

It was dark, the only light coming through the open door, and it took a moment for my eyes to adjust. Ferris headed to a table covered by a large piece of cloth and moved it out of the way, revealing a concealed trap door. He lifted it, and the smell of sewer filled my nostrils.

"You will need my help, as there are a lot of corridors," Ferris told us. "There are no torches, but I know the way through the darkness."

I found it odd he already knew his way after allegedly only a couple of times but said nothing. I pulled the flashlight from my bag, turned it on, and invited him to climb down the ladder.

His eyes grew wide, his mouth agape, and he stared at the source of steady, white light I held in my hand. It took him a few moments to recover, and with trembling feet, he climbed down. I kept my gun on him, and with the torch between my teeth, I followed him into a tunnel. The light revealed a corridor wide enough to fit two people side by side. The ceiling was about three meters from the ground, supported by wide slabs of wood and pillars every few meters. It looked stable, but I still wouldn't want to be caught inside if there was an earthquake.

Once Alana joined me, I signaled Ferris to lead the way.

He hadn't been lying, and only five minutes later, we reached a bifurcation. Based on my observations and the distance traveled, we had to be somewhere between ten to fifteen meters away from the main gate.

"This one," Ferris said, pointing to the tunnel on my right, "will get us next to the stables near the gate. The other one will get us to one of ou…the houses the thieves use for storage."

"Which one is shorter?" I asked.

"The one on the right, but now I think it will be full of soldiers, and there's a greater chance of being discovered." He hesitated, giving me an odd look that I couldn't place. "I think we should take the other one."

I looked at Alana, who shrugged, so I made a gesture for Ferris to take the one on the left.

Alana and I followed Ferris through the tunnel until he reached a set of stairs covered by a trap door. Ferris climbed first, followed by me. Alana waited at the base of the stairs until there was enough room on the ladder. Ferris punched the door once, but it didn't give way.

"Sometimes it gets stuck," Ferris said apologetically. He hit it again two more times when it finally shot upward. I pointed my flashlight through the opening, but I only saw a couple of beams supporting a wooden roof.

He climbed out first, and I followed on his heels, again holding the flashlight in my teeth. He moved a few steps away, next to a couple of wooden crates, and turned, watching me with an odd smile, as I gave Alana a helping hand.

Something hit me from the side, compressing my elbow into my ribs, and I was catapulted through the air. I landed on something hard, with a loud crack. My head hit the thick wood, my vision blurred, and everything spun around me. Someone grabbed my hands and tied them behind my back. My feet were also bound together, and someone put a cover over my eyes.

I felt my body lifted off the ground, and a short while later, someone dropped me, like a sack of potatoes, on a cold stone floor and took the blindfold away. I opened my eyes to see a wooden wall in front of me. I heard another thud next to me, and then the sound of a door being locked as everything faded to pitch black.

18

"Duncan?" Alana whispered.

I tried to move, but pain hit me like a rushing train coming out of a tunnel. I groaned. My entire right arm felt like it had been hit by a wrecking ball, and a hot iron poked my ribs when I tried to move.

"Where are we?" I asked through clenched teeth, trying to master the pain.

Her voice came from the darkness surrounding me. "They moved us to another room. I think we're in the basement of the house. When you helped me up, someone hit you with a log, and you hit a crate. I tried to help you, but they hit me in the back, threw me to the ground, and bound my arms. But I have a knife I got from your kitchen. I'll cut both our ropes."

I nodded and felt my brain swimming in my head, hitting the sides of my skull. *Why did I nod? She can't see me.*

Alana's soft steps shuffled near me, and I felt her palms

going over my body. She stopped for a moment when she found the ropes behind my back and the ones tying my feet. Cold fingers caressed my cheeks, then forehead until she reached my temples, and with slow movements, they began a gentle massage, and the pain receded a notch.

Warmth spread through my body. "Mmm, it feels good."

"Don't fall asleep. Stay awake."

"Why?"

Heavy steps approached from the other side of the door, and a beam of light slid under the crack.

"Keep your hands behind your back," she whispered and disappeared into the surrounding darkness. The light grew in intensity, and the footsteps stopped just outside. I heard a rattle of keys, and searing light exploded, blinding me.

I closed my eyes and blinked a few times until my eyes adjusted.

It was a small, empty storage room. Next to the door were two men, one with red hair and a short beard to match it, and the other with long, curly, black hair. The first one held my backpack, and the one behind him carried a torch.

"I see ye're awake. Good," said the one holding the backpack, his gaze fixed on me. "Ye know, Ferris said I should kill ye." I didn't say anything, so he continued. "But if ye tell me what these are, I won't. Maybe I'll even let ye go."

He must have thought I was born yesterday. No, once I wasn't useful, he would kill me. And Alana.

The man put my backpack down and opened up the zipper, watching me intently. I don't know what he saw, but a vicious smile crept on his grisly face.

He took out a bottle of water with deliberate movements and nodded in my direction, waiting for an answer.

I contemplated fighting him, but I had no chance without any weapons, even if Alana joined me. Both of them were armed, and I had a suspicion I had fractured a rib, or at the very least pulled a muscle. Those two would kill me before I took a step. I needed to buy time.

"Water," I replied in a dried voice.

He grunted and picked up the next item, a rechargeable lighter.

"You use it to make fire."

"How?" Curiosity was evident in his voice.

"You press on that button, that small red square, and it will create fire."

He studied it, then extended his arm farther away from his face, and pressed it. A purple electrical arc appeared, and he almost dropped the lighter to the ground. The man tried again, and this time his hand hovered a few centimeters away from the purple light.

"I don't feel any heat."

"It's different from your torch, but it will make fire."

"Hmm." He put it down, next to the bottle of water, and took out my gun.

My heart lurched in my chest, and fear constricted my throat. If he shot Alana or me…then an idea flashed through my mind.

"What is this?" His eyes studied the pistol.

I took a small breath to steady my voice.

"It shows pictures, drawings."

"How do I see them?"

"There is a small hole. You can look through it..."

"I don't see anything," he complained, holding the muzzle toward him.

"You need to press on that switch next to your right thumb." I hoped with all my being that the safety was off.

Thunder inundated the small room, its blast worthy of a cannon, and was followed by the heavy thud of a human body. The bullet must have penetrated the skull and reached his brain; the body remained there, unmoving. I tried to push myself up, but a sharp pain in my ribs made me sink down to my knees. Alana, though, was faster, and something flashed before my eyes, the knife heading straight for the heart of the second guy. I had no idea where she kept it.

The thief was agile and moved out of the way, the blade grazing past his tunic, hitting the wall and clattering on the floor. He pulled a sword and took a step toward Alana, who retreated to a corner, with nowhere else to go. He raised his sword, ready to strike.

I dived, ignoring all the pain, and grabbed the gun, now lying at the dead man's feet. I turned on my right side, pointed the gun, and fired. The bullet hit him in the shoulder, and he staggered. In an instant, Alana was next to him and poked his eyes. He cried out in pain and took a step back, hitting the wall. The sword clattered at his feet. Alana dropped to the ground, grabbed the handle, and with a lightning movement, sank the blade into his chest, near his heart. The body twitched once and sagged to the floor.

"We have to move quickly. The fire will spread." While rock

covered the ground, the walls were made of wood, and the fallen torch ignited the one across from me. I had been too absorbed by the fight to notice it.

I grabbed the bottle of water and the lighter, threw them in the backpack, and followed Alana out of the room, closing the door behind me. Heavy smoke was already coming from under it. As I swung the backpack onto my shoulders, my ribs screamed in protest, and I had to put a hand over them to alleviate the pain. *Nice one, Duncan.* I took the phone out from my breast pocket—luckily it didn't suffer any damage—and turned on the flashlight function.

I saw the trap door, the one Ferris had used to get out of the tunnel. Across from it were the two crates I'd seen earlier, except one was cracked from my impact with it. On the far side was a set of stairs, going to the upper level, guarded by a heavy looking door. Alana was the first to climb them, and I followed, struggling to ignore the growing pain in my ribs.

"Reid, what's going on?" Hurried steps followed, and the door opened to reveal a man with a black eye patch, holding a knife in his hand. His momentum carried him forward, right into Alana's sword. She twisted, and the body continued its innate movement, past her. I stuck to the wall, and the corpse tumbled down the stairs, swallowed by the rising smoke.

The room above was small and empty, except for a table and four chairs on the door's left side. The table, though, was filled with bags full of silver-looking coins, and next to them stood four golden goblets. On our right was a window with a view of the street, and next to it, the exit.

"Let's get out of here," urged Alana.

"Should we see if we can find other clothes? These look like rags."

"You want to go down into the fire? I don't see any around here."

"Sorry, my head still hurts."

"Let's move. We don't have much time."

It was the last house at the end of a narrow alley, which ended with a tall stone wall. The neighborhood was deserted, except for the people running and shouting in panic at the other end of the street. They didn't pay us any attention.

"I think Orgetorix's army is here."

"Well, if they're busy with that, then they won't mind us. Where to?" I hoped she knew the city because I was clueless.

"Let's head toward the temple."

"And do you know where it is?"

"We'll see."

I reached the end of the street but stopped as another group of soldiers marched by, each holding a spear and a small wooden shield. Alana pulled me into a nook in the wall until the men passed.

"It was several years ago, and I haven't been to this part of the city," she confessed. "We need to find higher ground. The temple is the tallest building in town."

Alana went in the opposite direction the soldiers had taken. The streets were packed with people hurrying to their homes or to whatever safe places they had. Merchants pulled the produce inside, a group of women thronged in front of an inn with a white horse sign hanging above the door, and kids ran to their parents' open arms before hiding behind closed doors.

Everyone was too busy to give a second glance to two beggars dressed in rags. After a few turns, we arrived at a large fountain with a horse's statue in the middle. The pain in my ribs burned, and I sat on the fountain's edge to splash some water over my face. The cold felt good and refreshing, and the burning sensation receded a notch.

"There." She pointed through the buildings on the right, at the silhouette of a three-story house, shaped like half of a pyramid, with a tower on top. "That's where we need to go."

I grinded my teeth and followed her through narrow roads until I reached an alley across the wooden double doors of a massive building made of stone, the tallest structure I'd seen since arriving in this time. The thin tower looked very much like a lighthouse. In full armor, eight guards with spears, swords, and metal shields guarded the entrance. I did a quick mental calculation and realized I didn't have enough bullets. And even if I did, I could only take out three, maybe four, before Alana and I would be overrun.

"Alana, I don't think we can get past them."

"No, we can't," she said bitterly. "Having so many guards there, and more inside, means the trial has started. We must hurry."

"Hurry where?"

"I remember a side entrance. Follow me."

Alana took a roundabout way through an adjacent street until she reached the temple's left side. A small door, guarded by only one guard, stood between us and the temple.

"I had hoped this wouldn't be guarded." She bit her lip in frustration.

"I could shoot him," I offered and was disconcerted by how quickly I had suggested to harm or even murder a human being.

"No, we don't want to kill any of them. They're not our enemies."

"Then what are we supposed to do? Talk to him?"

"If we have to, yes. Let me think."

How can we get past one lonely guard? If only it was night and he slept. Hmm...sleep. Yes, that's it.

"Actually, I have an idea," I rummaged through my backpack until I found what I was looking for. "Do you think we can get close to him?"

"Possibly. Why?"

"You'll see. It won't kill him, but it should buy us a few minutes. Kind of like your poisonous darts, but less lethal."

She gave me a long look, then took off the hood, pulled the makeshift cloak around her to hide the clothes. "Wait until he's not looking in this direction."

Alana exited the alley, and she looked around, a confused expression on her face; then, as if seeing the soldier for the first time, she hurriedly approached him.

"What's going on?"

I recognized the panic in her voice. *She would make a great actress.*

"Everyone should be inside their homes. What are you doing out? Don't you know there's an entire army at our gates?" shouted the guard.

Alana let out a cry of fear. "An army? What will we do? I—" She didn't finish because her knees gave way, and her body started falling. The soldier had good reflexes, and his arms shot forward to catch her. He missed my approach and the two electrical prongs headed for his neck.

A stun gun is an excellent self-defense weapon, even if an attacker has grabbed you. You won't feel the effects, and the moment contact is made, the opponent will be incapacitated and feel disoriented. Then, in only a few seconds, all his blood sugar will be transformed into lactic acid, which will make him weak, without any energy to move or stay upright.

Usually, three seconds is enough to stop an attacker. I counted to six until I removed the stun gun from his neck, and he slumped to the ground, dazed and near unconsciousness. I took his sword to have a backup, in case I ran out of bullets. I didn't know how to wield it, but it was better than nothing.

Alana opened the door, and after she peered through, she helped carry him inside. "No need to raise the alarm too quickly," she said.

I was in a dark, empty antechamber, with only one other exit in front of me.

"This way, and be quiet," Alana whispered. She put her ear to the door, listened, and a few seconds later, opened it carefully, without a sound. It led to a long, narrow hallway, filled with torches every few meters. On the right side, between the torches, were three doors, and behind each, I heard people talking, their words muffled.

"We need to reach the third door. It's the one leading to the hall where the trial is held," she murmured in my ear, her words barely audible.

She put a finger over her lips and tiptoed to the first door. It was slightly ajar, and I saw a stand full of spears. It looked like a small armory. Next to it, two soldiers, in battle armor, their backs to us, inspected one of the weapons. Farther away, there was a group of soldiers with axes and shields. No wonder they didn't need more guards posted at the entrance; they had an entire army inside.

Like a ghost, Alana passed and headed to the next. I took a silent, deep breath and followed as quietly as I could.

The second door was open, and I saw a line of servants, each holding trays filled with food and drinks. They were waiting to be inspected by one of the four guards in front of a large archway, blocked by a wide wooden door.

Alana made a gesture, and she sprinted silently until she reached the other side. I ran after her, but in my hurry, the blade I was holding hit the stone wall with a loud clank. I winced.

My breath stopped in my chest, and I closed my eyes, hoping no one heard it.

"Hey," I heard a shout. "There's someone there."

I opened my eyes to see Alana's frightened look. The sound of people running assaulted my ears, and I turned to see the soldiers pouring out of both doors.

"Run!" Alana shouted over the noise of weapons being drawn and launched herself toward the third door, which was closed, but I hoped not locked. I was hot on her heels, with a hand pressed over my ribs, and I reached it a second after she opened it, the soldiers only a few meters behind me. I slammed it shut as soon as I got through, put my back to it and closed my eyes, letting out a deep breath, expecting to be pushed aside by the mob.

When nothing happened, I opened my eyes and wished I hadn't.

A dozen men faced us, their swords drawn, blades gleaming in the light cast by the torches spread around the room.

The whole situation reminded me of a movie scene where two thieves try to rob a bar. Except the bar is full of cops, and the thieves' puny threats are met with dozens of weapons.

I laughed, a deep, hearty laugh, which made my ribs ache. I didn't want to, but I was tired, hungry, injured, and there was nothing I could do. Seven bullets against a dozen swords, held by people in battle armor and a veritable army behind me. I also had a sword, but I had no idea how to use it, compared to people who had grown up fighting with one. If I was to meet my end here, at least I could face it with a smile on my lips and Alana at my side.

Everyone, including Alana, turned to look at me like I was a madman. The moment didn't last long, and several soldiers took a step forward.

"They're with me," thundered a male voice. It was a voice I knew, a voice I'd last heard a few days ago. It was Ambenix's voice. *This is the first time I enjoy hearing him speak.*

The soldiers stopped but didn't put their weapons down. One of them, an older man somewhere in his forties, turned to face Ambenix, who was opposite us, on the other side of the room. The flame of the torches reflected on the soldier's shiny scaled armor like it was a mirror.

"You can't have more than three people with you." The man had a tone of command in his voice.

Ambenix stared at him, and I thought he was going to ignore the soldier's words.

"Fine, I'll leave my men here. Does it satisfy your rules, Lucterius?" There was a note of challenge in his voice.

Lucterius looked at me, then Alana, before nodding and sheathing his sword. "Very well, you may pass."

Ambenix made a gesture for Alana and me to join him, and he walked toward a massive double door, embroidered with golden threads around its edges. Two of his men remained back, but another figure started after him, hiding his face in a hood.

The sea of soldiers parted, and Alana and I hurried after Ambenix.

"Don't make me regret it," he whispered through clenched teeth, loud enough only for me to hear him. The guards opened the massive doors, and all four of us stepped through into a large hall surrounded by tall stands, similar to floor lamps, with ceramic vessels on top, from which flames illuminated the room.

An immense round table, shaped like three quarters of a circle, stood in front of us, with twelve massive wooden chairs like thrones around it. Eleven men filled them, their gazes on a tall man with thick blond hair standing in the middle, his back to us. He wore a green cape with golden embroidery that flowed from his shoulders to the ground. Behind ten of the chairs were three people, each armed with an ax.

On the chair across from us, on the far side of the room,

stood a man with black hair, bushy eyebrows, an olive complexion, and a white toga with two broad purple stripes. Behind him stood three men wearing red cloaks, golden helmets, and short swords at their belts. I had seen enough movies to recognize who they were. They were Romans.

Two seats to his left, wearing a black robe, stood a tall man, a hood covering most of his face. The two gleaming eyes focused on me. His hand stroked his short, black beard, and he inclined his head in my direction. I nodded back. Behind him stood only one man, dressed in a plain brown robe, tied at the middle by a white rope. It struck me he was the only guard in the room with no apparent weapons.

"You've all heard the accusations and what Orgetorix intended to do," said the man with the green cape in a powerful voice, which resonated in the entire hall. "He even brought his army to scare us. But we can't be easily frightened. We will stand united against any and all enemies." He paused to look at the gathered leaders. "I say we should vote and give Orgetorix what he deserves. What every murderer deserves," he continued and pointed to the man standing to his right, closest to the door.

On the chair closest to me, wearing a silky dark-blue knee-length tunic, sat a man in his early fifties with rust-colored hair, a round face, and steel gray eyes. I recognized him. Orgetorix didn't say anything, didn't move, but kept looking at the man in front of him.

"Vercingetorix, we've only heard what your captain, Lucterius, told us," replied the man to Orgetorix's right. "He could be lyi—"

"I hope you don't intend to accuse Lucterius of being a liar," interrupted Vercingetorix, his voice threatening.

"No, I wanted to say he was misinformed," the man quickly backtracked. "For all we know, a servant may have written those words and then used Orgetorix's sigil to make us believe he wrote them. Why didn't Lucterius give us the name of who gave him the letters?"

"Because I've asked him not to," shouted a feminine voice next to me, which I recognized immediately. *What is she doing here?*

Standing next to me behind Ambenix, Tarrah pushed her hood back and looked around the room. Everyone turned to look at my group. My gaze had remained on Vercingetorix, and his eyes widened the moment he noticed Alana.

"All the words I sent to Lucterius are true," said Tarrah, her head held high. There wasn't an ounce of fear in her features.

"You ungrateful child." Orgetorix's voice dripped with venom. He stood, the chair tumbling away behind him. His face was red, and his eyes were full of rage.

"I'm not afraid of you anymore. After what you've done to me, I hope they burn you and your soul to ashes." Tarrah's disgust was evident in her tone.

Orgetorix took a few steps forward, his intention clear. He raised his hand to strike Tarrah. My body tensed, but before I could move, Alana intervened and batted his arm away, leaving a thin red line on the back of his hand.

"How dare you touch me. You'll die for this, you filthy whor—"

"I am Alana, daughter of Helix of the clan—"

"Helix and his entire line are dead," uttered Orgetorix through gritted teeth, loud enough to be heard by everyone in the room.

"You've murdered my parents, and you've killed my people, but I survived, despite your attempts. I hope you burn alive!" Alana spat in his face. A feeling of immense pride swept over me. Sometimes spit hurts more than a punch.

Orgetorix took a step back, his hand grabbing the handle of the sword at his belt. He completely missed the giant fist thrown by Ambenix, who sent him sprawling to the floor to count his teeth. One of his guards rushed to help him, while the other two men faced Ambenix, ready to strike. The giant ignored them.

"You attacked my people," he thundered. "I, Ambenix, invoke my right as chieftain to challenge you to combat."

Silence fell, but I had the feeling it was the calm before the storm.

"Go back to your village. You are not welcomed here. You cannot challenge without proof, and from what I see, you have none with you," said the man who had earlier defended Orgetorix. His trimmed brown beard matched his hair, and he wore a silky yellow shirt, with an ax dangling at his belt. His dark eyes were filled with contempt.

"Casticus," grumbled Ambenix. "Don't worry, your time will come as well."

"You'll pay for this. My men will skin you alive," said Orgetorix, massaging his jaw.

"Do you think I'm afraid of your army out there?" Ambenix countered. "I brought mine as well."

"How many? One hundred? Two hundred?" laughed Orgetorix. "I have ten times more men than you."

"But not warriors. Your army is made of, what, carpenters, shoemakers? People you forcefully carried from your town? Each man I have is worth ten of yours."

Orgetorix scoffed. "You came for nothing. You're not even allowed to vote."

"All the chieftains are allowed to participate, even if they can't vote," intervened Vercingetorix, who kept a hand on the golden hilt of his sword. His voice was calm and steady, but his blue eyes told a different story.

Orgetorix sneered, then turned his gaze to Alana.

"Even if you are Helix's daughter..."

"She is. I know her," interrupted Vercingetorix. "And she has the right to be here, to represent her people, same as Ambenix." He had made the statement sound like a challenge.

"Her people are no more," countered Casticus.

"Because he killed them," shouted Alana, pointing to Orgetorix.

I knew it was a risk, but I put a gentle hand on her shoulder. *If she loses her temper here and provokes a battle, I'll die next to her.* I half expected Alana to ignore my gesture, but her body relaxed and she took a step back, coming closer to me.

"Again, no proof!" Casticus challenged. "Just like this entire charade. You called us here based on made-up stories."

"How do you dare to accuse my friend of being a liar?" shouted Vercingetorix, any pretense of calm gone. "I have known her for many years, and if she says it happened, then it did." His fingers gripped the handle tighter.

"You are a foo—"

"Dear Casticus," said the man in the white toga, and put a hand on his shoulder. I hadn't noticed him move away from his chair. Immediately, Casticus bowed his head and took a step back.

"I think it's best we all take a few moments to rest and go back to our seats. Let's have some food, and then listen to what the new witnesses have to say. I'm sure everyone here can judge if they deserve to be listened to or not. Isn't that so?" His voice was conciliatory, but his eyes were hard. I didn't trust him.

"It's good it was just a suggestion, Maximus, as Caesar has no power here, and I would hate to cut your head and send your body back to him," said Vercingetorix, a threatening note in his tone. He had said it loud enough for everyone to hear. "Just because Casticus invited you, it doesn't mean you have a saying in our matters."

Maximus's eyes flashed with anger. "I am well aware of what my role is at this council, but let me give you a piece of advice, young chieftain. Things can change, and it's better to have the Romans as friends rather than enemies."

What a snake.

Vercingetorix's hand closed into a fist, but instead of striking the Roman emissary or drawing his sword, he took a deep breath and turned to face the council.

"Let's have some food and wine and listen to what they have to say," said Vercingetorix.

The doors opened, and the servants I'd seen earlier entered the room, bringing plates filled with bread, cheese, fruits, and drinks. The other people, including Orgetorix, Casticus, and the Roman envoy, retreated toward the table, filled with fruits, cheese, meat, and roasted vegetables.

"I never thought I would see you again, Alana," said Vercingetorix. He approached and gave her a brotherly hug. "I heard about what happened but had no idea who was responsible for such a thing. I asked my men to search the area, but they found nothing, and I feared the worst. I'm glad you're alive and well."

"Tyrenn saved me," Alana told him. "We fled to a faraway village, where we hid."

"Ah, that old fox," Vercingetorix said fondly. "I've never seen anyone else even close to his swordsmanship skills. How is he?"

Alana closed her eyes for a second, and a tear rolled down her cheek. I understood her pain; I knew how it was to lose a parent.

"He died two days ago," she said, her voice strong, despite her grief, "killed by Orgetorix."

Vercingetorix put a hand on her shoulder and lowered his gaze.

"Tyrenn was a good warrior. I'm sorry for all the things Orgetorix has done to you, but I promise he won't get away this time."

"Of that, I am sure," Alana said, her eyes burning with fierce intensity. I got the feeling there was more behind her words but didn't know what.

"And who is this?" Vercingetorix said, his gaze falling on me.

"He is Duncan, my friend," Alana introduced. "He saved me from Orgetorix's clutches and helped me get here." I should have been happy she had called me friend, but something inside my stomach turned into a knot.

"Very happy to meet you, Duncan." Vercingetorix offered his hand, which I shook. His grip was firm and true. "Now, if you'll excuse me, I have a trial to finish. Please wait outside until you are called."

Alana bowed her head slightly, and I did the same.

I looked toward Tarrah and Ambenix. Ambenix was too deep in conversation with two other chieftains to notice, but Orgetorix's daughter smiled and nodded at me. Though she'd been afraid before, there was no danger to Tarrah here, among the other leaders.

I followed Alana into the antechamber. This time, none of the soldiers challenged us.

"Can you please come with me? Vercingetorix asked me to show you to your rooms so you can freshen up and wait until you are summoned," said one of the servants as he bowed in front of us. Behind him stood two guards, their eyes fixed on us.

Alana frowned slightly but inclined her head and made a gesture for the servant to lead the way.

I exited through another door, opposite where Alana and I come from. It led to a room with a dusty smell, where a man with a brown robe, his back to us, stood in front of a floor-to-ceiling set of shelves filled with scrolls. He turned to look at us, but before he had a chance to ask any questions, the servant escorted us through another door, into a poorly lit hallway.

"Hey," said Alana to the servant, but he continued walking as if he didn't hear her. "Hey," she repeated. "Are you sure this is the way?"

The servant didn't reply but instead continued walking. Alana stopped just as a door opened, and three Romans in red tunics with short swords at their belts came through. Behind them was another man whose face I knew. Ferris.

One of the Romans moved to grab Alana, but she ducked behind his hands, spun, grabbed the back of his tunic, and pulled. The soldier hit the ground hard. Another one tried to pull out his sword, but Alana blocked his hand before the blade cleared the scabbard and punched him in the throat.

My hand flew to the pocket where I had the gun, but before I could pull it out, something slammed in the back of my head, and I fell. I saw the last Roman grabbing Alana, and then Ferris covering her nose with a rag.

The last thing I heard was, "Leave him, someone's coming," and the lights went out.

19

A foul, pungent odor woke me up to see a man with a black hood, feverish eyes, and a short black beard with white strands leaning over me. He had something close to my nostrils, which reeked of cat pee.

"How are you feeling?" He retreated, the smell going away with him.

I groaned. *Where am I? And what's this smell?*

"You should feel better soon. I took care of your injuries."

My memory started coming back and a shiver ran through me.

"Alana?"

"They have taken her. You have to go. There isn't much time."

With his help, I stood and leaned against the wall.

"Who took her?"

"Maximus ordered Alana kidnapped," he explained.

Fear spread through me.

"Why?"

"Power, why else?" he answered with a shrug. "I can only assume he wants a seat at the council. He wants Rome involved in our internal matters. I suspect he kidnapped her because he wants to force her to marry him or someone he controls. Then he would be in position to claim a seat at the table. Backed by one of the Roman legions, it would be impossible to stop him."

I wasn't interested in their politics. My main concern was Alana. Everything else could burn for all I cared. An idea flashed through my bruised mind.

"Why don't you raise the alarm, tell Vercingetorix or someone else to stop them?"

"Because even if I convince them she was kidnapped, and even if they would agree to send riders after her, we still have an army at the gates."

"Can't the soldiers stop them from getting out of the city?"

He shook his head. "I suspect the kidnappers used the thieves' tunnels and had horses waiting for them. No, from the stories I heard, even if they're half true, you're her best chance."

Stories? What stories? "At least, do you know where they'll take her?" I shook my head to clear my thoughts.

"Yes, I'll give you directions and tell you how to get outside unseen. But you must hurry. And when you see Alana again, tell her I know what she did, but her secret is safe with me. No one else will know the truth." Before I could ask what he meant by that, he went on, explaining about a secret passageway that led to the side of the castle facing the woods. I had to go around it and find the bridge over the river. From there on, I had to go west.

"Who are you?" I asked, preparing to leave.

"One of the druids. Now hurry, time is of the essence," he said and disappeared in the shadows, his voice a distant echo.

Something in his voice and behavior made me trust him. That and I had no other ideas on how to find Alana. His instructions had been clear and the streets were mostly empty, so I swiftly arrived in front of the house at the edge of the wall surrounding the town. I knocked three times, paused, and then one more time. The door opened, and an older man in dark green robes with a pointy hood opened it, looking curiously at me.

"He who possesses the knowledge knows nothing," I said, following the druid's instructions.

The old man studied me, nodded, and opened the door further.

"I need to get to the other side," I said and stepped inside a dark room with a musty smell. It looked like a small antechamber where three pairs of shoes waited for their owners.

The old man didn't reply but motioned for me to follow him through a door on the right.

He brought me to a storage room with empty shelves on the sides and wooden crates next to the front wall. Without saying a word, he lifted a lever placed near the floor, hidden between two of the boxes, and the part of the wall I was facing started sliding, revealing a hole big enough for someone like me to squeeze through. On the other side of the tunnel, not even ten meters away, was the forest.

I thanked him and crawled through the hole until I was one meter away from the edge, where I stopped and listened. A few seconds later, without hearing anything nearby, I sprinted toward the protection of the trees, hoping no one skewered me with arrows. No one did, and once past the tree line, I headed to where I'd left the RV. It wasn't until I reached the vehicle that I realized my ribs weren't hurting anymore. *That druid did more than just wake me up.*

The sun had begun to set, hues of orange blazing through the azure sky, so I hurried to my laptop and plotted a course for my last remaining drone to survey the area around me. I had to find a way to reach the bridge behind the castle that wouldn't put me in the vicinity of an entire army. *I already lost so much time.*

"Yes!" I exclaimed when the relayed image showed a path through the forest that led to the bridge. Far away in the distance, I saw a few dark pixels, moving away at speed. *I'm coming, Alana.*

I drove until late into the night with very few breaks, constantly checking my tablet until the drone sent me an alert. Off the main road, hidden behind the trees, were fourteen orange dots.

That's a small army. There was no way I was able to save Alana from thirteen kidnappers. I covered my face with my palms.

Think Duncan, think. I had a drone, a gun, and an RV.

Sounded like the beginning of a joke. There was no fire to distract them with my drone, I didn't have enough bullets, and there were too many trees to drive where Alana was. The only thing I had going on was the element of surprise. It wasn't enough, but I had to try. Surely they must be tired from all the running.

That's when it occurred to me, and I slapped my forehead. *That's not thirteen soldiers. Half of them are horses. They had been running for hours, they were radiating heat, that's why they were all orange. That means there are only six kidnappers.*

I had tried to avoid killing people, but now there was no other possibility if I wanted to save Alana. With seven bullets, the odds weren't overwhelming against me.

I took the night vision binoculars, my battered vest, knife, and gun, and hoped it would be enough.

Everything was dark, with the occasional hoot and howl, and if I hadn't had my drone, I would have driven right past them. I tried to mimic how Alana moved but without much success. In my ears, every step I took, every branch I stepped on, sounded as if someone screamed, "Here I am!"

But I didn't hurry, and soon enough, I reached them. The horses formed a circle around the group of people, and inside it, seven dark mounds rose from the ground. *They must be sleeping.*

I didn't know if they had a guard, but I decided to play it safe and assume there was at least one person awake.

For the entire time I drove, searching for them, scenarios had played in my head of how I would rescue Alana, but now, when faced with the actual possibility, my mind was drawing a blank. If I approached them, the horses would give me away. If I waited, morning would arrive, and everyone would wake and see me. If I acted now, I had the advantage of seeing in the dark.

For a brief second, the clouds parted, and the pale moonlight illuminated through the trees, the place where seven people slept. In an instant, I recognized Alana, her lengthy hair scattered over the makeshift pillow, and her hands and legs tied together. I looked around to make sure I had enough space for what I needed, set the sights on the first soldier, and fired. His body remained there, lying on the ground, while everyone else, except Alana, stood, swords in hands. Alana, hands and feet bound, looked left and right, and for a brief second her gaze lingered in my direction. My heart swelled even though I knew she couldn't see me. The horses started neighing and pattered the ground with their hooves, then ran away in the night.

Two more shots and two more silhouettes fell. I had four bullets left and only three kidnappers. *This will be a piece of cake.*

I moved to a nearby tree to avoid being detected by the flash caused by my gun's muzzle and saw one kidnapper darting toward Alana. I hurried to stop him, but my first shot only caught his arm. He staggered but continued moving, so I shot again, this time in the head, and he dropped to the ground, at Alana's feet, like a tree hit by lightning.

Preoccupied with him, I didn't see when a tall shadow headed toward me until it was too late. I shot without aiming, and the bullet must have penetrated his body as I heard a grunt, but I felt the impact of something metallic in my chest, pushing me back to the ground, and my binoculars flew away, leaving me blind. I shot again. Then again, but the third time, the gun clicked empty. The massive shadow dropped over me, his head hitting the bridge of my nose, and stars exploded all around me.

I strained myself and pushed the corpse away from me. *Man, he's heavy.* I wanted to remain there, exhausted, but there was still one kidnapper left.

With a supreme effort, I staggered to my feet when I felt something slide across my abdomen and arm. Burning pain seared through my left forearm, and I stepped back, just as a blade whizzed past where my head had been. I lost my balance and fell to the ground. Painted on the moonlit sky was the dark silhouette with a raised sword, ready for the fatal cut.

The gun was somewhere in the bushes, but even if I had it, it was empty and I didn't have enough time to pull out my knife. I felt the area around me, to no avail. *How come I landed in the only place in the entire forest without any sticks around? Only leaves, dirt, and...Oh.*

My right hand flashed forward, and I threw a handful of dirt in his face. He shouted in surprise and covered his eyes with his left hand, buying me a short time.

I placed my left foot behind the leg closest to me, and with my right, I kicked his knee. It propelled him backward, and his back hit a tree with a loud thud, his blade flying away into the darkness.

Without waiting for him to recover, I pulled out my knife lunged, aiming for his heart. Before the blade touched his flesh, he punched my wrist with enough force to crack the bones. I shouted in pain, and my knife dropped to the ground. I felt his hands grip my throat, pressing in, squeezing my airway. Terror swept over me, the memory of the last time I had been choked still fresh in my mind, and I panicked. I thrashed, scratched at his hands, but to no avail. He had slammed my back to the tree, and I felt his thumbs digging into my throat.

"Not so powerful now, are you?" said a voice I recognized. *Ferris.*

Rage coursed through me, and with only a few moments of air left, my brain frantically searched for a solution. An old technique my dad had shown me when I was younger flashed through my mind. My left hand reached across to grab his bent left elbow, then pulled with all my remaining strength. His body twisted like a whirligig, his hands flying away from my throat, and because of the spinning force, he landed with his back on me. I immediately put my right forearm around his neck, grabbed my wrist with my left hand, and squeezed, leaning backward.

He thrashed for almost a minute, and then his movements slowed down until he went limp. I kept the choke for another few seconds, for good measure, and then I let Ferris's body slump to the ground at my feet.

I picked up the knife and considered cutting his throat but decided against it. Alana was there and fear gripped my heart. *What if she was hurt?*

The moon was again on my side, and two dark objects glinted in the darkness. *My gun and binoculars.* I collected them and hurried to Alana's side. She was breathing and her wide eyes stared at me. I swiftly cut the ropes and she stood and looked around her.

"Are they dead?"

"Yes."

She gave me a hug. Her body felt warm, and I wanted more, but my battered body said *later*. I groaned in pain.

She took a step back. "Are you hurt? What happened?"

"It's nothing. Can you walk?" She nodded. "Good. Let's leave this place."

From nearby, a long howl cut through the silence. A wolf was ready to hunt. Memories from when I was a kid, with my dad hunting in the woods, came crashing down, and a shiver ran through me, like an electric current through water. I froze.

"Duncan, what is it?"

Somewhere nearby, I heard movement.

"The wolf," I whispered, afraid I would attract its attention.

"He won't hurt us." Her voice was full of confidence.

Despite her assurance, I used whatever reserves of energy I had left and hurried to the RV. Inside, I collapsed with my back to the closed door, exhausted.

"You're hurt. Why didn't you tell me?"

I didn't have the energy to reply and let the darkness close in.

~

Sounds intruded into my blissful abyss, and I opened my eyes to see the white walls of the RV bedroom. I tried to stand and felt like every muscle in my body had been depleted of energy.

"Don't get up," Alana said. "Here, drink this."

I didn't even look at what it was. I did as she commanded and felt a warm liquid spreading through my body, invigorating every cell, every muscle. I felt like a man dying of thirst when he receives the first few drops of water.

"Thank you for coming after me. Again." A sweet smile danced on her red lips.

"Anytime." I took one more sip.

"You need to recover. Your injuries were rather severe," Alana said and pushed a strand of hair over her ear. "Also, we should leave, as they'll probably send people after us."

I pushed myself out of bed, waited until the world wasn't spinning anymore, and headed for the driver's seat. Alana came and sat next to me.

"Where to?" I had no idea where I was.

"Follow the road. Let's see if we can keep a promise we made to a little girl." Her face broke into a grin.

A crackle of thunder announced the rain, which started splashing over the windows, like the waves of a rough sea.

"Close your eyes, and I'll put on some music," I said and launched a playlist from my phone. "Coming Home" by Keith Urban started playing in low tones, in sync with the bobbing vehicle. With this rain, I didn't dare increase the speed to more than ten kilometers per hour.

"You amaze me with everything you say and do. I haven't met anyone quite like you, Duncan."

"Well, I can safely say I've never met a girl like you—or more appropriately, a woman like you. A smart and gorgeous woman, with excellent doctor skills, who knows how to handle weapons, and feel free to stop me anytime." My gaze met hers and she smiled, then turned to face the windshield and closed her eyes.

A few minutes later, a gentle snore resonated from my right.

I drove until I saw a familiar clearing, the place where Alana and I first met, and stopped the car. The battery was at less than one percent. She was still sleeping, and I didn't want to disturb her. I went to take a shower and remove the bandages she must have placed while I was asleep. The wound on my forearm was fully healed, like it hadn't been there at all. I got a fresh change of clothes, burned the rags I'd taken off, did a quick sweep of the floors and the couch, and ate a sandwich.

Alana was still in the chair, her blond hair falling over her face and nose, almost like a blanket. I slowly caressed her face and moved the hair out of the way. She woke up instantly and looked at me, my palm still touching her cheek. She pressed her palm on mine.

"I dreamt about you. That you left to a faraway land, where I couldn't follow," she said in a soft voice.

"I won't leave you. Not now, not ever. I promise."

She rose, her gaze boring straight into mine.

"Nor I, you." Alana took my palm and pressed it to her lips. They were soft and warm, like a fire in the cold of winter.

An uncontrollable shiver went up my spine. I'd never felt anything quite like it. It was like the anticipation when you're faced with a delightful mystery waiting to be solved. And once you unlocked it, it would give you immense pleasure, like nothing you'd ever tasted.

She motioned to the side window. "The rain stopped. I need to get into the woods and collect a few things."

She headed to the door.

"Wait." I couldn't resist anymore.

She spun and faced me, staring into my eyes. I cupped her head in my palms and kissed her. The moment finished sooner than I wanted and she pulled back, her eyes beaming.

"I'll be right back," she whispered and turned to leave.

I felt my head spinning, my legs melt into the floor, and the next moment, she was outside. I caught a glimpse of the door swinging back, and my face headed toward the cleaned floor.

"Ouch," I exclaimed, awakened by a sharp pain in my head. I stood and rubbed my forehead until the pain receded, but not by much. I felt the need for fresh air. I pressed down on the handle, closed my eyes, inhaled the morning's clean air, which had a soothing effect, and stepped out, right onto something firm, like pavement. The background noise wasn't made by insects or birds, but by something else, something I knew very well. Traffic.

"What the f—" I froze when I raised my gaze and saw what lay in front of me.

It was the CERN building.

∽

I RAN like a madman into the building and bumped into Sergio, who was just badging in.

"Are you back so soon? I thought you'd be somewhere in the Alps for the entire month. Or maybe you're interested to know how the experiment went? It took us a week. We just finished it and are waiting for the preliminary data."

"I need to talk to you. Something strange happened," I said, trying to catch my breath.

"Okay, come into my office."

On our way there, I tried to tell him about time travel, being transported into the past, but he shook his head.

"It is impossible," said Sergio dismissively in his heavy Italian accent, taking a seat in his comfortable-looking leather chair.

"I'm telling you, it wasn't a dream," I argued.

He took a deep breath and seemed to consider what I'd said during the last few minutes. A decade older than me, Sergio was in charge of a project designed to test data transmission over immense distances using quantum entanglement, or what Einstein referred to as "spooky action at a distance." The experiment had the potential to advance our understanding of quantum physics beyond what we currently knew was possible and allow information to be instantly teleported across the globe or even in space. Or at least that's how he described it to me when I first met him several months ago, when I joined CERN for my internship. He had tried to explain it in greater detail, but most of it went over my head.

"Duncan, why don't you tell me everything from the beginning? Like you Americans say, the long version," Sergio relented. He took his "attentive" position, and his fingertips lightly tapped together.

"Thank you," I said in an exasperated tone, my palms up, fingers pointing toward him. I took a moment to compose myself and remember how it all began. "It all started when I woke up in the RV after the party..."

I spent the next couple of hours telling him everything I

remembered. Uncharacteristically for him, he didn't say anything, just stood there, listening to everything I'd said.

"And that's when I came running into the building," I finished and let out a long breath.

Sergio stood there, in his chair, palm under his chin, looking at me. Then he took a deep breath and stretched.

"I need coffee. You know, this is the best story I've heard in a long, long time. You should write a book."

"But it's true! And it wasn't a dream."

"Come on now, Duncan, you are a brilliant young man; otherwise, you wouldn't be here. Don't you think it's more plausible you came back early from your vacation and had too much to drink last night?" he said with a laugh. "It's a lovely story, but I don't see the reason you persist in telling me it's true. How can it be true?"

"I don't know. Maybe it had something to do with your experiment?" I asked, grasping for straws.

"That's a good one!" Sergio laughed. "You know the experiment is designed to test only how subatomic particles can be sent over great distances and doesn't work at the scale you're suggesting. It can't transport you across the globe or in time. It's designed to send only quantum information."

"But would it be possible, in theory?"

"No. What happens at the quantum level stays at the quantum level."

He must have seen something on my face, probably disappointment, because he continued. "Okay, let's do an exercise. Let's say it's possible. It's well known there is a link between an outside observer and the behavior of the quantum particles. If you somehow can influence their state or movement, then you may be able to have them act in a particular way that you desire. And in theory, it can transport you to far distances in an instant. That's the whole idea behind quantum entanglement. Distance and time don't apply to them. Now, about what you said at the beginning, regarding the language spoken. Everyone thinks similarly because, at its core, the thoughts are the same. Electrical impulses. Only the way they are expressed through words differs. Neuroscience is not my area of expertise, but I assume that somehow, the brain waves can be picked up by an external receiver. Another brain. Think of it as a form of telepathy. You can understand and possibly communicate with someone, even though you don't know their language."

"So, it's possible?" I asked.

"In reality, no," Sergio said, instantly dashing my hopes. "In theory, many things are possible. And bear in mind, I didn't take into consideration a lot of other things, regarding the energy required, distances, laws of physics that are broken, and so on. I'm sorry to say, Duncan, but you probably had a very vivid dream, and that's all that it was. Just a dream."

"But I remember all the things that happened."

"Duncan, let's be serious for a moment. You know very well that the simplest answer is most probably the correct one. What do you think is more plausible? That you teleported and went through all those things, or that you were too drunk last night and slept in the RV?"

I shook my head in disbelief. A slow feeling was creeping into me; I knew it, and I hated it. Doubt.

"I would suggest you go home, get some rest, and then you

can go back to your vacation. Your story was fascinating, but now I have some work to do. I need to look over the data."

I nodded, but I wasn't focused on what he said. *Is it possible to have imagined everything so clearly, an entire battle, people murdered, people I killed? And the noises, the smells, the pain, the gentle hands that helped me, Alana's face, her kiss?* My head swam. I felt dizzy and reached out with my hand to a wall to keep me steady.

"Are you okay?" asked Sergio, his voice expressing concern. I nodded, afraid that if I spoke, I would throw up. "Do you want me to call anyone?"

"No, I'm fine. I'll go rest," I managed to say and hurried out of his office and the building.

The fresh air cleared my throat of the bile I felt in my mouth. *It's impossible. Everything felt so real.* I went back to my RV, dark thoughts swirling over me.

There, on the stairs, behind the closed door, I sank to my knees and wept.

I don't know how long I remained there, tears flowing freely on my face, but I remembered a smell, a faint one. It was an unpleasant odor. To my right, there was a bin, and with trembling hands, I opened it. Inside, in a white plastic bag, were two pairs of dirty shoes. My heart exploded, and I inhaled deeply, letting it course through me.

It was all true, it wasn't a dream, and I had proof. I wanted to go back and show the shoes to Sergio, but after a second thought, I decided against it. For him, it meant nothing, even though it meant everything for me.

I drove the RV back to my apartment in Geneva, and after a

quick meal, I started investigating. My mind was filled with questions. *Was I in the same universe? Where had I been?* I spent hours checking my documents, Googling, going to the library, and researching history books.

From the names and descriptions I found, I gathered I had been transported back in time a couple of thousand years. What I did find about the period made me smile. Orgetorix had been an aristocrat among the Helvetii tribe, and they resided in what was now Switzerland. His attempt at seizing control over all the other tribes had been exposed, and during his trial, he had died mysteriously. Some sources even mentioned people believed he had poisoned himself. I remembered the druid's words. *Tell her I know what she did.* The histories had been only partially correct. He had been poisoned, but he hadn't done it himself.

When I completed my analysis, I concluded that all the things I knew were the same, and nothing had changed during the week I had been away. I should have been happy; instead, a chill ran down my spine.

Either my actions had no major impact, or what I did was precisely what was supposed to happen. It was late in the day, and I didn't want to go down the rabbit hole and consider the implications of what that meant.

When I returned home, it was already dark. I stopped by my mailbox and then went upstairs to have a shower.

The hot water had a calming effect, and I studied myself in the mirror. Only a faint pink line remained on my left arm where the blade had cut me.

I looked at the mound of history books I'd checked out and

decided they could wait until the next day. Instead, I browsed through the mail I had received the past week. The only interesting item was a note saying I would be audited. The letter also mentioned an investigation into how I won at lotto. Concern washed over me, but I was too tired to care. If I had to make plans to leave the country, I could do it tomorrow. I turned off the lights and went to bed.

My phone buzzed with a message, just as darkness enveloped my mind. With sleepy eyes, I checked to see what it said.

HI DUNCAN. *Just wanted to let you know that I have reviewed the initial data, and I found something odd. We'll probably rerun the experiment in a few days. Enjoy your vacation. --Sergio*

THE NEXT FEW days were a whirlwind of activity with preparations and research. I started receiving notices from lawyers, and even the police, about the launch of an investigation into my activities related to winning the lotteries. I ignored all of them.

Finally, the day arrived. I had spent so much time selling most of the things I owned and preparing for what I hoped would happen, that when I parked in front of the CERN building and turned off the headlights, a feeling of dread washed over me. *What if it doesn't work?* I had gambled everything I had on this night, on this one moment.

I took a seat on the couch with a can of Coke in hand and stared at the tar-like sky. Lightning flashed somewhere in the distance, briefly illuminating the threatening dark clouds looming over me. I closed my sleep-deprived eyes. If my last gamble didn't work, I was finished. Everything I had was with me inside the RV and would be taken away when the police found out the truth. *What was I thinking?*

Alana's face appeared in my mind. She smiled and made a gesture for me to follow her through the meadow's high grass. I took the first step, and things started spinning, like I was sucked into a black void, and from all around, a dark silky veil enveloped me.

I blinked my eyes open to see the sun's golden rays inundating the inside of the RV. My neck felt stiff, like I had fallen asleep with my head on the table. *It's morning.*

A jolt ran through me, and I jumped from my seat and stumbled, but managed to grab the door's handle to steady myself. I closed my eyes, opened it, inhaled the morning's fresh, crisp air, and stepped out...right into something wet and mushy.

My eyes shot open and fixed on what lay ahead. The majestic Mont Salève, Geneva's impressive home mountain, rose like a balcony over me, its green forests and gray rocks a splash of contrasting color on the azure sky. I took a few steps and looked around me, taking in the natural beauty of the place, the vibrant green of the grass and forest. I was alone. I was where I needed to be. *I've done it.*

I turned and headed toward the RV. During my research, I had spoken with an Italian archeology professor who had found some writings about how the Romans had tried to infiltrate themselves into the Gauls' internal affairs by making an alliance, through marriage, to obtain a seat at their council. The son of a Roman governor was supposed to marry the daughter of one of the Celtic chieftains. But the marriage never happened.

I knew it was a long shot, but it was the only lead I had. I knew where I had to go. The same place where all roads led—to Rome. If needed, I was prepared to fight an empire to save the woman I loved.

MESSAGE FROM THE AUTHOR

If you liked the book and want to know more about Alana and Duncan, please consider leaving a review. I would love to read it.

Thank you!

ALSO BY ANDREI SAYGO

SOMEDAY, SOMETIME, A GENIE AWAITS

A down on his luck historian, William meets an enigmatic woman at a coffee shop in London. Her fascinating stories spark the beginning of an adventure that leads him to the banks of the Nile river.

But his past catches up with him, and William is left to die alone in the Sahara desert. What happens next will have you wonder and second-guess yourself until the end.

If you liked the *Inception* movie, surely you'll enjoy this time travel book.

ZOX SERIES

A high-tech thriller with a hint of Sci-Fi à la Stargate. Fans of Mr. Robot and Jack Reacher shouldn't miss this. Hacking. Secret agents. Alien AI. This book has it all.

DC COVEN SERIES

An inexplicable attraction draws Robert, an IT guy with a secret, to a witch marked for death. Witches, magic, secret organizations, martial arts, and invisible assassins. Robert has no idea what he gets involved in.

If you want to be reminded of the best of Cassandra Clare's *The Mortal Instruments*, *The Da Vinci Code*, *House of Night*, and *Harry Potter*, then this series is for you.

THE SQUEAMISH VAMPIRE

Meet Dave. Dave has been a vampire for two days. By accident. He thought the first day was fabulous; now, not so much. Dave is thirsty, but can't stand the sight of human blood. Oh, what he wouldn't do for a pizza or a cheeseburger...

In his hunt, he meets James, a resident illusionist in one of the town's hotels. James has his own problem. He had met a witch at the local coffee shop, but in a moment of weakness, he refused her advances and fled. Now he badly wants to find her to ask for a second chance.

Together they will form an unusual alliance and face a host of mundane and supernatural obstacles in their quest for the things they desire the most. Can they find them before sunrise?

Printed in Great Britain
by Amazon